I0736399

Eerie River Publishing
Box 99900 HP 157 673
RPO Stanley Park
Kitchener, Ontario, N2A 0H1
Canada
Eerieriverpublishing.com

ISBN 978-1-998112-09-8

This manuscript is a work of fiction. In the novel, alongside characters who are pure fantasy and are products of the imagination and do not constitute a reconstruction of actual events.

Edited by S.O. Green
Cover Design Grady Earls

THE VOID

BOOK ONE OF THE FANG RIPPER SERIES

NEEN COHEN

EERIE RIVER PUBLISHING

The Void is dedicated to the fabulous human being who watched animals pull red berries from a bush, and perhaps noticed their increased energy and ability to function. You blessed human who then began the process of providing us with the elixir of the gods, ie coffee. This book is dedicated to you and your continued gift to the world.

For Frankie and Carter. Every word I write is dedicated always and forever to you both.

PROLOGUE

Hidden in the gaps of the rain, the Void wove its insidious ink through the darkness and closer to the beating hearts of humans.

It had not needed to break free. Its cage, the source of so many pains and agonizing moments, had been opened. It had slithered free, but kept itself hidden in shadows, fearing the error would be too soon discovered. The chaos had hidden it as it slipped out of the building, the prison where it had been held.

Now, it was free. It had escaped the land between the clouds in a rush of water, tearing its body into shreds of blackness, droplets of oily putty falling from the tips of slithering tentacles.

It was unseen by the humans of the land below, who had long ago unlearned the truth of their myths.

Where were those naïve creatures now? The small humans who dared to call it myth?

It didn't matter. The Void would sniff them out, take its time, enjoy the fear and destruction.

It had dreamed of the carnage during its imprisonment. The desire and determination to kill every human that crawled on the earth, the ones responsible for its capture, was all that pushed it through the days of fire and lightning.

This earth would be the Void's, and the humans running rampant would learn the meaning of true fear. The pleasure of inflicting the torture ignited the fire in its belly once more.

Humans—the thought spat out in its mind—how they thought of themselves as something more than cattle. As though they were alone in this world, on top of the food chain. The Void would have scoffed had it not been reduced to this temporary slither of itself.

The streets were absent of those scurrying creatures. They hid behind brick and mortar, as though the power of rain and wind could not blow their structures down if it desired. The sound built as the rain fell harder and faster, the wind picking up traces of the Void and scattering them further than it would have liked.

It hissed from its newly forming mouth, calling together the other ink-dripping tentacles of itself. The noise set the dogs of the neighborhood to barking. Slowly, parts slithered toward each other, and it began to reform. The hacking gurgle that escaped the undeveloped mouth sounded nothing like the laugh the earth had heard in eons past.

But that mattered not. Once reformed, it would again rule and terrify this world.

It twitched from its indulgent, fiery plans. Starvation flooded its weakened mass.

Discovering it could slip to the earth as a trail of dark ichor, broken into pieces, had been fortuitous. It did not remember, but much had been lost over time. Soon the others would follow, escaping through their cages and dripping through the rain as it had shown them.

First, it had to be whole again. It had to be ready to lead. It had to feed.

Curling its newly formed fingers, the Void felt bones crack into life, bending the encasing flesh, a mottled grey and black shell that darkened as more pieces came together, sucking and tearing through the rain.

Black wings, dark as obsidian, creaked like drying leather as they soaked up the polluted water from the sky. It remembered all its old forms and took from them the parts it most enjoyed.

The silhouette made the night look as midday. A figure with outstretched wings.

It was a true darkness the world had forgotten, but would never forget again.

The Void saw with newly formed eyes—three for now, but it could call upon more if needed—the first petty human through a nearby window.

Three would be enough to frighten.

Craig got up to pee. The bloody rain, three days in a row, and he felt like an hour hadn't passed without him needing to pee yet again.

He looked out the window and instantly regretted this ritual.

Frozen, with his dick still in his hand, he watched as thick globs of ink moved on their own out of the puddles of rain and couldn't turn away.

His breath seemed heavy and loud in the small bathroom. His eyes stung from his refusal to blink. When he couldn't fight the pain in his eyes any longer, he blinked. In that moment, the beast completed its transformation and stood, silhouetted against the skyline.

A sound, like the kind a strangled cat would make, issued from his mouth.

He blinked again and the beast was gone.

But the raised hairs on Craig's arms, his limp penis, told him more than he wanted to know. This was not some midnight imagining. He'd seen a monster, and Craig knew without a doubt that it had seen him, staring and immobile, as he watched its reanimation.

"Beast..."

The word dropped from Craig's mouth in a whisper before he left the bathroom and raced to the insufficient safety of his bedroom.

The Beast opened its mouth, its bulk hidden beneath the window. A smile of jagged bumps and small, sharp teeth split across its face.

"Beast…" The copied word scratched out between black tongue and raw throat. "I like it."

It was going to be almost too easy. It watched the human as it scurried away from the window into the depths of the building. Hunger pulled, and it jumped to the windowsill of the now-deserted bathroom. It had been so long since it had feasted.

The Void heard the wheezing beyond the room. It didn't bother to quiet its footsteps or shrink to stop the sound of its wings and claws scraping along the walls of the narrow hallway.

The heartbeat of the human raced, the sound of air rushing in and out in short gasps.

At the doorway, it stopped and waited for its meal to see. The Void had expected a scream, but the terrified silence was just as rewarding.

Slowly, it crept up the wall and over the ceiling, scratching flakes of paint down onto the carpet, until it stopped over the bed and the still body of its prey.

Opening its mouth, it was finally rewarded with a scream.

The Void laughed and dropped down onto the man. It wrapped its wings around him, easily trapping the flailing limbs. This human did not have a good survival instinct.

Sharp claws on the tips of its wings crunched through the human's shoulders and pinned him to the mattress beneath. The poison was slow. It had time enough to enjoy the pain and horror of its feed.

"Hello, Feast."

The Void let out another blackened laugh. It joined its prey's screams in a cacophony of chaos. It was a beautifully horrific chorus, improved with the sound of tearing flesh.

The Void's razor-sharp claws peeled the first layer of meat from the body beneath it, then the next. Each piece it consumed with slurps and moans as it filled the emptiness within and rounded out its silhouette into the nightmarish shadow of a balloon animal gone horribly wrong.

Blood dripped down over its chin as three eyes morphed and bulged to five. With this new sight, it could see the veins carrying the blood beneath the skin that remained.

The Void, consumed by the sating of his own desires, enjoyed hearing each new snap of bones as he disarticulated his meal. Small, jagged teeth gnawed fingers, grinding them to a white powder, before sucking out the marrow of the arm bones.

Outside, the rain grew heavier, louder, as thunder and lightning echoed outside of the apartment.

The Void noted the increase in tempo, but nothing would stop it taking its time to enjoy its first kill.

Its first feast, in lifetimes.

CHAPTER 1

The shuffling in the seats behind Blue might as well have been a roar in his ears. His eyes narrowed at the woman. A pair of burly guards dragged her by the arms from a small door recessed into the back wall. It was the only wall in the large, cavernous room not obstructed by hundreds of Skyans, come to see the results of the trials, in their macabre curiosity.

He couldn't blame a single one of them. Hadn't he come for a similar reason?

The room itself had once been beautiful to him. The clear, domed roof gave an unobstructed view of the cerulean-blue sky above. When the clouds lowered, and the light brushed in just the right way, fingers of a lover's caress, a rainbow of colors would flood the room and fill Blue with a sense of immortality and the freedom of the skies.

It was the largest room of the building, allowing those from all the clusters to gather. But now, it was too close, the crowded room too loud to his ears. The sky beyond was weeping a thin mist of rain, sliding down the curve of the roof like tears on a cheek.

The woman, the prisoner, stepped into the small cage on its dais. It sat in the center of the suddenly hushed crowd. All eyes were laser-focused on her. Her long, blonde hair, nearing white, hung limply around dirt-smeared cheeks and the deep grey eyes that had once reminded him of a coming storm. Purple colored the skin beneath her eyes, and her cheeks were sunken with the bones protruding.

Those eyes—once so familiar, but now as distant as a stranger's—avoided looking at him and their children. He tore his own gaze away and looked above her, to one of the four diamond-shaped jewels that rested on shelves halfway up the walls.

The one behind her head was white. He knew it would not stay that way.

Blue's daughter gripped his left hand so tight the tips of his fingers were beginning to whiten. His son, who sat to his right, pushed his father's hand away when it was offered. Moments like these, it was hard to believe they were the same age. Just thirteen years and yet here they sat, silent with backs straight. So much older.

He ached for those days, now lifetimes ago, when he could wrap them in his arms, hold them close and promise them it would all be okay. When he believed those words were more than just platitudes.

What could he say or do to comfort them now? He had shown up without much doubt of his wife's guilt, but a small flame of hope continued to burn in his chest. It was a fool's hope. And it was a hope for his children, no longer for himself.

He had wanted them to stay home, to spare them the horrors this trial would bring—the looks, the whispers, the rumors—in the hope it would wipe this day from their memories, but it had been no use. At the mere mention of it, his son had become enraged, screaming obscenities and demanding to attend. His sister said nothing, simply stepping beside her brother, face unreadable as ever. Her actions spoke louder than any words could.

He should have stopped them, became the dictator his son accused him of being, but in the end, he was fighting his own battle, and losing the love of his life with it.

So, here they were, the entire family, watching the inevitable execution of wife and mother. Her own mother was nowhere to be seen. If she were there, she had not deigned to come to the pew for the family of the accused.

It was day seventeen of the trials, and the Guardian leaders, known as the Four, sat with slumped shoulders and heavy-lidded eyes.

It was an honor to be on the Council of the Four, one that came with both power and longevity.

Blue knew all about that honor. He'd been removed from the Council of the Four the day his wife had been arrested. He itched at the fresh scar near the crook of his elbow. The strength waned more obviously in Blue's replacement then the other three.

It was the last call of the day, just as Blue knew it would be.

"Fang-Ripper." The widest of the Four stood, keeping his eyes on the piece of paper in hand. "You are accused criminal twenty-nine of the infanticide trials. You have confessed to thirteen acts of inappropriate use of our people's crystal shards, and ten cases of torture of juveniles."

Fang-Ripper's nostrils flared as her eyes roamed over the crowd. "Those are your words, not mine."

So many Skyans had come to see justice done for the children of their race. Blue's eyes closed when his wife finally looked at him.

He could forgive her for the crimes to their people. What he could not forgive were her crimes to her own family, or the secrets she had kept and the consequences he would have to pay for them.

"Do you deny your guilt?"

"I took the children, and I made them better."

Blue watched Fang-Ripper's hand rise to her chest, fingers searching to clasp something no longer there. He clasped the pendant she had given to him moments before the door to their home was forced open and his world was turned inside out.

Slowly, as though stuck in a thick syrup, he opened his eyes as the roar behind him became thunderous with the stamping of hundreds of feet. Individual words bled together, until nothing could be discerned except the anger and the outrage.

Parish, the oldest of the Four, and once Blue's closest friend and confidante, stood and slammed his palms down on the desk. "Enough!"

The Guardian's palms slammed upon the desk a second time, and that finally did the trick. Perhaps not instantly, but the sounds dulled and soon silenced.

"You say you made them better," Parish continues, "but you

have provided us no explanation when questioned. You have given us no reason to believe your words. In truth, what you did was torture until death the next generation of our people. You, madam, are sick. Perverse. The very worst example of what a Skyan can be, what our people are capable of, and you deserve nothing short of death. And so it shall be. Your sentence is death, to be carried out immediately."

Blue's daughter squeezed his hand and he reacted, squeezing back for just long enough to reign in his anger. She continued to cling to him. Surprisingly, his son had leaned closer to his side, not quite touching but brushing his father's coat.

Today, he would fail them again.

The cut was clean, a black, crystalline shard dragged across Fang-Ripper's slender neck.

Fang-Ripper kept her head held high until the blood dripped, slow and agonizing, out of the cut, stark against her pale skin.

When she began to choke, a hacking cough and gasp that echoed around the silent crowd, neither of her children looked away.

CHAPTER 2

Green light streamed through the wall of windows. Kiera leaned back on the third-floor staffroom bench and sipped her coffee as the storm drew closer. Her office was a large rectangle overlooking the serpentine river that cut through the suburb. The kitchen was her favorite place, not just because of the coffee machine, though that was a big draw, but also for the amount of light that flowed in, even now.

That hypnotic, green light danced across the long table, the uncomfortable benches, and the few armchairs squashed together at each floor-to-ceiling window. Each crack of thunder, each flash of lightning, made her flinch, shoulders coming together as though to make herself a smaller target. The sound of rain against the building grew louder, a roaring musical tattoo—drums, trumpets, cymbals.

They'd needed rain. The news had gone on about the drought for weeks now, but it was such a heavy, sudden downpour. There had been nothing on the weather app this morning. She wouldn't have come in early, or at all, if there had been.

She shivered, despite the warmth of the coffee. So why was she smiling this time?

The hair rose on her arms and at the back of her neck. Green meant hail, right? Could a storm be too much for the earth to take? The river was already rising against the bank, threatening calamity.

And still, she smiled between each sip of coffee. Must have been something in the air.

Still, glad I didn't race back for the train now.

She sipped on her bitter black fuel, feeling vindicated as she watched frozen chunks of ice join the fat drops of rain smashing against the reinforced, double-glazed windows.

She looked at her phone, tapping her index finger against the back. She smiled at the scar that ran across the skin between her knuckles. One of her souvenirs from fencing class.

The green light deepened to a dark grey. The pummeling on the building grew louder, drowning out all other noise. The lights flickered.

Kiera pushed off from the bench and left the kitchen. Back at her desk, in her seat, her cubicle, she pushed herself back and rested sapphire blue Doc Martens up on the desk. Her little bit of 'fuck you' was normally hidden beneath her uniform of long, black pants and 'professional' white blouse.

The others wore different shirts, a useless way of individualizing themselves. Kiera stuck with the shirt with the embroidered sigil of the company over her left breast for pure convenience. These were not the kinds of clothes she would have ever bothered to purchase for herself.

She brushed cold fingers over her arm, prickling the hair on her skin as she looked beyond the office's wall of glass. At least the claustrophobia was less than her library assistant job two years before. It had been in a dark room in the middle of the library, no windows and dust for days.

Of course, three floors up, these windows didn't open, but at least she had a view.

The lights blinked out. Darkness settled over her.

Fuck!

With the power out, no more coffee. At least she'd already made her first cup.

The whir of computers and ducted air-conditioning died as a

thunderclap made Kiera jump in her seat. She slapped her feet to the floor and gripped the edge of her desk.

"That was close…"

Her laughter echoed in the empty office as her heart thudded in her chest. The adrenaline pumping through her veins was her favorite fix, made her feel lighter.

She chugged on her coffee, gasping as the still-too-hot liquid burned a trail down her esophagus.

The battery-operated clock on her desk illuminated green dashes that told her it was a little after 7am.

Was anyone else stupid enough to come in today? Usually, Kiera resented the others who came in and got the bulk of their work done in the stupid o'clock quiet, but the dark and stillness pressed in on her. One other person would have been nice, maybe.

She could wait out the storm. She *had* to wait out the storm. Fear threatened her enjoyment of the darkness, so she stuffed it back into the pit of her stomach where it belonged.

Outside, it looked as though the sun had yet to rise. She knew the fallacy, because she had drunk her first cup of coffee watching it come over the horizon while she sat on the shitty balcony of her one-bedroom apartment, the place that cost enough to make her aunt almost cry when she told her.

As it was, Aunt Em had clung to her fingers, and all but begged her to stay, to live on the farm and be safe. She hadn't mentioned Kiera's history—the voice in her head, the nightmares, the sleepwalking— but it had radiated in her eyes and the concerned crinkles on her face.

Kiera had been ready. The voice, the nightmares, even the sleepwalking were long gone. Years gone.

So why were they in her mind now?

Turning her back on the torrential downpour, Kiera stood and looked over the partitions, like a cityscape in miniature, streets and blocks, a walkway like the river running through the middle. The desks were pods of six, the cream and brown color a mix that reminded her of movies set in the Seventies. Three desks at the end were hotspots, with nothing personal to indicate sole occupants like the rest of the pods.

But even the static desks held minimal whimsy or personality, except for Josie's desk and its multitude of crystal pyramids. They scattered the surface and threw rainbow lights over the dreary walls of their day job.

Kiera's own desk had three stress balls, things she had never needed at any previous job. The purple dragon was her favorite. She spoke to it more than the fairy or the bridge. The bridge was her free memento from the sunset climb of the Story Bridge over the Brisbane River. The climb itself was immortalized in the photo frame beside it. Her five-year-younger self wore a big grin, despite the hideous blue and grey jumpsuit she wore.

Kiera laughed and flicked the photo of her face.

"Ah, so young. The climb wouldn't do anything for me now."

Sky diving, daredevil rock climbing, fencing, axe throwing—everything and anything she could find. Except for spelunking. That shit was terrifying. She couldn't imagine anything giving her a fraction of the thrill that bridge-climbing version of herself had experienced.

"Except maybe climbing it in a storm."

Kiera shuddered at the mere idea, though she felt a smile tug at her lips. She'd never have the chance to climb the bridge again. Her contract was nearly up and her plans to head north were sorted. Josie was the only one she'd miss. The last two years had felt longer than most. She couldn't remember the last thrill she had, unless she included Hannah. Hannah had been fun at least.

Kiera shook her head of memories.

She just needed more adventure. Brisbane had lost its charm long ago. She needed more.

For now, she would settle for coffee.

She looked at the screen on her phone as she plonked it on the bench beside the sink. She chewed her lip, convincing herself she wasn't worried her phone hadn't rung yet. Aunt Em hadn't called yet, hadn't called when the storm began.

She always called.

The pounding of rain continued to envelope her as she put her cup under the machine and hit the worn, grease-stained button. Nothing happened, and for a moment Kiera just stared at the machine, head tilted to one side. Another thunderclap made her jump. She facepalmed.

"No power, idiot."

"What?" Kiera looked around, hope and fear warring at the idea of finding someone behind her. "Oh, for fuck's sake."

The voice was back? The voice was back! No. It wasn't possible. Therapy and pills, all those appointments and treatments. The voice was nothing more than the result of trauma. Losing both parents. It couldn't be back; she'd taken her pills that morning.

But even Kiera knew she was lying.

Before the thought could germinate into further panic, her phone pinged with the slow buildup of the *Star Trek: Voyager* theme, her favorite TV show, one her Aunty Em would watch sitting beside her, holding her hand too tightly or wrapping her arm around her shoulder and pulling her close so all Kiera could smell was kerosene and paint. She forced in a deep breath, let it out slowly, plastered a shaking smile on her lips and snatched the phone off the bench.

"Hey, Aunty Em. About time, I thought you weren't even going to check on me this storm. Like you just don't even care." Her tone was wooden, forced frivolity in the words. She was rewarded with a soft chuckle down the line and her shoulders dropped a little from her ears. "How you doing?"

"Oh, you know. Crazy as always." Aunty Em's Aussie accent faded into the background, the British one that hinted at her undiscussed past taking over.

Something was bothering her. Kiera tapped her fingertips on the edge of the bench as the silence stretched.

"Are you safe out of the storm?"

"Yeah, I'm fine." Kiera let out a breath. She could deal with her storm worries; she'd been doing so since she could remember. "I got to work early this morning, to finish a project." Em didn't need to know her normal routine. "I'm all safe and tucked away in the building."

"Why would you go in when you knew the storm was coming? It isn't safe to drive in these conditions. You know it's not. You know..."

"I know. Of course I know. But it wasn't on the weather app, Aunt Em. Besides, I took the train in this morning. I'm safe. I made it before the storm hit. I promise, you don't need to worry about us. *Me.* You don't need to worry about me."

Kiera didn't remember the crash that had killed her parents and left her with a disfiguring scar, when she took her shirt off at least. Her fingers trembled over her chest, feeling the rope of scar tissue beneath the material. Her Aunt remembered the crash all too well.

"I'm okay. It's just a little freak storm. I won't go anywhere, I promise. Besides, it'll probably just blow itself out soon enough."

Deep slow breathes came down the phone line.

"It's okay, I promise."

"What's happened, K?"

"W-w-what—?"

"What's happened?" Aunt Em—stern, serious parental figure, Aunt Em—was now on the other end of the line.

Kiera felt like she was twelve years old again. "I heard the voice."

"You know the voice is just your conscience. Have you seen your doctor recently? Do you need a refill on your medication? Perhaps the dosage needs to go up."

"I know." Kiera laughed, nodding to herself and pretending the prickle in her eyes was anything but tears. Hell, she would have been happy to have a sudden case of conjunctivitis. "And yes, I've seen the doc and got my refills. It's okay. It was just the once."

"And you are safe inside? You'll definitely stay inside, no matter what?"

"Of course, I'll stay inside."

The heart attacks her aunt would have had if she'd known how many light showers Kiera had danced in during her life, just to prove she wasn't scared of a little rain. Who wanted to feel like the Wicked Witch of the West?

The silence stretched.

"More nightmares, K?" Aunt Em asked.

Kiera closed her eyes as another crack of thunder rattled the glass in the frames.

Memories of storms wrapped up in Aunty Ems arms while she told fantastical stories about her paintings flooded her mind while the silence stretched like taffy. It had been a long time before Kiera learned that Aunty Em's paintings were based on Kiera's own nightmares.

"No," Kiera answered, pain starting behind her eyes. A common enough occurrence when the interrogations came. "I haven't had any."

"Not too long now and you'll be off on another adventure, huh?" The tension was a plucked violin string, but at least Aunt Em was trying.

"Yeah."

Kiera pushed herself up on to the staff room table, shuffling her feet on to one of the uncomfortable, plastic chairs. She leaned forward, forearms resting on her thighs. One hand hung loose in the air while the other kept her phone pressed to her ear.

"How far away are you going this time?" Em's tone caused an instant lump in Kiera's throat.

"Aw, Aunt Em, don't get like that. I always let you know when I get somewhere. And I visit as often as I can."

Liar!

Kiera choked back the gasp, desperate for Aunt Em not to hear it.

"Not heading this way yet then. I didn't think so."

The light dulled further. Kiera spun to see a brief flash of something falling from the sky. A wooden something.

"No, no, no, no, no, no!"

It had looked like the hull of a ship, but that was crazy. She hadn't fallen asleep, or... Maybe she had? But she didn't have the nightmares anymore.

"One 'no' would have sufficed." The tinny voice rang distant as the phone slipped away from Kiera's ear.

"Sorry, gotta go. Love you." Kiera pressed the red button on Aunt Em's growing panic and tossed the phone on the table. "There isn't a ship flying in the storm. There isn't a ship flying in the storm."

She muttered it like a mantra, like it would change anything.

And I'm just your conscience.

"Shut up, Jiminy."

You were talking to Aunty. How did she know I was back, hmm?

"I'm not asleep."

Kiera couldn't tell if she was certain or surprised. With her nose pressed to the reinforced glass, she tried to see the ground where the 'ship' had landed. Streaming rain and mist blocked the view of the street below. She forced her shoulders to unclench and laughed as she stepped back.

Another echo of thunder clapped.

Not thunder. A scream.

"No, it was thunder. Why the hell am I talking to you?"

Had it been a scream? A scream that was far too close for comfort?

A blur of green slipped through the raging clouds, moving closer by the second. Kiera backed away from the window, liquid fire rushing though her veins. Tendrils of iridescent green and blue, like the branches of a weeping willow, followed behind a jade green dragon. A dragon with horns like twisted, dead branches and a textured chest of what could be mistake for vines and leaves. It's beak glinted silver in every flash of lightning.

"No..."

A ship, followed by a dragon. This couldn't be real. Dragons didn't exist. This was Brisbane for god's sake, not some fantasy realm in a Peter Jackson movie. Brisbane. It was beautiful, yes, but it was a town pretending to be a city, in a country that was little more than a puffed-up island. Dragons and flying ships did not belong here.

Kiera's feet moved while her mind struggled to catch up. She raced to the foyer and groaned. She rolled her eyes as the light for the elevator remained dark.

No power, moron.

"Yeah, thanks."

She headed for the fire escape doors. In the back of her mind, she felt Aunt Em's panic, but there was a dragon and a flying ship. There was no way she was staying inside.

She could deal with the lecture later. Better to beg forgiveness then be denied the adventure.

CHAPTER 3

The three flights down took far too long. Breathing hard, Kiera pushed into the ground-floor foyer and ran to the glass door. "What is this company's obsession with glass?"

She looked out at the water rolling down the hill, easily ankle deep by now. Taking one last glance down at her boots, she shrugged and pushed open the door.

Sound boomed against her ears. It was incredible how much a few sheets of glass could muffle the rage and rush of nature. Stranded cars were pushed out of their spaces, starting to drift down the street.

"Okay, a little more than ankle deep."

She turned left, up the hill, keeping as close to the building as possible. Water sloshed into the tops of her boots, soaking through the bottom of her pants. It was deeper further out, and the idea of what could be lurking beneath made her shiver more than the cold water. The force of the rain kept her face pointed toward the rough, red brick.

She turned at the edge of the building and headed to where the impossible thing had fallen past her view.

She hadn't believed it. She had hoped, but not truly believed.

"Did I hope it was true, or hope I was crazy?" she muttered, as she kept moving forward.

Who says you can't be both?

"Not helping."

A small laugh made her stop in her tracks. She shook her head.

The voice was just her imagination, and ignoring it was the best way to get rid of it again, just like the therapist advised. Besides, it was the least of the day's craziness, the least of her current concerns.

There, between her office and the river, was a boat like nothing Kiera had seen before. It had no sails, and the wood looked frail and old, ready to collapse at the next onslaught of rain, and yet it still stood, the same color of ancient wood she associated with the trees at the botanical gardens. It seemed to throb, like it had a heartbeat. Kiera rolled her eyes, because she wasn't poetic, and a ship couldn't pulse. It was just the persistent rain warping her perception. Still, how had a ship this size gotten in the middle of the road?

But then there was the dragon, an entirely different sight to behold.

Its head swayed back and forth, its scales a gem green, jade or emerald, nothing at all like her friendly purple stress ball. She had been wrong in her initial appraisal of its size. It was large enough to have carried several riders on its back, though she doubted it would allow it, even if she could imagine them clinging to the thick vines that scattered it's back.

Through the haze of rain, the dragon looked like a twisted sculpture made from roots and vines, earthy greens and browns, with a sharp bark and a sharper bite. The dragon snuffed air from its nostrils. Dirt washed from its head, turning the rivulets of rain cloudy like a weak cup of tea. Two horns, the grey of a paperbark tree, sprouted thorns like rose stems as they curved up and back from its head. The horn on the tip of its nose reminded Kiera of a triceratops.

Wings flicked and snapped at the rain and air. Between the bones of the wings, lit from behind by the flashes of lightning, draped the sheer greenness that had reminded Kiera of the leaves of weeping willows. Up close, the membrane looked far more delicate, though she doubted it would be.

When it slammed its tail down, the ground trembled and drops of water pelted all around it.

Is this what earthquakes feel like?

Kiera froze, even in her coldness, as her eyes met the dragon's. Large, black ovals, shining as though it could see into and through her in the space between heartbeats.

Movement beneath the dragon pulled Kiera's attention unwillingly away from its investigation of her. There, waving a staff over seven feet long, fire raging from the end of it, stood a man with salt and pepper curls on his head. He was large, with broad shoulders and a dirty, brown trench coat that flapped in the wind, whipping around his body. His boots were a baggy looking brown leather halfway up his legs, a mere shade lighter than his pants. His lower face was covered in a grizzled beard.

Kiera choked back the laughter.

"Oh my god. It's a bloody dragon-fighting pirate."

There's a problem with that?

All thoughts of laughter left Kiera as she ignored the re-shattering of her mind and studied the man closer. Something else was wrong. Kiera looked down at her own feet and back to the man's.

"Bloody hell, the water ain't touching him."

She was certain the voice in her mind was giving her a slow clap.

The man's hand that wasn't waving the flaming staff, rested on the hilt of what could only be a sword—an actual freaking sword. Through the haze of the relentless rain, the flames on the staff looked as though they burned a thin, watery violet.

How did it still burn? How was he dry?

Kiera's eyes blurred as she looked for something to explain, to answer her questions. She bounced her attention back and forth between dragon and man, unsure which was more intriguing to her.

There was a thick blackness on the dragon's front claws that washed away like the dirt on its face. The watery rivers glinted a stained pink. Kiera's breath caught in her throat as the tainted water touched her boots

It's not dirt.

"Is it blood?"

The voice was mercifully silent as bile rose, burning the back of Kiera's throat.

She turned back to the pirate; anything was better than the blood. His mouth moved, but the words were lost in the downpour and wind, snatched away from her hearing.

He inched closer to the dragon. The river rushed beside them, rising as the water from the street flowed in past Kiera's ankles, the roar of it adding to the overall chaos.

Kiera's breath was heavy from her open mouth, the sound too loud in her ears. Movement flickered to the man's left. He had a companion. She was tall and leather-clad, with short-cropped, dark red hair. If the man saw her, he made no indication. Instead, he took his hand off the hilt of the sword and reached toward the dragon.

Time slowed, and for the smallest of moments, the idea of suspended time flashed through Kiera's thoughts. But nothing could control time. Not even a dragon, surely.

Still, in that moment, Kiera pondered. Would the dragon meet the man, push his snout into the outstretched hand, like a cat might with their owner?

Then the man's companion moved.

With a screech, the dragon pulled back from the man's touch.

"Winger!"

The man's scream came too late. The companion froze, caught in the dragon's stare.

Kiera watched as the dragon snuffled and moved with speed that defied its bulk. Front claws, vine-twisted, snapped forward. It reminded Kiera of a movie she had watched as a child with a man who snatched flies out of the air. She'd forgotten the name of it, and that thought itched at the back of her mind. Insane that anything could distract even the smallest part of her thoughts.

But then her thoughts stopped dead in their tracks. The dragon effortlessly plucked the companion, Winger, from her feet and shook her like a ragdoll, tearing flesh with its claws, breaking bones with the force it swung her around, then tossed her aside. Kiera wished she had blinked. That would have been all it took to miss this horror.

Red rain burst forth. Winger's lifeless body dropped unceremoniously on the ground in front of the dragon. The beast snarled before it jammed the claws on its wings into the asphalt, cratering the road, and pushed itself off from the ground. The gust of air forced Kiera back toward the wall as the dragon flapped its wings and took off.

The glass of the office building cracked and exploded inwards as the dragon's wings beat air at them. Someone was going to be red-faced explaining that one.

A bubble of nervous laughter caught in Kiera's chest, the pain gaining momentum, until the wind from the beating wings forced her down to the ground. The rain grew heavier, louder, and fiercer.

Water soaked through her clothes and flooded over into the tops of her boots once more. She looked up just in time to see the dragon fading into an unidentifiable speck. The green light that had come over the world when the storm began receded as the dragon disappeared into the distance.

It was so fast.

The man's voice boomed like thunder, but the words, if they were words, didn't translate as adrenaline spiked in her veins.

Her instinct for flight finally kicked in. She pushed herself back to her feet. Her knees stung as water seeped into the myriad of grazes beneath her pants.

Kiera turned to run back inside, but stopped dead in her tracks when a body floated by. It looked like that of another warrior, being carried through the currents of the receding flood waters. She wanted to run, but she was frozen. The large man ran towards her, his voice still booming, screaming at her in words her brain could not put together.

It didn't make sense. None of it made sense. Kiera backed up against the wall of the building so hard a piece of mortar stabbed into her palm.

Blood, that's real. Pain, that's also real.

The man reached for the body, holding onto it before it could be washed away.

"Wake up girl and help me!"

Bile touched the back of her tongue. The rain lulled to a soft mist.

"Help me!" he roared.

Kiera looked around.

"Me?"

You idiot. Who else could he be talking to?

"Who else would I be talkin' to?" His voice rumbled in harmony with the storm ebbing away. "I need 'er out the rain. Me ship's too far away."

"She's alive?"

"Not for long if you keep stuffin' about. Now. Help. Me!"

She knew when not to argue. Well, maybe not all the time, but right now, she was at a loss to find words at all.

Following his directions, she grabbed the girl by her knees and helped carry her into the lobby of the office. Kiera's stomach roiled each time she looked at the girl's face, images of the redhead being crushed in the dragon's claws repeating in her mind. They could have been sisters with the same short, cropped hair and sharp cheekbones. With the mix of water, blood and mud smeared through it, Kiera couldn't even be certain of the color.

They laid the body on the white-tiled foyer floor. The stark contrast between it and the dirty appearance of the woman caused a small pulse of pain behind Kiera's right eye. She winced and the man, a head taller than Kiera, took off his brown trench coat to lay it over the girl's body, up to her neck.

Kiera began to tremble.

He shoved a small round wafer into her hand. "Eat this."

She laughed.

"Eat it!"

She placed it on her tongue. In moments, her body didn't just feel warm, but dried, her clothes following suit with the heat from her body.

"Well, that's handy."

"It ain't handy; it's necessary." He jerked his head toward the door next to the elevator. "What's back there?"

"You mean the carpark?"

"Good." He disappeared back out the front door, leaving Kiera alone with a strange and damaged woman who might or might not actually be dead.

A woman Kiera was too scared to touch again.

CHAPTER 4

Kiera jumped when the old man's head popped out of the door to the garage. "Hurry up."

A laugh she had little control over escaped her lips. She looked away to the front door and then back to his salt and pepper head.

"Hurry with what?" she asked, once she'd refocused on his face.

His eyebrows rose in impatience, then he rolled his eyes and kicked the door open further. His frame filled the entire doorway, hands on hips, a silhouette from an old fairy tale Kiera half-remembered.

"Any chance your name is Odin?"

"What? No, it's Blue. Now, hurry up. I need ya ta help me bring 'er aboard. Take 'er home."

"Aboard?" Kiera frowned and tilted her head.

"Christ, being with these humans has made you as stupid as one of 'em. Come on."

Again, his words brooked no arguments.

Wait, made me as stupid as a human? I am *a human.*

Another chuckle from the back of her mind sent shivers up Kiera's spine.

She barely had a hold of the woman's legs before he directed her to begin walking backward into the garage. She almost dropped her grip when her eyes adjusted to the gloom. Blue grunted as the body shifted in his arms, Kiera's own grip slipping at the sight in front of her.

The wooden ship filled the bulk of the garage. A grey car in one of the corner spaces would never be the same again. The nose of the ship had pressed it against the furthest wall, the driver's side window little more than spiderwebbed glass around the edges. A few last shards fell with a tinkle onto the driver's seat.

Kiera started laughing again. This was by far the craziest dream she had ever had. Sure, it was better than the nightmares, but this still won the crazy contest, hands down.

The pirate shook his head and kept walking. His movements pulled the unconscious—hopefully not dead—woman and Kiera behind him.

Kiera stared around again looking for some gaping wound in the staff garage as she followed Blue aboard. "How did you get it in here?"

Blue narrowed his eyes as they placed the woman on a small cot. He sat down on a small, wooden box and his eyes drilled into Kiera.

She held her breath, waiting for the fragile construct to break beneath his weight, but it held. The box, just like the ship, was far stronger than it appeared. At least, she hoped.

The ship was long and thin, a cabin at each end forming a slightly raised platform, with two small steps that led to a wooden steering wheel and a dark, waist-high pillar beside it. The pillar was sleek and obsidian, with rounded corners and veins of colors she couldn't pin tracing patterns beneath the darkness. It looked smooth and Kiera imagined the cool touch against her fingers as they itched to reach for it.

"How long you been down here, Guardian?"

"Guardian? What the fuck are you on, old man?"

"Hmm..."

Blue stood back up and headed to the end of the ship where the pillar and wheel stood. The wheel was so ordinary it made the black stone of the pillar stand out that much more. Kiera struggled to drag her eyes away from it as it shimmered, despite the limited light in the parking lot. She turned in a circle, taking in the crates that covered half the deck. Most were pushed up against the sides, with some stacked on top of each other. There were a few, obviously used as chairs, arranged around a barrel.

"There's no sails."

Yes, that's the only strange thing that's happening right now. Open your damn eyes.

"Course there's no bloody sails. Definitely been grounded for too long. Hope you ain't lost yer air legs, cos we gotta get goin'."

"I'm not going anywhere in this thing. Especially if there is any chance in hell of running into another dragon, seeing as that one was definitely not warm and fuzzy."

Kiera crossed her arms and planted her feet against the deck of the ship. She could feel her fingers trembling beneath her folded arms. They were hidden from view. It wasn't like this was the first time she'd bluffed her way out of being scared.

But had she ever been both this intrigued and scared at the same time?

"What moron ever say they were warm an' fuzzy?"

Kiera felt her cheeks heat up thinking about the purple dragon still sitting unsqueezed on her desk. Knowing her luck, it would tumble out of the smashed windows and land upside down with her name, written in black Nikko, announcing her ownership. Except he didn't know her name.

He didn't even know she was a bloody human.

"Gotta get Winger back to the leaders, and you back home. Protocol exists for a reason. Something you've well forgotten it appears." He continued to mutter under his breath. Kiera thought it sounded something along the lines of, "If you'd ever known them to begin with."

That became irrelevant when the boards beneath her feet shuddered slightly.

"You can't just kidnap me." Kiera knitted her eyebrows at the pirate, voice rising to a pitch that hurt her own ears.

There was curiosity and then there was downright stupidity. She had just seen a woman ripped in half by a dragon.

"You ain't no kid, Guardian. Now sit down and shut up. Getting you back is here or there to me, protocol or not, but Winger don't got time for your shit."

"My name is Kiera, not Guardian." Her words didn't have the

same strength as she looked at the pale woman, covered in blood and mud.

"Fine. Sit down and shut up, Kiera."

Kiera sat down on the nearest crate. The warmth of the wood beneath her was a comfort that made no sense. She rolled her eyes. It's not like they could get out of the garage. No point getting upset.

You idiot. You didn't think it could get in here either, till you saw it.

"Where are we going?"

Blue opened his mouth and snapped it shut again. With a shake of his head, he turned his back on Kiera and smashed his hands down on top of the black pillar.

Kiera watched, head cocked, as Blue rocked his hands back and forth on top. His fingers rose and fell from the obsidian stone in a way she imagined a pianist's fingers might, though she couldn't find the pattern of the music. The veins of color she had discerned within the glossy stone shone brighter as Blue's hands played along the top. His palms pressed so fiercely against the pillar that the backs drained of color, turning them near translucent, veins popping light blue against the whiteness.

The sound started in Kiera's ears, and she flicked her hand, like she was trying to shoo away a mosquito. It grew louder.

This was no mosquito.

Kiera followed the sound to its origin. Her eyes stopped on Blue and the pillar. The sound of wind joined the buzzing, and the deck beneath the now-bouncing balls of her feet moved and shuddered. Kiera's fingers gripped the box beneath her. Her legs would not stop moving. Her heart raced in her chest and her head swiveled back and forth, wondering which way to go to get off this bloody boat.

Then, color joined the noise.

Shadows wrapped around the ship and blocked out the carpark and the door that led back to her office building. The door back to that old life. To safety.

"Why didn't I run when I had the chance?"

Because you feel more than you can remember.

"Great. Thanks for vaguing that one up for me."

Spatters of light grew brighter, and Kiera smiled as the blackness lightened to a deep, indigo blue with pinpricks of white.

"Are they stars?"

Kiera hadn't realized she voiced the question aloud until Blue answered.

"Dust."

It wasn't too late. They weren't outside yet surely. Squinting, she was determined to see how the ship got out of the carpark, hoping for another chance to get the hell off.

But, in the blink of an eye, the darkness began to fade. Kiera stood and turned in a circle on the deck of the ship. Blue sky surrounded them. She stood and gripped the railing on the side of the narrow vessel, then looked down. Deep grey clouds surrounded the bottom of the ship, small streaks of light soundlessly flashing within. She looked up and saw a second layer of clouds above them, with enough space between the two to fly a fleet of kites.

Kiera flapped her mouth a few times before stumbling back and sitting heavily on the box once more.

"This isn't a dream."

You're only just realizing that?

"Shut up."

Yeah. A chuckle that made Kiera shiver. *That's never going to happen again.*

What the hell was going on? Kiera gulped in air, not quite able to catch her breath. A lump had formed beneath her breast and her blood roared in her ears. Stiff and tight, her back felt like a rod had been lashed to her spine.

Blue stepped away from the wooden pillar and moved, his limp pronounced, toward Winger's still body.

With a loud gasp, Kiera finally pulled enough air into her body, her shoulders rounding and drooping forward.

"Can you help her?" Kiera asked, focusing on the strangers.

Her kidnappers?

"She's breathin'." Blue's breath was loud and slow, the gruffness in his voice lighter. "Gotta take her to the Four. Their Healers'll get her back on her feet." The last of his words escaped between clenched teeth.

"Are you okay?"

Oh, stop being so human.

I am *human. What do you expect?*

"I'm fine." He collapsed onto his own box with a pained, "Ummph..."

"Don't you have to steer the ship?"

Blue ignored the question and closed his eyes, leaning back against the railing. After a moment, he opened his eyes once more and leaned forward. With slow movements, he alternated between tugging up the left leg of his pants and making bigger the rip that had split the side of the material. Kiera's mouth hung open a little as she noticed the dark stains around the edges of the original rip and spreading down the fabric, landing in fat drops of crimson on the deck of the ship.

"Shit..."

Unable to take her eyes from the wound, Kiera noted the muscle tissue visible through the gaping tear in the flesh.

"We need to wrap that up," Kiera said surprised her voice didn't quiver.

"Aye."

Blue made to stand back up. Kiera jumped to her own feet and pushed him back down, not so gently. A low growl emanated from Blue's throat.

Fear turned to anger. She had never been the kind to just sit on her arse like some pathetic damsel in distress waiting to be rescued. "Just tell me where the medical kit is."

"Medical kit?" He laughed, shaking his head. "What do you think this is, some fancy human hospital?"

With closed eyes, Kiera let out a slow breath before responding. "You know, bandages, gauze, something to help?"

His eyes narrowed, but he stayed seated and pointed Kiera to the end of the ship away from the helm.

"In the hold."

Kiera blinked a few times before she noticed the hatch in the floor, a half-meter or so in front of the cabin.

"Downstairs?" Kiera asked, after forcing down the sudden

thickness in her throat. There was a reason spelunking had never made it to the bucket list.

"A ladder. No stairs on my ship. Second door on the left, everything I need'll be in the box on the wall."

Kiera, alone in the ship's interior, had every horror movie she had ever seen flood her mind. Every time she had screamed at the screen at the stupid token female stepping into the dark unknown alone.

At the bottom of the stairs was a hallway with doors on one side and round windows on the other.

Portholes? Is that what they are called?

The darkness fought against the light streaming through the open hatch above her.

What the hell was she doing? This was a little quick for Stockholm syndrome, surely. But, was Blue really her enemy?

Well, he did *kidnap me.*

He also chased the dragon away. What would have happened if he hadn't?

Kiera ignored the voice. Why the fuck was Jiminy back, now of all times?

Letting out a slow breath, she found the door and opened it into a small room that held a hammock at the back, and as promised, the box—a medicine cabinet, for all intents and purposes—on the wall. The bandages weren't white, but ignoring years of first aid training, she grabbed two and a collection of small bottles that looked like they might help.

The climb back up the ladder was harder with the bottles and bandages but she made it, letting the hatch slam back in place before she walked, stumbling slightly at the jerky movement of the deck, back to Blue.

This ship is rocking like we're in the middle of a storm.

If you say so.

The voice, once a rarity and now verbose, made her body tense and her skin tighten as though she were suddenly being dunked into an ice-cold pool in the middle of winter.

Her aunt had always called it her conscience. It had been easy enough for her to believe. The voice only ever spoke when Kiera was making a big decision, or about to get herself into some deep trouble. She could usually rely on the fact it never vocalized during her adrenaline sports.

But something had shifted. It was stronger and much closer to the surface, more...real. It had felt different from the moment she heard it in the office.

And that's the thing making me feel crazy. Not the dragon, the pirate, or the sky ship.

You aren't crazy.

Kiera scoffed. Why wouldn't she believe the voice in her head telling her she wasn't crazy? Shaking her head, ignoring the heat in her chest, she scanned the deck and made her way to where Blue had moved.

He sat beside Winger, who lay on what looked like a small cot. She was covered in blankets, small circles of blood seeping through where her shoulder hid beneath. Winger's head turned and Blue nodded at words Kiera couldn't make out, a whisper of a voice that wrapped about Kiera and made her feel like she could jump off the side of the ship and fly alongside.

Don't try it.

She wanted to tell the voice to shut up, but the words snagged on the myriad of questions in her mind.

"I have your bandages." Kiera swallowed. "They aren't exactly clean though."

Blue winced as he leaned back, snatching the items from Kiera before she could protest. "Good."

"You must be Kiera." Winger's eyes fluttered her way and a small smile played on full lips turned pale by blood loss.

"Yep, Blue's abductee."

Kiera smiled, trying not to stare at the blood that coated Winger's chest as she shuffled, the blanket sliding down her body.

"Blue?" Winger's voice was sharp, like the snap of a dead tree branch.

Blue shrugged.

An ally? Will she help me off?

Depends what you mean, the voice purred, mimicking the sultry tone Kiera herself had used in more than one club.

Kiera felt her stomach writhe as though a snake was waking. *Seriously, now?*

"Why don't you show me that leg so we can get you healed, and I can pretend you aren't both whispering about shit I know nothing about."

She turned to Blue whose silver eyes narrowed at her, before he revealed the leg already wrapped in the off-white bandages.

"You got hurt, Blue?" Winger laughed, and then cringed as the pain knifed her. "You owe me five turns."

"Turns?"

"I see what you mean, Blue." Winger tried to sit up but fell back down on the cot, coughing and hissing, the noise muffled by clenched teeth.

"What's actually wrong with her?"

"She's got dragon poison in 'er."

Kiera looked down at Blue's leg, the ripped material flapping slightly. "Do you?"

"Nah, I only got the claws. Deeper wounds..." His nostrils flared as the ship suddenly shuddered, like a car going over a speed bump. "... but only the wing tips carry poison. Strongest poison I've ever known."

"Will she survive?"

"She'll be fine, s'long as we get 'er back to the Four. They got potions that'll pull the poison right out."

Kiera nodded, but her eyes were drawn to the blue sky that stretched around them.

"Ya got questions?" Blue asked, as he walked to the wheel of the ship and moved it slightly to the left.

She laughed and forced back tears, as she stepped up beside him. "Just a few thousand."

"I've got some of me own, come to think of it." He scratched at his beard as he nodded toward a crate behind a pillar that had hidden it from view on Kiera's previous scan. "Take a seat while you can. Not entirely sure what'll happen once we get to the Guardian City. You've certain spun shit into a web, girl."

Kiera chose to ignore the 'girl' comment. Pick your battles, Aunt Em had always said. So instead, she focused on the question she wanted to ask and smiled as images of Aunty Em's paintings danced across her memory. Nightmares that teased at the edges of her mind, stole the warmth from her lips.

"There are cities in the clouds?"

"Mmmhmm..."

Blue focused on steering the ship, though Kiera felt his eyes drilling into her on more than one occasion.

Unwilling to look back, she kept her eyes on the horizon.

Is it a horizon if the sea is made of clouds?

CHAPTER 5

"**Y**ou want to find it, don't you?" the Guardian asked, his voice sharp and loud; a crack of a whip. "That vital piece missing from what you once were?"

He stood in front of the cage where the Void was being held. Cold iron bars lined the cage. Large, perhaps, to the Guardian, the barred roof the height of his chest, but to the Void, it compressed its true shape and form. Between the bars, a pale, blue light flickered rhythmically, in a pattern that tormented and teased the Void. It had reached out once, wanting to touch the color. The pain that had shuddered through its body had been the one and only warning it had needed.

Others of its kind were not so fast to learn, or not so patient. Either side of its cage were lines of other identical prisons, filled with the mulling impatience of its brethren. Throughout the enclosure that housed the multitude of cages, screeches of anguish echoed. Threats and promises were wrapped in the noise.

The Void did not speak, did not answer the Guardian.

The Guardian slammed his spear against the metal bars keeping it in check. It felt the darkness within flare but quickly reeled in the anger and fury. He would not show it to this disgraceful thief. He would never allow him the upper hand.

The cage was only for now.

"Yes," he finally answered, his own voice matching the darkness of his warden.

"And can you find it?" the Guardian snarled.

"I will."

The Void would say anything to get out of the cage and stretch to their full capacity; it was no exception. It once had a name—Matriol, Martlon perhaps—but that no longer mattered. It was part of something bigger now. So many of its siblings graced the cages surrounding it now, filling the hold of the Guardian's ship. It had taken this Void awhile to understand the sway of the enclosure, but the rhythmic rocking explained more than the Guardian knew.

Such foolish creatures, these men.

"Look, Void."

It hadn't noticed the Guardian had stepped back, and now held out a pulsing, orange crystal in his hand.

"My heart..."

The Void choked out the words. Hunger ached and churned in every space of its being.

"Find me what I need first, and then I shall return it to you."

"Liar."

"Perhaps. But is it worth going against me? I could simply smash it now if you'd prefer." The Guardian lifted the precious item above his head, ready to slam it to the floor beside him.

"I will find the cave." The Void's voice, weakened in the fear of its heart's destruction.

"And?"

"And show you the way. But I want it back. I need it back."

"When you have helped me, I will help you."

"Then let me go find it."

"First, I need you to get something else for me."

"What?"

The Guardian smiled and the Void almost liked his captor. The darkness inside him called to its own, as he explained what the Void was to collect.

"They will sense me long before I can collect them."

"I'll send the distractions. You just worry about the Four." The Guardian spat the title of those who would presume to rule him.

The Void took note of the Guardian's disgust.

One never knew when something like that could be used to one's advantage.

CHAPTER 6

Kiera's skin itched. The view was sickeningly endless, the lull of movement beneath her feet only increasing the roil in her stomach. The only time she had felt anything remotely akin to this was on her one and only cruise in open water, with no land in sight. The three days had been mostly spent vomiting and wishing for death. She could jump out of planes, throw herself off cliffs, but sailing seemed out of her comfort zone. Not quite as bad as spelunking but pretty close.

Without the help of the medicine they had given her on the cruise—it hadn't helped much anyway—she busied herself with movement. She paced nervously, biting the skin on the side of her thumb, trying her best not to look out over the railing.

Which worked until a small sparkle winked on the horizon, catching the corner of her eye and her attention.

Land. There was land on the horizon. She managed a smile at the odd sight. An island in a sea of clouds. The comparison to the seas on earth were undeniable. Dread washed over her as she waited for the nausea to roll around in her stomach. She breathed slowly and continued to wait.

Nothing. Not even vertigo. Her wary smile slid into something far more genuine.

Still too far ahead, closer to the lower layer of clouds than to the top, Kiera saw the air shimmer. The sparkle she had originally seen grew larger. She chanced a quick glance to Blue. His eyes were focused on the same growing light, his face a stony and angry mask.

Kiera blinked rapidly, as though that would bring clarity to the distant object.

"Shit." Blue could have been mistaken for a bear, the growl more noise than word.

"What is it?"

Flames. She was certain now. The light was the dance of orange flames against... Was that wood?

"It's a bloody attack."

"Attack? Attack on what?" Kiera asked, her heart beating in rapid staccato. "Is it another dragon? The same dragon?"

"Dragons are the least of a Skyan's problems."

"Skyan?" Her voice emerged a fraction higher than normal but she couldn't just tell herself to calm down expect that to change. Not now.

"Our people." Blue's words were forced out between clenched teeth.

Kiera's face felt numb, all sensation lost as though the skin had been ripped from her skull. Her eyes focused on the blazing, now-clear ball of light in front of them.

"We gotta help." He looked over at Winger, his frown deepening. "But we don't really have time for this."

"Time for what? What the hell is going on, Blue?"

It was strange how familiar and comforting his name was on her lips. Blue like the sea. Blue like the sky. She would have laughed, if the tension weren't a metallic bile at the back of her throat.

"Void attack."

Blue turned and headed toward Winger. Kiera followed, far enough away to not seem like she was eavesdropping, but close enough to hear what was said. She hoped.

"Void attack, Winger." Blue's voice, while stiff and gruff, somehow softened. Kiera wondered at their relationship. Perhaps familial?

Winger shuffled back, sitting up against the ship's railing, hands fisted in the blanket at her chest. Her face paled, but her eyes locked on Blue's and she nodded slightly. "I can hold on."

"What about her?" Blue asked, pointing at Kiera, hand still

splattered in a mixture of his and Winger's blood.

"Take her with you, idiot." Winger laughed, which started another coughing fit. The wheeze she pulled into her lungs reminded Kiera of her time working as a tea lady at the hospital. Two, maybe three, jobs before the most recent.

Not so current now, Kiera imagined.

"She'll get herself killed. She's useless."

There were many things Kiera was easily able to shrug off—derogatory insults about her gender, her sexuality, her country attitude and habits—but being called useless was waving a red flag in front of a bull. Her wandering thoughts vanished under the metaphorical red in front of her.

She stepped forward and pulled Blue's sword from the scabbard that hung on his hip. It was heavier than the ones she had handled before, during fencing lessons and the annual medieval fairs, but her muscles recovered quickly, strengthened from the rock climbing. When Blue turned, curses spewing from his lips, she had the point lifted and aimed at his throat.

The chuckle from behind Blue brought a smirk to Kiera's lips, feeding the flame inside of her.

"I am not useless, old man," she spat.

"We'll see about that," Blue grunted, but his eyes sparkled.

"So, can I keep this one?" Kiera asked, as she lowered the sword. Blue snatched it immediately from her loosened grip.

"Over my dead body."

"You can take mine." Winger's voice was soft, but strong enough that neither one of them could refuse her offer.

Blue pulled out a sword from beneath the cot. It was beautiful. A large, white stone winked from the pommel. Without warning, he threw it toward Kiera. She smiled and snatched it out of the air.

"Your clothes'll get ya killed."

"Been telling the boss that for years," Kiera smirked, and then let out a sigh. What was the point of using humor to quell the fear swirling in her guts if no one got the joke?

Blue stared at her with furrowed brows.

"Got something else I can use?" she asked, tilting her head and pursing her lips.

"Me daughter's old clothes might fit."

"Daughter?" Kiera's eyes flashed between Blue and Winger, both quickly denying that was their relationship with strained laughed and shaking heads.

Blue has a daughter? Can't wait to meet her. I'm sure she's just wonderful after being raised by a father with Blue's rough attitude and impatience. The daughter of a pirate. Simply. Can't. Wait.

Jiminy chuckled in the back of Kiera's mind, reacting to her sarcasm. Well, at least someone understood her humor.

After a quick wardrobe change—she refused to wear the ruffled shirt first offered—Kiera was decked out in the tank top that had been beneath her work blouse, and pants that fit a little too snuggly on her hips, but didn't cut in to her skin or quite reach her ankle.

Blue held out a brown leather jacket in the same style as his own. "You need ta protect yer arms."

"I'm good, thanks," Kiera replied distractedly, as she gazed over the railing.

The flames that had been indistinct earlier now loomed close enough she could feel the heat, or at least imagine she could. The fire consumed the ship's cabin on the top deck. The ship itself was obscured with heat haze. It was at least three times larger than the ship she stood on.

"Suit yaself."

Kiera watched as Blue navigated the ship around the fireball. Flames licked up to the clouds and she couldn't have sworn one way or the other if they touched the sky of this world between the clouds. Her curiosity of the world vanished as screams and crashes reached her.

"Stay beside me," Blue spat.

Kiera nodded, felt comfort in the grip of Winger's sword, and watched as Blue jumped over the railing of the ship. She raced to the railing just in time to see Blue landing, knees bent, on top of the clouds the ship seemed to float on. The soles of his boots were swallowed up in the white cotton candy of the cloud.

What the hell?

"You'll be alright." Winger's voice was strained, the words coming slow and short. "Trust yourself."

"Trust myself." Kiera climbed up on to the railing, sitting on the smooth wood and letting her legs float out over the cloud sea below. "Yeah, right. But shit, what else am I supposed to do?"

Stay here and pretend you aren't dying of curiosity, you weirdo?

"Fine," Kiera huffed out.

With clenched teeth, anticipating something unpleasant, she pushed herself off the railing. Her feet landed and juddered a little, knees bending in reaction. Opening her eyes, Kiera laughed.

Blue was halfway to the burning ship, and the laugh died as she remembered she was supposed to be following, running toward the burning vessel.

Smoke warped her sight and threatened to clog her throat, but she pushed herself forward, running behind Blue, catching up with less trouble than she expected. The ground beneath was soft, a sponge that took her weight with ease and pushed back, like the memory of pounding on a trampoline as a kid. The gap between her and Blue lessened, and she was relieved to see the outline of a ladder on the side of the ship. Blue bent his legs and jumped, grabbing a rung on the ladder almost halfway up.

Kiera didn't trust herself to jump, but clambered up as fast as she could. Blue's boots disappeared over the railing only moments before Kiera followed.

"Drop the child!" Blue ordered, as Kiera's boots landed with a thud on the burning ship deck, three steps behind him.

He stood in a stance reminiscent of Kiera's fencing classes, sword raised, body turned to the side. She stepped out from behind him, intent to mimic his stance. Her arm fell when she saw what he was facing, only just remembering in time to keep hold of Winger's sword.

In front of her was a figure, darker than midnight, the true absence of color. But it was more than that. It didn't just lack color; it *stole* the color from around it, a fading echo left like a tormented halo around its shape.

And oh, its shape was another horror of its own. A twisted

perversion of humanoid, its limbs bent the wrong way, and in one hand it held a child's head. A small, blonde-haired child no more than three years old. At Blue's words, it had stopped bringing the wriggling toddler towards its maw. The mouth was elongated like a snout, sharp, white teeth bright against the monster's darkness.

"And why would I do that?"

The monster's voice was the slither of a snake over brittle leaves, crunching and snapping. The insidious tendrils of sound wormed their way through Kiera, the darkness leaving its trail behind. Kiera bit back a scream that tasted like bile on the back of her tongue.

"I won't ask again, Void."

Blue stepped forward, sword held in front of him. The Void's laughter was worse than its words, scratching down Kiera's thoughts like nails on a chalkboard.

She could do nothing but watch as Blue rushed forward, sword swinging down toward the arm that wasn't holding the child. As Blue drew closer, the Void morphed, its slick, black form shifting and writhing. A long blade extended from it and met Blue's sword mid-swing with a deafening clang.

Blue twirled toward the Void, as though the two were dancing and he were the damsel being wound in. His back toward the creature, his body blocked the sharp blade from the screaming toddler still gripped in the monster's other hand. It was a misshapen limb ending in too many fingers, black tentacles of oozing tar wrapping around the child; one around the neck, two others across the face, three clutching the child's skull, the blonde hair seeming white compared to the darkness of the Void.

Not stopping a beat in his dance, Blue flicked his wrist, and his sword came up, slicing the black tar of the Void's arm in half. The child's scream, renewed with fresh terror, pierced the air as it fell free toward the deck. Blue scooped the child against his chest and turned back toward the Void, raising his sword again, just a little too late.

The Void's blade sliced at Blue's shirt sleeve and cut into the skin beneath, causing him to stumble back. With a grunt, a rumble like thunder in the distance, Blue found his footing once more and lifted his sword as though his arm was not gushing blood and staining his shirt. The child continued to sob, though the high-pitched squeal turned into a hiccupping sniffle.

Kiera watched the writhing limb on the ground. It reminded her of a worm as its front rose from the ship's deck, swaying back and forth as though sniffing out its destination. The Void howled, but Blue stepped forward and brought his sword down once more, cutting the blade from the end of the Void's second limb.

"Skyans and their cities are protected." Blue's voice boomed like a wizard from a fantasy movie. "You are not welcome."

The Void's screams turned to a gurgling laughter. "Your army is shrinking, Guardian."

While they spoke, Kiera watched, mesmerized by the darkness of the Void, drawing her attention as it pulled color in from around it. A new limb extended from the Void's bulk. It bore elongated claws, longer than those that were on the now-still arm.

Blue didn't step back, didn't react to the new threat that drew toward him. Heat rushed through Kiera's limbs, her heart racing in her chest.

She stepped forward and, mimicking what she'd gleaned of Blue's movement, she slashed out. It wasn't a delicate movement, minimal and precise like she'd learned from fencing lessons. There were a lot of swings, movements previously unknown and yet strangely familiar. Each time she copied one of Blue's strikes, her body copied with an ease that it shouldn't. Not without training anyway.

But it felt so good, like sleeping in one's own bed after being away in a hotel for too long.

Kiera's arms ached as her breath came fast and loud. Sweat beaded on her skin before she lifted her boot and stomped down on a still-wriggling limb.

Blue's heavy hand on her shoulder made her jump.

He nodded. "Good work."

She smiled, and a far more pleasant warmth spread through her. His hand dropped and she turned to face him.

Stop!

The smile and warmth fell away instantly as the tip of Blue's sword flew at her head. At the last moment, she realized it wasn't coming at her eye but just over her shoulder. The sound was a tar-sucking wetness and she wasn't too ashamed to admit that she yelped.

As quickly as her legs were able, she rushed out from between Blue and the Void that now gurgled at the tip of Blue's vibrating sword.

"Never turn yer back on the bastards. Lesson one."

"Thank you," Kiera gasped.

Blue nodded again. He was covered in a sludge of black ichor and blood. "Time to go."

"Where's the kid?" Kiera looked around, only now noticing the child was no longer in Blue's grip.

He jerked his chin up and she shifted just enough to look behind her. People covered in soot were dousing the fire. The child gripped the hand of a woman, watching as the fire was brought under control.

Kiera couldn't form words, too many thoughts stopped any taking root as her limbs became leaden with the aftermath of adrenaline. She had just enough strength to nod as she followed Blue back to the ship.

CHAPTER 7

Kiera was quiet. Jiminy was quiet. Blue was quiet.

She slid down against the side of the ship, pulling her legs to her chest.

Blue strode over to Winger, as though he wasn't bleeding from several new places, as though he hadn't fought a creature of darkness and horror and saved the life of a small child, let alone the others who had been cowering somewhere in the ship before they arrived. She watched, blinking, thinking without thinking. When he strode back to her, she didn't move or avert her gaze.

"You good?" he asked, two small lines appearing between his bushy eyebrows.

Kiera blinked for a moment at the question. Was Blue actually concerned for her? Finally, she nodded and the stiffness fell from her shoulders with a breath.

"Is Winger?" she asked.

"She's weaker." He turned away, before the words were all out of his mouth. "We are going to the Four now."

Kiera shivered, her teeth clacking gently together, watching the rise and fall of Blue's wide shoulders. "What will they do with me?"

"I dunno," Blue answered, with a small shake of his head, the salt and pepper curls bouncing slightly at the back of his head.

"Let me stay with you." Where the fuck had that come from? "You can train me to fight those things."

Blue didn't answer.

He walked to the helm and stayed there.

The vibrations beneath her slowed. Her butt was numb, her leg muscles cramped, and she wobbled to standing on her way to the railing of the ship. Kiera had hoped to see land on the horizon. The stretch of cloud sea that continued in front of her made her lean heavily on the rail and wonder if there were any actual land up here. Perhaps it was all just ships in this claustrophobic world.

Was the headquarters of the Guardians, the place of the Four, just another, bigger ship? And what an ominous title. Were there actually four of them? Four of what, exactly? She wanted to ask the questions; she wanted to know. But while Blue had saved her life against the Void, he didn't exactly welcome the inquisitive type.

Kiera squinted as something appeared on the horizon. Her heart thudded in her chest. The last time she had seen something small in the distance, it hadn't exactly turned out to be a rainbow. But as they drew closer, she let out a laugh. She should have been shocked, but really, what more could be thrown at her today?

Be careful what you wish for.

Jiminy's voice held hints of mockery, and a little warning.

"It's an egg, because why not? A transparent egg floating between the clouds, and made of bloody glass no less. It looks like a freakin' snow globe. So the Skyans all live in an egg-shaped snow globe. How the hell do the ships dock?"

All Skyan cities are transparent shells, but mostly they are in small clusters, cities smaller than this, all connected through doors of sorts.

"Why do you know all this? How?"

I know a lot of things, K.

"Do *not* call me that."

Kiera sensed the roll of Jiminy's eyes in her mind, but the voice thankfully remained silent.

Kiera swallowed over a lump in her throat as they drew closer to the transparent egg. She had underestimated the size, that was apparent. But while the shell was indeed see-through, there didn't seem all that much for Kiera to actually see, except a forest that stretched to the top of the egg and ended two-thirds down, where they were met with a deep, brown dirt.

Whatever she had been imagining, a forest wasn't the first thing that had come to mind.

She looked around, searching the horizon for other shapes. In the distance, three lumps appeared on the horizon. Had she been on the earth, she would have taken them for mountain peaks.

She hadn't realized she was smiling until Jiminy spoke up again.

You are terrifying.

Kiera smiled wider, guessing at what the voice would be thinking. "Why?"

You know why.

"Oh, come on, how can you not want to explore the world up here? How many clusters of cities are there? Do they correlate to the land below? Are there maps? Are they all forests? Do they actually know what a city is supposed to look like? It's the ultimate adventure, Jiminy."

She laughed low in the back of her throat and felt the tightness in her muscles ease slightly.

Sure, just a pity about all the Skyans. And the Four don't exactly take kindly to things they can't explain. Jiminy paused, but Kiera sensed there was more and waited. She wasn't disappointed. *Things like you.*

"Me? Why would the Four care about me?" Kiera's joy slipped from her lips. Jiminy remained silent. "I'm a human. They know about humans, right?"

Pouting, she turned away from the mountainous landscape and turned back to the Guardian Headquarters.

She could see finer details as they drew closer. The dirt was veined with roots and the ground was covered in green grass that reminded Kiera of days in the country after a week of rain. Days with Aunt Em. She missed her family and concern gnawed at the back of her mind. Aunty Em would be in a panic. Despite the promise of an adventure of a lifetime, she did have to get home. Didn't she? Before Aunt Em did something irrevocable and stupid.

But Kiera couldn't drag her eyes from the looming site in front of her. She couldn't stop herself imagining more adventures aboard this ship. If she were honest, she *ached* for the adventures.

But her stomach gnawed at the thought of meeting the Four. Why would Jiminy even know these things?

Kiera tightened her stomach muscles, and her fingers gripped the railing as they drew closer to the shell wall that wasn't showing any signs of cracking or weakness.

"Keep yer hands down and don't touch anything," Blue called out, as the front of the ship entered the shell. "Keep yer mouth shut as well."

Kiera pulled her hands from the railing and nodded, though she hadn't turned toward Blue to know if he had bothered to note her reaction.

She threw a quick look over to Winger and held her breath. The injured woman was paler than earlier, and Kiera waited for her chest to rise again. She strained her eyes to see the slightest movement. Finally, relief engulfed her as she detected a marginal rise.

They weren't too late.

Letting out a breath, Kiera focused again on the front of the ship as it pushed further through the transparent eggshell. She let her tension drop. The shell collected against the deck of the ship like a waterfall being lifted by a hand. Kiera shrunk in a little and cringed as the shell drew closer.

The tingle at the edge of the shell was cold; Kiera's teeth chattered as she passed through. It brushed her arms like a sheet slowly pulled up over cold skin, tickling and teasing, raising the fine hairs on her body to attention. She worked at uncurling her fists. They moved slowly, even after they'd begun to rub at her bare arms, wishing she hadn't scoffed at the coat Blue had offered her earlier.

Her arms stopped rubbing, the cold forgotten, as she focused on the city within the shell.

They had pushed through the line of trees, so few despite the density they appeared to have from the outside. A whole city waited within to welcome them inside, or maybe not welcome them. Damn Jiminy for making her worry. This visit wasn't about her; it was about healing Winger.

Taking a deep breath, Kiera took in the white, red and green light that glinted back at her from walls that looked as though they were made of diamonds, gems, colorful stone. Most of the buildings were low to the ground, three stories high at most, with a few rare spikes that stretched closer to the top of the enclosure, although as Kiera looked up, she couldn't see exactly where the shell ended and the sky above began.

"Something's wrong."

Blue's voice carried over the quiet of the ship and the city that surrounded them. Kiera turned, seeing the man crouched beside Winger, who sat up in her cot.

"This isn't normal?" Kiera asked.

Her fingers, rubbing once again, did nothing to relieve the deep cold as drops of rain began to fall from heavy, dark clouds that hadn't been there moments ago.

"No!" Blue's teeth clenched. He stood again, with a low grumble, and headed back to the wheel.

"What's happened?" Kiera followed.

Blue ignored her and navigated the ship through the buildings until they stopped in front of one of the tallest. At first look, Kiera saw the beauty of the aqua gems of the buildings. As she looked closer, she noticed the cracks along the walls and the sheen of dust and darkness that muted the color. She couldn't even imagine how shiny the building would be if it were cleaned and cared for.

The ship landed with a thud and judder. Kiera's knees bounced and she rocked slightly forward but managed to keep her footing. She would have punched the air if the tension surrounding her didn't feel like a weighted blanket.

Kiera watched, shaking her hands and arms out, while she bounced on the balls of her feet. She wasn't needed as Blue bundled Winger into his arms. He cradled her like a child, something precious and delicate, easily broken.

With the ease of a much younger man, Blue jumped over the railing, Winger clutched tightly to his chest. Kiera followed, the call of the strange city, of being near Blue, pulled at her chest like a hook, and she was caught.

The effort of keeping up with Blue's long stride caused a stitch in her side. She was fast forgetting any confidence she had once had about being fit and healthy.

The front doors of the tall building opened with a shove of Blue's shoulder. Winger shifted, straining against his grip, trying to push herself out of his arms.

"I can walk, Blue."

Blue ignored her, as Winger's face scrunched up once more, and her eyebrows knitted together.

With pain or worry?

"Put me down." Winger's voice was louder than Kiera had heard it before.

"You ain't strong enough," Blue said.

"I know where the healing tonic is kept. Put me down, Blue. She can help me."

Winger jerked her head toward Kiera, who dashed to Winger's side and helped her out of Blue's arms. She kept her upright, holding on as Winger leaned into her.

"Winger?" Blue asked.

His eyes flicked to Kiera, then over his shoulder, down the long hallway where dust motes floated in straining bands of light. But his attention fell again on Winger when he turned back.

"Go find out what's happened, Blue," Winger answered, in a tone that brooked no argument. "We don't have time to screw around. You need to find the Four, because they have some damned explaining to do."

Blue and Winger nodded to each other, a conversation spoken in a glance.

Kiera's chest ached and a pain long-forgotten emerged. She jerked her head away. For as long as she could remember, she had been an outcast. Unpopular and awkward, the butt of every joke. It didn't take long for the kids at school to figure out she was different, especially when she didn't know that Jiminy was just her imagination, something no one else had, something she shouldn't respond to aloud, at least where people could hear.

She had convinced herself long ago that what others thought

didn't matter. But the longing within her chest refused to go out. Smoldering burst into flames seeing a connection between these two strangers. Just once, she wanted to find a connection, a true connection. One that wasn't conditional. One that didn't turn into betrayal. One that didn't have secret tears that tried to be hidden in the middle of the night.

Always feeling alone had a way of pulling her apart. Being able to trust someone with her very life... She couldn't even imagine how that might feel.

She shook her head, trying to keep the melancholy from taking hold.

She would help save Winger from more pain, whether she was one of them or not.

Kiera followed Winger's directions through abandoned hallways, as the woman rested heavily on her shoulder.

When they had taken more turns than Kiera had been able to keep up with in her head, she found herself standing in a small room with an unexpectedly low ceiling. It was the first small thing Kiera had seen since sailing through the shell of this place. It couldn't have been more than a three-by-three room, with a solid, stark white paint job and shelves that lined three of the four walls. In the center was a thin, narrow bed, the bedding atop as white as the walls around them. In truth, it reminded her of a doctor's office back home, sterile and impersonal.

Back on Earth, Jiminy corrected.

"What's the difference?" she muttered.

"What's that?" Winger strained in a half-whisper, gasping for breath to force the words out.

"Nothing, sorry."

"I just..." Winger sat on the edge of the bed, "I need to rest a moment first."

Kiera stood beside Winger and faced the fourth wall, the one not lined with shelves. The one that wasn't an actual wall at all. It was a constant movement of flowing water. The bubbling could have lulled Kiera into believing she was down at the creek, near the waterfall at the edge of Aunt Em's property. Except her eyes were open and they were mesmerized by the alien site.

The wall was a crisp blue that Kiera associated with tropical islands. She traced the path of individual drops of water as they flowed upwards, culminating in a froth of white at the corner of the roof.

"Blue's right, ya know." Winger took a deep breath and winced in pain. "You are definitely one of us."

"How can I be one of you when I don't even know who you all are or what you do?"

"You want a history lesson? Okay." Winger nodded. The breathiness in her voice had lessened, but it wasn't as strong as Kiera could imagine it would be when the woman was healthy again. "Here goes.

"The world's been here far longer than you humans think. And back then it was dark and terrible, Skyans were slaves to the monsters of the skies."

"The dragons?" Kiera asked.

"Some think so." Winger nodded, a smile that didn't look happy touching her lips. "But there were others. History says there was one creature, the original Guardians, who stood with the Skyans against the others and gave them the gifts we have today."

"What gifts are those?"

"Crystals."

"Crystals?" Kiera laughed and raised her eyebrows. Images of old women with long hair, tie-dyed dresses and large rings flashed through her mind.

"Yeah, crystals. You gonna keep interrupting?"

"Sorry."

Kiera gave her best 'I'm annoying but adorable' smile. Winger nodded.

"The crystals were given to the Skyans to pull them out of slavery, on the condition we used the powers to also protect the humans on Earth. It was an easy enough deal to make, and so our elders made it.

"There were twelve crystals given to the Skyans by the Guardians. Six were given to the leaders of the Skyan tribes. They were pressed into their bodies and passed down through their bloodlines. The full crystals give powers of longevity and strength. Each individual who receives the full crystal may also have gifts unique to themselves. Those six became the elders of our people, the first of our Guardians, named after the creatures who gave them the gift. Over time, they dwindled to four, and became 'the Four'. The strongest of our people. The other six crystals were smashed, and the slivers used to help fight our battle with the beasties, to keep both Skyans and humans safe. They were also used to help all Skyans find a way to stay within the clouds, and find a life beyond slavery."

Kiera let the words float around in her head. Truth rang within them, though it was easy to see she had been given an extremely brief outline of a people who used magic crystals to survive and fight beasties.

Winger pulled Kiera away from her thoughts. "Take me to the upfall."

She nodded, remembering again why she was there, and shuffled forward. With each step, Winger leaned heavier on her shoulder. They drew closer, the energy was insects crawling over and beneath her skin. Kiera's breath shortened and her hands trembled.

Stop! You can't get closer.

Winger's fingers gripped Kiera's shoulder. Kiera winced as nails pierced her skin. "Stay with me, kid."

Stop, K. Don't let her near the upfall.

The insistence in Jiminy's voice scratched at Kiera and made her falter in her step.

"What do I do?" Kiera asked.

"Nothing, I'll do the rest," Winger replied, as though the question were to her. She stepped away from Kiera, moving closer to the upfall.

Please, K. Stop her, NOW! Jiminy screamed.

Kiera bit her lip. Her conscience was never kind. Had never *been* kind. She hadn't known it even knew the word 'please'. Reaching out, Kiera's fingers wrapped around Winger's wrist, her heart thudding in her chest. Winger didn't turn or acknowledge the touch.

She held on while a kaleidoscope of colors fizzed around Winger's arm as it pushed through the upfall.

"Winger?" Kiera's voice echoed loud around the small room.

Not even a flinch.

"Winger!"

Kiera began to pull the woman back. Her conscience was some weird level of crazy, but she knew, that voice inside of her knew, this was not right. Something about this was all kinds of wrong.

"I'm okay."

Winger blinked and pulled her arm out of Kiera's grip as she drew her other arm back from the upfall. Her fingers were blue and shriveled like she had soaked in an ice-cold bath for too long. They were wrapped around a small, blue vial.

"I got it." Winger's voice was choked as though she held back tears.

Kiera sighed, her shoulders relaxing, but the relief was short lived.

Too late.

"What? Too late for what? What the hell do I do?"

Winger ignored the question, if she even heard it at all, which was something Kiera wasn't certain of. "I don't know what happened here."

She stumbled. Kiera moved faster than she knew she was capable of, catching Winger in her arms. She gripped Kiera's bare arms, falling into her embrace and pressing her fingers, along with the bottle, against Kiera's skin.

The cold she had felt before was like a summer's day compared to that touch. For a moment, Kiera wondered if the bottle would peel her skin away with it. It reminded Kiera of the time she got freeze burn while defrosting the freezer.

"Blue isn't all he seems."

Winger pulled away, standing on her own once more. Kiera was relieved for the distance of fingers and bottle, and sighed when her skin remained intact.

"I'm sure he's a fluffy, cuddly bear."

"Ha," Winger's laugh stopped when a cough took over. With a deep breath that sounded as painful as the expression on her face morphed into, she continued. "He has been good to me, but you need to be careful. I had to help him. Once I knew, I couldn't just forget about it. It's our job to make it right, not to let it all keep going, no matter the cost. But I didn't do enough."

Her words came out in a rush, though her eyes bored into Kiera, demanding she pay attention, and take her words seriously.

"Okay, I'll remember, Winger." Kiera smiled, but she couldn't quite keep it on her lips. Her eyebrows knitted together. "Everything will be alright. You have the healing tonic now. You will heal, you will feel better, and you can tell Blue anything you need to."

"Promise me you will remember to be careful, to look deeper," Winger begged, drawing Kiera again to the panic that seemed to dance in the strange woman's eyes.

"Yes, okay." Kiera would have promised Winger a kidney to stop the woman talking with an intensity that made her skin crawl. "I promise, I'll remember."

"And remember me? I just want someone to remember me."

She pressed a leather band into Kiera's hand while her eyes moved from Kiera's and narrowed in on the closed door of the small room.

When did the door close? Had Winger closed it when they came in?

Stop her, you idiot.

That was more like the voice she had always known. But once again, Kiera was too late. Before she could grab the vial, Winger unstoppered it and tipped it to her mouth. The closed door slammed open like a wild animal had crashed into it. Splinters of wood cascaded around her as Blue barged into the room.

"No!" Blue's voice was guttural as he leapt toward Winger, knocking the vial to the ground. The glass shattered on impact. Yellow vapor rose from the shattered remains.

Winger collapsed back onto the bed, eyes rolling up toward the ceiling.

"What the hell ya done? Ya just killed her!"

"I... I didn't kill her!" Kiera felt the tears prick her eyes and slide over her cheeks. "We came for medicine! You said to get her medicine, and that's what I did!"

But you knew. You knew I was right.

The voice wasn't accusing; it was simply stating a fact. Kiera even detected a resigned shoulder shrug in the words it didn't say.

"How stupid can ya be?"

"I'm not stupid. Winger told me what she needed me to do. You left us to look for it. How was I supposed to know this wasn't what she was supposed to be going? It was supposed to heal her."

"Heal her?"

Blue threw up his hands and turned around as though unable to look at Kiera any longer. For a moment, the silence in the room was broken only by the soft trickle of the upfall.

Kiera's legs could no longer hold her up and she crumpled to the ground, turning her head away from the blank, open-eyed stare of Winger.

"Dinna ya see what it did just by touching it? Dinna ya feel all the warnings telling you to back away?" He turned back to her, looking down and shaking his head. His words had lost the volume and strength, but not the disappointment. "Is that why they grounded ya? Because ya got no bloody sense?"

"No, I escaped."

Kiera stared up at the man looming over her, hands covering her mouth. She sat back on her ankles. She blinked and let the tears slip from her eyes as she watched Blue shake Winger gently. Her body flopped back and forth.

"You silly kid, there's nothing we couldn't have worked out."

Blue's words were interspersed with sniffles as his shoulders shook and he dropped to his knees. The sobbing echoed around the room and guilt lodged in Kiera's chest while bile rose in her throat.

Before she could force the nausea down, the contents of her stomach splashed on to the stone beside her. On hands and knees, she vomited until she was dry heaving, her nose running and sobs tightening her chest until it ached and burned.

Her breath was a gasp and a shudder. There was adventure and then there was this crazy shit.

The hand was a hot touch on her back.

"Up ya get, girl. We gotta get out of here before anyone finds us."

From the corner of her eye, she saw Winger's still body and swallowed down the urge to start retching all over again.

"I'm so sorry, Blue," she blubbered, still on the floor. "I'm so sorry.

I didn't know. I didn't know it would kill her. I didn't mean to kill her."

"We gotta get going." He sounded more like the Blue she had known so far, not the sad, broken voice of a man who had lost a friend.

Kiera met his eyes. "I didn't kill her, Blue."

"I know, kid." His voice was a gentle balm, but his fingers dug into her arm as he pulled her away from the upfall, the room, and Winger's corpse.

He led her through the warren of turns and dropped her arm only when they were back in the main hallway where they had originally separated.

She turned right, feet taking her in a direction she had not thought about.

"Whatcha doing?"

"I, um..."

She could have sworn that was where she needed to go. But as she looked down the hall, several more closed doors leading off the long corridor, she saw it ended with floor-to-ceiling double doors. Not the way out. She still wanted to go that way, wanted to push open those doors and reveal the world within. That hook behind her bellybutton pulled her toward them.

Blue's hand gripped her arm again and pulled her away from those beckoning doors. "Hurry up."

Their feet crunched in a tattoo on debris as they stepped out of the building. On the way in, she had been too busy trying to keep up to notice that the ground was littered with paper and leaves, small beads, and broken glass.

It's a ghost town.

Kiera shuddered as she shook off Blue's grip.

Blue slowed and their eyes met. After a quick shrug and shake of his head, he turned and continued silently toward the ship. It stood where they left it, filling up the gravel road that separated the buildings on each side.

Kiera wanted to look away, explore more than the one building in a city that shouldn't exist. Instead, she followed in Blue's wake.

CHAPTER 8

"Blue."

The voice was high-pitched and stern, as similar to Blue's as it was different.

Blue slowed his steps and, with one hand, pulled Kiera behind him, wrapping the other around the handle of his sword. They stood halfway between the building to their right and the ship to their left.

Blue turned and Kiera followed suit. She stared into the face of a wraith-looking man with dark, sunken eyes. His clothes were a parody of Blue's, everything faded and baggy, with several darned patches and loose threads searching for escape. Pants and boots, a long-sleeved shirt with tattered cuffs and wet, blood-colored stains that made Kiera swallow thickly.

"Jayson." Blue barked. "Are you responsible for this? What ya done this time? Where are they?"

"What have *I* done?" Jayson scoffed and shook his head. "What have *you* done, Blue? Where's Winger?"

"The Four, Jayson. Where are the Four?"

Blue spoke slowly as he took a small step, arms out in front of him. It reminded Kiera of Aunt Em when she would approach a spooked horse.

"Oh dear. How careless. Have you gone and lost your own leaders now?" Jayson tut-tutted. "But I guess it's to be expected. You never have been good at holding on to much have you, Guardian?"

Blue's hand returned to the hilt of his sword. "I will ask you one more time—"

"I haven't touched your precious leaders," Jayson snapped, cutting Blue off with a wave of his hand, as though the anger wasn't present in his voice. Then he jerked his chin toward Kiera. "Who's your new pet?"

"Pet?" Kiera asked, as she stepped out from behind Blue, hands on hips and eyes narrowed at the man throwing the insults.

"Ohh, she's a feisty one." Jayson's chuckle almost made Kiera want to scurry back behind Blue. Almost. She couldn't pinpoint exactly what it was about the laugh, but it felt like bugs crawling on her skin. "Even if she does look like a breeze could blow her over."

"Who the hell are you?" Kiera snapped, ignoring Blue's growl beside her.

"Oh." Jayson looked to Blue and then back to Kiera. His eyes narrowed for a moment on her before he bent forward in an overdramatic bow. "I am Jayson. A Skyan kicked out of the Guardians for daring to have my own mind." Standing back up, he returned his attention to Blue. "The Four are wherever they want to be, doing whatever they want to do. Just as they always have."

"The Four are the only reason you are still walking around a free Skyan. You will show them some respect."

"Respect is earned. You taught me that." Jayson spat out the words. "The only lesson you taught me that was worth keeping. You're a fool, still following rules that mean nothing. Even after they demoted you and used you as an example of what not to be."

Blue's words pushed through clenched teeth. "Give me one reason not to take you in chains right now, Jayson."

"I'll give you a few."

Jayson gave Kiera a wink. For a moment, his eyes narrowed before the cocky half-grin lit up his face once more. Behind the buildings came others, similarly dressed as Jayson; all rattier versions of Blue's crisp lines and sharp colors.

"Still can't fight your own battles, Jayson? I *will* find out what you've done."

"Your time is over, Blue. It's time for you and those old bastards to finally realize it."

Jayson opened his jacket and showed a bright badge beneath.

Kiera couldn't quite see what the badge was, except that it glinted. A bubble of amusement rose in her chest. The badge looked like some prop from an old western movie.

She turned to Blue, and the amusement died on her lips. Blue's face was frozen in a mask of anger, his cheeks reddened, his hands curled into fists by his sides.

"Now piss off. We have an investigation to do." Jayson tilted his head before leading the way for the group to head inside the building Kiera and Blue had just exited.

Blue waited until Jayson was out of view before taking the last few steps to his ship.

"Hurry up!" he snapped over his shoulder, as he got back on board and started playing the silent music again on the black pillar.

Kiera's mind swarmed. She tucked the bracelet Winger had given her into one of her pants pockets. She would remember her only for how she died. It was a sad thought, but it was one Kiera would never forget.

The air outside of the ship darkened, as though clouds were being drawn to them, wrapping them up in a deep blue swirl of color.

"Are they investigating Winger's death? Is that what that was about? I didn't kill her. You know that, right?" The words slipped out again, tears leaking from her eyes along with them.

"She did what she thought she had to. It weren't ya fault, but hells, didn't ya feel the dangers? No Guardian could be this ignorant."

"I'm not a Guardian. She said—"

"What? What did she say?"

Blue came back to where Kiera stood, towering over her. She felt her body heat at the attempted intimidation. She stood straighter and narrowed her eyes at the burly pirate. Her inner fire sparked to life.

"I didn't kill anyone. I'm not responsible for whatever shit you have got going on up here. I don't care about you or Jayson or the goddamned Four, whoever the hell they are. None of this has anything to do with me, and I don't want it to. Just take me back." She lowered her voice, stunned by the words that tasted liked ashes on her tongue. "Take me home."

The words were lead in her stomach, but the image of Aunt Em panicking rose to the forefront of her mind, and guilt smothered her fire. She had to go back.

Do you, now?

Blue's smile made Kiera want to slap him. "There's the Guardian."

"I'm not a bloody Guardian," Kiera snapped.

Blue scoffed and headed back to the helm.

"Gotta take care of the dragon before she does any more damage landside. Then we'll see."

Kiera let out a long breath and dropped her shoulders. The relief washed over her like the foam of a wave caressing sand. She wasn't a Guardian, so why was she so relieved that he hadn't called her bluff and taken her back?

Why indeed?

"Shut up."

The voice in her head laughed. *Haven't you figured it out yet? Really, it's about time you finally started listening to me.*

"I've always listened to you; I never had a choice. You're the one who's never bothered to answer any of the questions I've actually wanted answered."

Kiera closed her eyes. She had always feared being found out as crazy. She also knew insanity might be the easier option. Easier, but also dead wrong.

"Who you talkin' to?" Blue asked.

Kiera jumped, opened her eyes and found Blue's cocked head two feet away from her.

"No one," she muttered, and stepped away from the rail she had been resting against. "Are things always so dangerous up here?"

You can't hide that smile from me.

Blue walked back to the helm, looking over his shoulder and waiting for her to join him. He watched as she tried not to stumble across the deck.

"Things are changing. The Void's growing stronger. Used to be we'd see one every few years. Now it's every few weeks. Soon, it'll be daily. Guardians have been disappearing for months, but I ain't high enough in the food chain to know what's been happenin' with that. I didn't know Jayson had been brought back to the Guardians, and as a bloody investigator at that."

"What did he do?" Kiera asked.

"He's got too much rage and anger. He enjoys the killin' a little too much."

"You trained him?"

"What makes ya say that?"

"You taught him respect must be earned?" Kiera shrugged, trying to put pieces together when she only had a handful of a much larger picture.

"I don't know what's been happening here. Been away for too long. And now those who would, the Four, are missing." Blue snorted. Kiera wondered if maybe this was the longest speech he had made for a while, perhaps ever. "So, who are ya, girl?"

Kiera laughed and shook her head. "Now you bother to ask?"

"Don't answer then. But I won't have risks on me ship."

"So, you're going to tip me overboard?" The threat didn't ice her veins as she had expected it to.

"Tempting, but no. Once we deal with the dragon, we find me daughter. She always seems to know more'n me."

Kiera laughed. "Surely not."

Blue looked as though he were debating a smile, but then his lips turned down again in his usual frown.

"How do we track the dragon?" Kiera asked.

"I track the dragon; you don't need to worry about it. But while we wait, we go through the basics."

"Okay?"

Kiera fought the desire to ask more and nodded, wondering what would be considered the basics. An old pirate song came to mind, sung in the voices of small children laughing, with no understanding what a rusty razor could actually do to a belly.

Blue jerked his head toward the helm. "Come on."

"Where?"

"Always handy to have more than one skilled to guide a ship. Never know when you might need it. Place your hands on the pillar."

Kiera didn't reach forward. Instead, she swayed slightly to the rhythm of the pulsing veins of light. "What's it made of?"

"Obsidian," Blue answered.

Kiera smiled as the answer came easily to her mouth. "Dragon Glass."

Blue looked at her like she had sprouted three heads.

"That's what they call it on earth." She shrugged. "At least in all the fantasy shows."

Intrigued by the hum, she took another step toward the pillar.

"Bloody humans," Blue muttered. "Go on then."

The moment her hands touched the top, pain screamed inside her head. She fell back, landing hard on the deck, head pounding as though a storm-ravaged sea was bashing itself against a wall of rock.

Blue offered a hand and helped her to a sitting position.

"Have a drink." He pulled a small flask from his pocket and handed it to her. Taking a big swig, the warm liquid slid down her throat, taking with it most of the pain that roared inside her head.

She handed the flask back, her breath still coming too fast. "What was that?"

The silence lingered and she looked at Blue. He avoided her eyes.

"It shouldn't have done that." He scratched his beard before taking a swig of the flask and shoving it back into his coat. "I'm sorry."

"What happened?"

"I'm not entirely sure what happened to ya, girl, but we gotta get outta the city first." He placed a big hand on her shoulder and squeezed, as though trying to comfort her.

She didn't move as she watched him place his hands back on the pillar, slower than he had last time. While they pushed their way back out of the transparent enclosure, Kiera's head swarmed.

Jiminy popped up with his two cents. *Well, that was interesting.*

"What the hell was that, Jiminy?"

The voice in her head didn't answer as the ship took back to the undulating sea of clouds.

CHAPTER 9

Kiera could no longer see the Guardian Headquarters behind them when Blue left his position at the helm and called her over to where Winger had lain, poisoned and broken.

"You'll need to get used to wielding her blade. Shouldn't take ya long, seein' as you're a Guardian."

"I'm not a Guardian," she insisted, drawing Winger's sword and taking a few practice swings in the air. "What I am is a champion fencer, and a great basketball player."

"Yeah, yeah. Time to show me what you're made of."

Blue smiled, though there was something in his eye that Kiera didn't like. Had it always been there? She had no idea; she hadn't exactly had the luxury of stopping to truly examine the man. And right now wasn't the time either.

The sword felt good in her hands, and she was eager to let her muscles take over from her thoughts.

Hours later, sweat dripped down her back and the smile wouldn't fade from her lips. The only interruptions to their swordplay had been a few small breaks where she caught her breath and Blue played the pedestal. Each time she saw Blue touch it, Kiera shuddered at the memory of the searing pain, fearing it's return.

Her breath caught and his checking done, they continued to

dance around the deck. She took each instruction to heart and felt her cheeks warm when he nodded approval and called her a quick study.

What a sight they must have made, a woman with cropped brown hair, and a half-bald head holding her own against a man who really would look more complete if he had a peg leg and a parrot on his shoulder. The ring of metal on metal sounded like thunder calling to the horizon.

"Alright. Not as hesitant as I feared."

Kiera felt her chest warm and puff at the compliment. She found she liked the bloody pirate, for his gruffness as much as for his praise.

"I'm an adrenaline junkie. What did you expect?"

"You're a Guar—" Blue's words were cut off by a sharp jolt of the deck. "She's found us."

"She?" Kiera asked, her voice higher than normal.

"The dragon."

Her heart raced a little harder, and her breath was audible to her ears. "What? The dragon found us? How?"

"Hold on to something. We're heading back down."

Kiera growled at Blue's evasiveness and pulled herself along the rail of the ship until she found another crate. Her legs collapsed as she sat heavily on the makeshift seat, hands white-knuckled on the railing as she watched Blue alternating between the wheel and the pillar. The dark dust surrounded the ship again, blocking out the travel back to Earth.

Another bump came from the bottom of the ship as the sound of thunder surrounded them. Rain joined the cacophony of noise as Kiera's feet left the boards of the deck and she gave a small yelp.

"I thought we were tracking her?" Kiera asked over the noises of chaos surrounding her. "How did she find us?"

"We led her here."

"How?"

"The sound of swords," Blue answered. "You think all the fighting was just to alleviate the boredom? I invited her."

Kiera's chest heated at the stupidity of her previous reaction to Blue's praise. It was all about the dragon, not her at all.

The dust that still surrounded the ship didn't fade; it simply snapped out of existence, like the click of a finger. For a moment, she forgot about the dragon, the pain in her clenched fingers, and the absurdity of this entire day. Had it only been one day?

She shook her head and focused on the world they now sailed above. It was her city; she knew this view like the back of her hand. In her bedroom was a painted canvas of a photo she had taken on her one and only hot air balloon ride. It was an experience, but so slow that the adrenaline Kiera had hoped for never appeared.

In the distance, she could see her house. She traced the path from her home to where they were. Leaning over the railing, she saw the tops of trees, a forest that had no place being there.

"Blue, what the hell?" Kiera asked, after another bump from beneath lifted her feet from the boards of the deck.

"What?" Blue called back.

"Is that a forest? There isn't a forest here. I've walked through here more times than I can count. There isn't a bloody forest here."

"Course there is. You can see the thing."

"But how?"

"The world's a lot bigger than humans see. The magic keeps the forests and the creatures within it safe. Dragon's nest is probably in this one."

"They live on Earth?" Kiera felt her mouth go dry at the mere idea of it.

"Course they do. Where else would they live?"

Kiera had no answer for this. Instead, she found herself fixed on the tops of the trees as they drew closer to them.

There are forests on Earth where dragons live. She repeated the words in her mind over and over.

You're finally waking up child.

"Waking up?"

To the real world. And to me. Go back to the clouds, and I'll tell you everything. It's harder for me to reach you down here.

"Tell me now," Kiera begged, as the she strained to hear what the voice was saying. It was as though they were now at different ends of a tunnel, too far for the echo to reach her.

"If her nest is here..." Blue's voice snapped her out of her own head as he stomped over to where she stood. "...she'll follow us down."

"Do all the beasties live in the forests?"

"Don't be daft. Some of 'em live in the graveyards, and others perch in the mountains."

"Oh." Kiera blinked. What the hell was she supposed to say to that? She wanted to know about every single beastie that went bump in the night, while simultaneously wishing she didn't know about any of it.

You don't believe that. This is the best adventure you've ever had.

"Shut up."

But Jiminy was right, and Kiera knew it.

Motion and movement were all around her and she planted her feet, trying to ignore the sway of the deck beneath her boots. A smile split her face and her heart raced in her chest. Blue whistled between two fingers and Kiera laughed as the deck shuddered beneath them once again.

"Bloody dragon." Blue raised his sword, and nodded down at Kiera's sword hand. "Get ready."

"Get ready?" Kiera followed Blue's gesture and found Winger's blade already in her grip. It had felt like an extension of herself rather than something she'd taken hold of. "Ready for what, Blue?"

He didn't answer. Instead, Blue stalked to the far end of the ship, turned and raced the length of it. He barely slowed as he reached the tip and jumped overboard. Kiera gasped and moved from her place along the ship's side, stopping at the railing where Blue had leapt out into the open air. Her sword down by her side, she gripped the railing and looked down.

Beneath her, she saw Blue, still running. Beneath his feet was the willow tree dragon's back. The dragon's head was hidden somewhere beneath the ship, while a long tail swished back and forth. As Blue ran, his sword slashed to the right and left, slicing through the ridges she had noticed when she last came this close to the dragon. It's back lurched against the bottom of the ship once more.

Kiera jerked forward, almost over the railing, though her eyes remained fixed on Blue as he stepped onto the thick ropy tail of the dragon.

Blue raised the sword and swiftly brought it down into the flesh of the tail. It flicked up, and then he was flying past the ship, up into the air. Kiera followed his path, turning as he flew over her and landed, rolling back onto the deck.

A screech came from below and Kiera flicked around again, to see the dragon shrinking fast, heading down toward the forest.

"Now the fun begins," Blue laughed.

Kiera smiled, more from the surprise that Blue actually knew how to laugh. "The fun?"

Blue gave Kiera a crazy-eyed look, sword in hand as he stood legs apart in true pirate fashion. Kiera had to bite her lower lip to keep from laughing. There was a dragon; there was danger. She could feel it on the air like a mist of rain blowing in from the sea, but still she wanted to laugh.

If only he had that peg leg and parrot.

A laugh slipped out and Blue looked back.

"That's the spirit, girl. Gotta enjoy the hunt."

His words both relieved Kiera and sent a chill of horror tiptoeing up her spine.

He whistled again and they drew closer to the ground as they reached the edge of the forest. The tips of the trees passed by, and Kiera breathed deep of the fresh scent of crushed leaves and rain-soaked earth. As they crept forward, more of the trees became visible over the railing. The deck shuddered as the hull brushed along the ground.

"Wait." Blue disappeared into the cabin and returned with that jacket again, the one so similar to his own. "Put it on. And stay close."

Kiera laid the sword down on the small cot and slipped the jacket on over her singlet. It was warm, but a little too long in all ways, brushing the backs of her ankles and hiding all but the very tips of her fingers.

Blue nodded. "This is your responsibility now."

He threw her a green canvass backpack. It reminded Kiera of something you might find in an old army surplus store.

"What is it?"

"It's a bag."

"For what?"

"Supplies. You never went camping in your life on Earth?"

"Not really, no. I get enough of nature on the farm."

She knew she sounded petulant, but she thought she was handling her world being turned upside down pretty well. Even so, she slipped the bag straps over her shoulder.

"It's medical supplies. Never get off the ship without it."

"We didn't have it when we went on the other ship, or at the egg city," Kiera said.

"Egg city?" Blue scoffed and shook his head. "We were lucky we didn't need it then; I'm not taking any more chances."

Kiera rolled her eyes. The pirate had a bloody answer for everything. Nevertheless, she followed him over the railing.

CHAPTER 10

Light struggled through the thick branches and leaves as they pushed their way forward. Kiera's thighs itched as she struggled to keep up with Blue's pace. It was only now she realized why her fingers felt naked; she'd been absently opening and closing them as she followed through the dense forest. The sword was still on the bed aboard the ship.

It was too late to go back up and get it. She pushed down the gnawing in her stomach at the missing extension of her arm as she struggled to keep Blue in sight. She followed, her fingers tapping in increasing speed against her thigh, the alternative to playing 'open-shut them'.

Slipping her hand into her pants pocket, a surprising warmth of security washed over her as she found Winger's bracelet.

The rain followed them into the forest, and it didn't take her long to appreciate the light brown coat. Not just for protection against the rain, but also from the branches and debris that jutted out onto the path, as though warning her against going forward.

As the light dimmed further, she wrinkled her nose against the stench of rotten underbrush and damp animal scat. Broken branches hung limply from their trunks. Every now and then, Blue would stop and point out an indentation in the dirt or a scrape of bark from a tree trunk. He would point until Kiera looked and nodded.

She opened her mouth and was quickly met with a glare, a shake of his head, and a finger pressed to closed lips. She nodded again, this time biting the inside of her cheek from the laugh threatening to escape.

I'm following an old pirate into a forest that doesn't exist, to track down a dragon who looks like a tree trunk. The true definition of sanity.

But she continued to follow.

Soon enough, Kiera noticed the indicators of the dragon's passage before Blue pointed them out. She continued to look and nod at his direction.

I'm home. I can find Aunt Em. The thoughts came unbidden. *I can keep us safe.*

But the word was unfamiliar. Safe? Against dragons she could suddenly see? Distracted by her thoughts, she didn't see the twig protruding into her path. It gouged at her cheek, and she hissed out a curse.

Blue looked back with raised eyebrows. She touched her fingers to her cheek; they came away bloody. He nodded and indicated to her back, where the backpack had been a warm and reassuring pressure on her back.

Kiera nodded, but wasn't going to stop just because there was a little blood. She could use the medical supplies later. If there was a later.

Their pace increased again. Feeling the stab of a stitch in her side, she pressed her hand against her ribs and forced herself onward. Blue's soft footfalls upon soggy leaves boomed in Kiera's ears. He disappeared around a bend and her legs chose that moment to stop following instructions.

She looked around. The forest was from some kind of dream. No, not some kind of dream; one of her very own dreams. Nightmares. The ones that came only during the storms.

A rubber band tightened around Kiera's chest, and she failed to take in deep enough breaths. Trunks thicker than her body surrounded her, branches sticking out like accusing fingers.

"No, no no..." she whispered, and tried to focus on the drops of rain that slipped through the canopy of the forest and dropped down near her feet.

The familiar wet sound began to lull her back from the edge. But there, on the edge, drops were falling with an unfamiliar sound, not quite metal, not quite glass. She opened her eyes, one at a time, and looked around, searching beyond the closest trees. It was shiny, similar to the pillar aboard Blue's ship.

Her feet obeyed, reluctantly, and she made her way toward the light. As she moved, the light flickered, a flashing morse code in and out between the trunks.

A low hum, like static, only not so damned annoying, buzzed in her mind. She took another step. The pull was physical.

Another step.

"Oh."

Everything around her stopped, or so it seemed. The static in her mind overtook the noises of animals and wind. No longer could she hear the rain, and if Blue noticed her absence and called out, she didn't hear it.

In front of her lay a nest of straw and bone cradling a mottled egg. She had never seen its equal. It shone with more beauty than the pillar on Blue's ship, veined as it was in deep, red ribbons on a slick, black background. It was dwarfed by the size of the nest, but that couldn't minimize the egg's beauty.

She smiled at this lone egg. Had it been left behind, not as big as the others? She guessed so, if the depressions in the nest surrounding it were any indication. Kiera felt the scoff of noise as it bubbled at the back of her throat. She was aware of how it felt to be smaller than the rest.

Step away.

The voice was hard and strong. She hadn't realized how much softer it had been, before stepping onto Blue's ship. It hadn't become the annoying background hiss she had always known, but now it sounded downright angry rather than snarky or annoyed.

The pull of the egg was still stronger.

"No."

She wouldn't have stopped herself from drawing closer, hand reaching to touch the shell, even if she had that power.

Touch it, and there is no turning back, no going home. No more Aunt Em.

Her hand flinched, but she couldn't stop. The adventure of a lifetime beckoned her.

There was a disconnect between thought and action. Her mind swirled with the beauty, while her hands cradled the egg into her arms. Despite how small it looked in the straw and bone nest, Kiera couldn't cover the egg with both hands combined. It was larger than a football, though not by much.

Put it down, please.

Was Jiminy sobbing?

Boom! Boom!

The earth shook, saving Kiera from arguing. Quickly, she tucked the egg inside the canvas bag, nudging it as carefully as she could between bandages and gauze before slipping the straps back over her shoulders. She raced toward where Blue had disappeared.

Boom! Boom!

Slamming her hand against the nearest trunk to keep herself steady, Kiera came on a scene that stole her breath even more than the discovery of the egg.

"Come on now!"

Blue raised both arms and reached his left hand out to the large, green dragon. His sword wasn't in his hand, or his scabbard. Kiera scanned the surroundings. It was three trees from where she hid. She could reach it, so long as the dragon kept her attention on Blue.

His fingers were only inches from the dragon's snout when the large head shook back and forth, reminding Kiera of a horse still needing to be broken.

"Eeeasy, me girl. It's okay."

Blue's voice caressed the air, and for a moment Kiera forgot what her plan had been, the sound so strange from the gruff pirate.

She blinked, refocused and moved, as softly as her boots allowed, to where Blue's blade lay. It was only half a foot away.

Blue's fingers touched the thorn at the tip of the dragon's nose and his shoulders lowered, relaxing. Kiera smiled as she crouched. Her fingers reaching out while her attention remained focused on the place where human met myth. She could almost feel the heat, though she had no way of knowing it would be hot. Her fingers wrapped around the handle.

The dragon's head dropped and pushed forward; a breath escaped the beastie's open jaws.

"That's a good girl. It's time you have a rest."

Suddenly, the dragon looked up and headbutted Blue in the middle of his chest with enough force that he flew back, thin droplets of blood following in his wake.

"No!" Kiera screamed.

The dragon's head turned and pinned Kiera with those big, black eyes. Its jaws opened.

The scream pierced through Kiera's body. Her ears buzzed, dizziness washing over her for a moment. The dragon's jaw opened again, but this time the scream that followed was dulled, muffled as though trying to pass through a brick wall.

She cocked her head, anger and adrenaline rushing through her limbs, her chest moving faster in and out. She ran, before thoughts could turn her immobile. Her soundless footsteps gave the sensation someone else had taken control of her limbs, of her body. It didn't matter.

There was no time. There was no space for thinking.

Her throat burned as she opened her mouth. There was no sound but for a ringing agony in her ears. Her arm came down on the dragon's thorn, splitting the beast's nose and mouth down the middle. The sword vibrated in her grip, her fingers tingling as though blood had been deprived and was now rushing back into them.

Fire from the dragon's broken mouth raced above Kiera head. The heat made her hair curl and memories of sleeping too close to the campfire raced through her mind as her steps continued to fall silently. She scaled up a front leg of the dragon.

It wasn't so different to an extreme run really.

Her hand rose again and came down, just as she had seen Blue fight this very dragon's tail. The point of the sword pierced the back of the dragon's neck. Kiera ignored the fizzing sensation that increased in her hands as the dragon writhed beneath her feet. She held her footing as long as she could.

Before she could be thrown backwards, she rolled sideways, back down the leg, hoping the ground would be more forgiving. The sword dropped beside her as rocks and dirt slammed into her side, pushing the last of the adrenaline from her.

So much for a graceful landing.

She gasped, a rush of cold tingling up her arms as her breathing remained silent in her ears. The light dimmed further and faster. She lay, rocks digging into her hip and shoulder, copper joining the smell of rotten underbrush.

Blue's face appeared above her. It was red beside the tiki torch he held up, his mouth opening and closing over and over again.

Soundless darkness swallowed her.

CHAPTER 11

Kiera came to consciousness like a truck slamming into a wall. There was a buzzing, worse than any silence, that vibrated uncomfortably inside her ear. Cold air chilled her mouth and down her throat as she gulped it in. The dull light was still too bright as Kiera blinked a few times, adjusting to the unfamiliar room around her.

A woman stood next to her, leaning over as she opened a small jar and dipped in a long, slender finger. Sharp features were surrounded by purple, shoulder-length hair, almost dirty-looking in the darker shades and most certainly dyed from a much lighter color. A natural blonde, Kiera surmised from the pale eyebrows, grateful for the distraction to the pain and confusion.

The woman's lips were full and a light, natural pink. She wore a simple, off-white pair of pants with a similarly colored tunic that stopped somewhere along her mid-thigh. Her bare arms were almost as pale as the clothes. Kiera found hope of a personality beyond the beauty when color from the woman's right wrist caught her eyes. She wore a chunky, multi-colored bracelet that slipped over her wrist just a little as she moved around.

Kiera flinched and hissed as the cream-covered finger poked at her forehead.

"I guess death isn't so bad after all," Kiera tried to smile, though the effort seemed beyond her reach as her throat scratched out the words. "Though it hurts a bloody lot more than I had expected."

Kiera couldn't say the woman smiled exactly, but the corners of her lips quirked as she closed the lid of the jar and met Kiera's eyes. The woman's own eyes were a pewter grey, and strands of her hair were tucked behind large ears. Noticing Kiera's gaze, the woman quickly untucked her hair, hiding her ears, and gave a small cough.

"You aren't dead." Her voice was quiet but hard. "You may wish you were, once the cream stops working."

"What is that?" Kiera nodded her head at the jar still in the woman's hand. She instantly regretted the movement as the ringing in her ears increased to a pitch just under poorly played violin strings.

"It's a numbing cream, infused with healing herbs. It smells quite beautiful." She opened the lid again and offered Kiera a smell.

"I'm okay."

Kiera smiled, then closed her eyes as the buzzing took on an even higher pitch. When Kiera opened her eyes again, the woman straightened, shoulders and back stiffened.

"Where are you hurt?"

"It's okay," Kiera said, and took in a deep breath. "What type of herbs are they?"

The woman's lips pursed together, two small lines appearing between her eyebrows. Whatever she saw in Kiera's face relaxed her own enough for her to give a small nod.

"I found the herbs years ago when my father took me to Earth to see the forests. It took me awhile to find the right combination for pain relief and numbing, but I've had very good feedback since I started using it."

"Earth," Kiera said.

"Yes."

"Where exactly am I?" Kiera asked

"You are aboard Hesperus." The woman's eyes narrowed. "You don't remember?"

Kiera shook her head slowly, scared the ringing would spike again.

"Okay," The woman placed the small jar somewhere behind Kiera's head, out of her sight, then turned back to Kiera. "Hesperus is a Healer's ship."

Kiera sighed and closed her eyes. "So, I'm back in the clouds."

"Of course. Now, you've been in and out of consciousness for two days. I would recommend only light food to begin with."

"Two days?" Kiera tried to sit up, but a sting pulled at the inside of her elbow and the woman—the doctor?—pushed her firmly but not roughly back down to the bed.

"Yes, two days. And unless you play 'nice patient', you will be here a lot longer."

The woman raised a single eyebrow. Kiera could have sworn there was a challenge, even a dare in that look, for her to go against the advice.

"Okay, Doc, but why am I back up here?"

"I am Zarzy, not Doc." Zarzy spoke with a precise coldness that belied the intrigue Kiera found in the woman. "You are here because you took on a dragon, alone and without preparation. Acting like some daredevil hero." The term was not spoken with affection or admiration.

"Well, it's not like I've been given an instruction manual."

Zarzy's head cocked to the side as she looked at Kiera. "What do you mean?"

"Well, I'm not a Guardian." She pushed the words out on a sharp sigh. She was going to go crazy if she stayed here much longer. She needed to move. And while the buzzing in her ears had decreased, below it remained a dull throb, a vibration that made her heart race and increased her desire to get up and move. "Blue told me nothing. I have had exactly one day knowing dragons exist, and at this moment, I'm pretty keen not to have any more encounters."

"You aren't a Guardian?"

"No, I'm not. Blue didn't tell you?"

"Blue has a habit of not telling people what they need to know."

Kiera laughed, and when her eyes met Zarzy's, there was a moment where the Skyan's lips twitched into something that might have been the beginning of a smile, and Kiera felt heat through her chest.

"You saw the dragon and the forest though." Zarzy's words were slow. Did she think Kiera was a moron?

"Of course I saw the dragon and the forest. They aren't exactly small..." Kiera's words petered out as she spoke. "I... I hadn't seen the forest before."

"This isn't right."

"That I can agree with."

"So, you never heard of Skyans or Guardians before you met Blue?"

Kiera shook her head and regretted it instantly. That damn dull throb was insistent.

"Humans aren't able to see the beasties, or the forests. Anything that uses the magic of the crystals, actually."

"So then, why can I?"

Kiera clenched her muscles and considered sitting up again. Sharp eyes pierced her, as though predicting her thoughts. She relaxed back into the softness beneath her.

Zarzy took a syringe off a metal tray beside Kiera's bed, quickly wiped at Kiera's arm and jammed the needle in without so much as a warning.

"Ouch."

"Hmm?" Zarzy looked up, eyebrows raised.

"Ouch." Kiera repeated and looked down pointedly to her arm where the syringe was slowly filling with blood.

"Oh yes. This may hurt."

"What are you, a goddamn robot?"

"Perhaps." Zarzy removed the needle with more gentleness than she had used when inserting it. Kiera could have sworn the corners of those lips twitched again.

"Where's Blue?"

"He's back on Zephyrus, trying to find out what happened to the Four."

"Zephyrus?"

Again, Zarzy spoke slowly. "Zephyrus is his ship."

Kiera sucked her top lip into her mouth as she tried to piece together what the hell had happened to her life. She watched as the woman opened the jar once more and dabbed the cream on other areas of Kiera's body.

Zarzy's fingers skimmed Kiera's bare shoulder as she pulled the sheet from her chest and dabbed more cream on various parts of her arm. Each touch stung, and sent jolts through Kiera's body. She was suddenly aware of her own lack of clothing; her underwear was still in place, but the singlet she wore pulled too tightly across her shoulder blades and the scratch of the sheet against her bare legs as it moved made her tense.

Someone had changed her. Someone had seen her chest and the thick rope scar that ran down the center between her breasts to her navel. Was it this frozen goddess? Would she ask, demand Kiera to relive the horror of her childhood?

Before Kiera could let her mind fill with more questions, a heaviness pulled at her eyelids.

Her words slurred in her ears. "You drugged me?"

Zarzy's words were unapologetic. "The pain has increased, you need sleep."

"I don't..."

She couldn't keep her eyes opened any longer.

Several times, Kiera half-woke, cottonwool haze surrounding her senses, and a few times voices of others came in and asked questions of Zarzy as she worked. Her answers were cold, sharp, direct. It was a relief to know she was a bitch to everyone, and Kiera hadn't made some unknown error to be inflicted with her wrath.

"So, Blue just left me here, huh?"

Her words came out slow, her tongue scratching along the roof of her mouth. She wanted to ask. She wanted to pull off that Band-Aid of waiting, for the woman to ask about her scar, for her to show disgust at the disfigurement, but the words lodged in her throat.

Maybe it was someone else who'd dressed and undressed her. The thought made her shiver in unpleasant ways. If someone had stripped her and seen her naked, she really did hope it was Zarzy.

"He'll be back."

Zarzy spoke the words in the same flat tone, but it wasn't hard to see the hardening of her lips. She came closer and helped Kiera into a sitting position. Gently, she pressed a straw to Kiera's lips. Kiera sipped, water flooding her mouth and she groaned in pleasure.

"Thank you."

Zarzy nodded. "Blue will return once his Guardian business is concluded."

"You aren't a Guardian?"

"No." Her eyes met Kiera's and there was a warning, flashes like lightning strikes in the greyness.

"Okay. At least we have that in common."

"What do we have in common?" Zarzy snapped

"Neither of us are Guardians?" Kiera hated the hesitation and quiver in her voice.

"Do you think I'm an idiot? It was the first thing I checked. I would have even without Blue's insistence and presumption that I do not know how to do my job. But you are a Guardian. Just because you were grounded, for reasons we are still trying to work out, doesn't mean you aren't still one of them."

"How would I know if you were an idiot? Right now, you're sounding pretty close to one."

Kiera had had enough of the ice, no matter how much her body reacted to the woman's attractiveness.

"Your blood shows the markers of the crystals. You are a Guardian."

"What?"

Kiera grew cold. She knew the sensation and could imagine the color draining from her extremities. Was that what stopped Zarzy's hard stare and looked closer, as though taking a swim in Kiera's eyes?

"You really didn't know you were a Guardian?" The lines appeared between Zarzy's eyebrows. "You have no memory of being one at all?"

Kiera shook her head.

"I've never heard of a Guardian losing her memory. It's such a... human thing to do." Zarzy's face softened, and Kiera could see more to like in the soft lines. "But I suppose there is always a first."

Kiera laughed and shook her head slightly, instantly regretting the movement. Pain throbbed at the back of her head, but she hadn't felt anything like it before her involuntary nap. "I haven't lost my memory."

Oh, but you do *remember something. Where exactly did you escape from, K?*

"I remember things too well, even the drag—" Kiera snapped at the voice in her head.

"Dragon?" Zarzy supplied.

"Yes." Kiera closed her eyes. She remembered the dragon. But her mind fought to connect the dots. Scenes flashed, out of order, and there was something more. After the dragon... No, before? "Argh!"

"What's wrong?"

"There's too much," Kiera said.

"Pain?"

"No." Kiera opened her eyes and stared at Zarzy. After a moment, she shook her head. Sure, that dull low throb was still there, but that wasn't what was wrong. Was it? "Not everything is about pain."

The muscles in Zarzy's jaws jumped visibly, and for a moment Kiera wondered what the woman was thinking. But it didn't matter right now. Something important came in the flashes.

"There's too much in my head. This whole world. It doesn't make sense. It's not real."

"Would that be better? To continue to live not knowing?"

Kiera opened her mouth to argue and then slammed it shut again. Did she really want to go back to Earth and continue living that life, searching for another adrenaline rush?

Sure, that's what you've been searching for, Jiminy said.

"I killed it, didn't I?"

"Yes."

Images of black and red came to Kiera's mind. The dragon's scales. No, the dragon was green, like the leaves of the trees.

"I need my stuff."

Kiera closed her eyes, fighting against the inevitable pain, and pushed her legs over the edge of the bed. When Zarzy tried to push her back down, she placed her hand over hers.

Her head pounded in her skull, and she squeezed her eyes shut.

"Please, I have to find... To find..."

"What is wrong with me? Why won't my head stop hurting?"

I told you not to touch it.

Jiminy was pissed. There was no denying that.

"It's okay," Zarzy said. "Your things are safe. A little worse for wear, what with the dragon blood and dirt all over them, but they are safe enough."

"And the egg?"

Tears pricked at Kiera's eyes. She remembered now. And here she was crying over a damn egg.

No, she was crying over killing the egg's mother.

"Shh..." Zarzy's voice was the lull of the ocean.

Kiera's eyes flashed open. Strobes of light danced in ribbons in front of her face, Zarzy staring behind them.

As Zarzy eased Kiera back down to the bed once more, she raised a single finger to her full lips, the wave of her voice joining in with the exhaustion as they washed over Kiera again.

CHAPTER 12

The Four trembled and shook. Their bluster and bravado had not lasted long at all. They were in cages, in a line pressed against one another, just as it once had been.

Or would one day be? Time slipped backwards and forwards in its mind. It was consumed by anger and darkness, new and old wrapped together, the separation less distinctive from one heated breath to the next. The desire to take what called to it, what called from their very chests.

Matriol—it was sure now, its name had once been Matriol—stood in front of the cages where it had crammed the Four. They would be the last to rule the unworthy race of Skyans.

The one in the last cage to the right was different to the other three. His essence glowed a crisp blue. Matriol stepped closer. Wisps of white tendrils filled the space within the cage.

Strange, it thought.

It sniffed, pressing its face as close to the bars as it dared. There was no lingering essence of the bloody past that dripped from the very pores of the others.

Behind Matriol, its fellow Voids hissed and called. Some begged to be released, while others would have been happy to merely witness the torture and punishment of the Skyans' leaders.

"Let us out," a voice behind Matriol begged. "We could have so much fun together."

It turned and pinned the Void who had dared to speak with a look that would have sent human and Skyan alike scurrying away.

Another of its brethren, stronger and less scared, spoke up. "But you need us."

"And how do you figure that?" Matriol asked.

"Because your past is too close to the surface, Void. But together we can be stronger, and we can take these worlds as ours once more."

Other Voids murmured in agreement.

"Please, this isn't right." Behind it, the rasping breath of one of the Four spoke. "We were once friends. You are not like the monsters in the cages."

Matriol spun and turned back to the cages that held the Four. The words had been spoken by the oldest. His name was just out of reach. Matriol shook its head; his name was inconsequential.

"Friends?" Matriol hissed.

A vicious laugh slipped from between the cracking skin of the flesh that clung to it. It had slipped into the skin of a Skyan, so constricting, but there was a familiarity to it as well.

Were the other Voids right? Was the past too close?

It smiled and slid the spear through the bars of this 'old friend'. It could fix that.

The scream from the cage filled the hull of the ship, along with the hissing laughter of the Voids. It echoed and bounced back. Each time Matriol jabbed the spear into the weak flesh, the scream started fresh, and the laughter filled it up.

It would not be long before it found a way to get what it needed, and oh how it dreamed of doing more than this to that other Guardian, the one holding its heart in his hands. The one who had started all of this.

He didn't start this, Void.

That voice. As much as Matriol despised the knowledge, it knew the leadership in this other voice.

You can hear my thoughts?

As you could hear ours, if you bothered to listen.

The fact stopped Matriol in its torture of the Skyan's flesh. It pulled the rod from within the cage and held it up, the spear a head taller than its shrunken form.

We can do so much more together.

That voice of power promised flames and blood of retribution.

My heart.

They shall all be ours again.

Matriol laughed, and the other Voids caged around it joined in.

"I want to see his insides," Matriol snarled, allowing its form to widen and expand.

Enough.

The word was joined by a searing electrical charge through Matriol's form. The spear he held fell to the deck. Another electrical charge made Matriol scream. Over it stood the very Guardian it would drink the blood and suck the marrow from the bones of.

"Speak of the devil," Matriol snarled up at the Guardian.

One hand clamped around the more powerful spear, one that would never be given willingly to Matriol; the other gripped Matriol's orange, pulsing heart.

It would do this Guardian's bidding, but neither of them were stupid enough to think the balance rested on anything thicker than a vein of a human's body.

"Enough," the Guardian spoke again.

"But I have not completed the job you gave me. They have not given up the location."

"It is done." The Guardian snatched the lesser spear from the floor and brandished the tip toward the Void. Both tips crackled with the electricity they would release on impact. "Go find something else to play with. I have questions to ask."

"Below?"

Matriol didn't care about questions or finding the location, not any longer. The only thing it really wanted was being literally held over its head by this Guardian.

"Fine. Go below. What do I care about a few humans?"

The Guardian placed the lesser spear on its hooks on the wall of the hull and flicked his hand as though Matriol's continued presence was a flying bug around his ear.

Matriol left its fellow Voids to watch the torture of the Four.

Its mind turned to the cattle below. The defenseless creatures, so sure they were at the top of the food chain.

Shifting its solid form into a viscous fluid, it let the storm beneath carry it to the earth.

She was a confident human. One of those ones that laughed and shrugged when the others warned her of the dangers in the darkness. Of course, they were thinking of other animals, darker animals of their own kind.

"See you later, morons," she laughed, and skipped away from the group.

It slipped into the shadows, its prey unaware and oblivious to its presence.

Between lips more tar than flesh, it let out a small laugh.

"What the fuck?" She turned around and scowled. "Johno, fuck off. It ain't funny."

It laughed again.

"Fuck off."

A hint of hysteria touched her words; it breathed the fear like it were life itself.

By the time she reached her door, her hands fumbled for the key. It would never find its way into the lock.

Her scream was muffled by the ball of darkness it shoved into her mouth, turning her around and pinning her to the door of her home.

Her eyes were wide and filled with such terror, the pleasure ripped through it like a spasm. She gagged as the Void's fist that filled her mouth shifted and touched the back of her throat. But the gag turned into an impotent scream as Matriol twisted the claws on the tips of its wings and cracked the bones of her shoulders. She was pinned in place and still conscious.

It was impressed. Its last plaything had not lasted this long.

Slowly, it peeled the flesh from her body with teeth and tongue, chewing on the fresh meat.

She passed out long before it reached the stark white bone beneath.

He crunched a few bones between its jaws but left enough. Just enough to terrify the human race.

CHAPTER 13

The next time Kiera woke, the rage battling in her head had lessened to a dull grump. She still sensed that low throb, the hum of a machine she didn't know or recognize. A washing machine? A dishwasher? Close, but not enough.

She opened her eyes without pain, and even managed to sit up uninhibited by any things attached to her or anyone pushing her back down. She was alone.

The room was sterile and sparse. Two other beds lay to her right and a door to her left. A medical bay of sorts, if she were to guess. But the white she had imagined previously was no longer in sight. Had it ever been white, or was it just Zarzy's clothes and skin that had given the impression of the color and brightness of the room?

She hoped she hadn't imagined Zarzy, as the memory of stormy gray eyes stared into her own. They'd been angry, flashing with danger the last time Kiera saw them. Surely, she wouldn't have imagined a hottie with that much attitude and ice though.

The egg. Find the egg. Jiminy's voice interrupted unapologetically to her rambling thoughts. *You are its guardian now, and you are failing it.*

"What is this feeling? Is that why I'm hurting so much? Is the egg in danger?"

She was grateful no one else was in the medical bay to hear as the panic built in her voice.

Find the egg, K.

Kiera nodded and slipped off the bed. It was higher up than she expected, which really shouldn't have surprised her. Being short here was just as frustrating as on Earth.

Or was she back on Earth? She didn't think so. There was something different, more alive in each breath she took. And the voice in her head, Jiminy, was strong and alert.

"Shut up, I'm trying."

"Do you always talk to yourself?"

Kiera stopped looking at the ground around her and came face to face with Zarzy. The other woman rested her shoulder against the doorframe, looking into the medical room.

"So, you *are* real."

Smooth, Kiera. Real smooth.

"Yes." A smile flicked across Zarzy's lips. "Now, you didn't answer my question."

"Your question?"

"Do you always talk to yourself?"

"Lately, it seems to be happening more and more."

Zarzy didn't smile but simply nodded. Kiera forced herself not to roll her eyes or explain she was joking, though technically she wasn't.

"You remember our last conversation. That's good. Do you remember the dragon?"

"The dragon. Yes." Kiera looked down at her bare feet, wiggling her toes for distraction. She wanted her boots, her clothes. She wanted that damned egg.

"How is it possible you don't believe you are a Guardian? You fought a dragon, on your own."

Kiera's words came out on an incredulous laugh. "Barely! I've been knocked out for days."

"You survived. Without training, if you are to be believed. It's unheard of."

Kiera narrowed her eyes and scowled her best 'don't fuck with me' look. "Because I can defend myself, I'm now a liar?"

"No, what I'm saying is that no one in all of my networks has ever heard of any Guardian losing their memory before."

"That's because I'm not a bloody Guardian."

Except, you are now a guardian to the egg, K.

"I mean, honestly…"

Kiera threw up her hands, ignoring Jiminy. She paced back and forth in front of her bed while Zarzy continued to lean against the room's doorframe, arms now crossed over her chest.

Damn you, sexy biceps.

"I mean, look at me. I'm a stump of a human, whose biggest claim to being a streetfighter is decking Paul in Fifth Grade, and then getting punished for a week because of it. Everything else has been learned from hours of training and it's all nice and civil, as much as throwing punches can be. I'm no one's Guardian."

THE EGG!

"But you *do* know what a Guardian is."

Zarzy stepped forward, pushing herself off the doorframe with a languid ease that heated Kiera's belly. She waved her hands in the direction of the chair beside the desk, shooing Kiera into it.

"There's a pretty universal definition. Besides, it's not hard to figure out. Guardians protect and…you know, *guard* shit." Kiera searched for logic. "And besides, Winger mentioned it."

"Ah. Okay, one mystery solved. I knew Blue wouldn't have explained." The crease in her brow was adorable, though the flash in Zarzy's eyes was a whole new level of pain. "What exactly did Winger say?"

"You know she's dead?" Kiera whispered her question.

"Blue mentioned it," Zarzy replied.

"She told me about the history of the Skyans."

Zarzy lifted a single eyebrow. For that, Kiera would tell her whatever she wanted.

"She told me how the original Guardians gave Skyans the crystals to help guard them and humans alike, from the dragons and other beasties."

Zarzy's lips pursed, and she nodded. "Ah."

Kiera scoffed a sound that offered another fleeting smile from Zarzy. "You want to explain that 'ah'?"

Gently, with a softness in her touch that belied Zarzy's icy features, she lifted Kiera's arm and pressed two fingers against the upturned wrist.

The woman really was a mystery, and that mystery intrigued Kiera.

"So, you are a doctor then, huh?" Kiera asked.

"I'm a Healer," Zarzy replied, without looking up at Kiera's face

Kiera rubbed her fingers across her temple. The low hum was fast becoming a pound once more. "And that differs to a doctor how?"

"I use magic, herbs and other items that help the body, unlike the butchers you have down on Earth."

The moment passed quietly as Zarzy's light fingers danced over Kiera's skin like a musician playing a melody. She checked scratches and wounds that now looked little more than grazes. Lastly, she checked Kiera's ears. Kiera was unable to hold back the shudder as the gentlest of touches ran the outside of her ear, down to the triple piercings she had in the lobe.

If Zarzy had noticed Kiera's shudder, her voice betrayed nothing. "You certainly do heal like a Guardian."

Kiera couldn't hide her smile, and even managed a small wiggle of her butt where she sat on the chair. "But you are starting to believe me?"

Zarzy didn't say anything. Instead, she stood up and nodded, her fingers now circling Kiera's wrist.

"You are cleared to leave the healing rooms. But can I show you something?"

Wait. Was their actual hesitation in the confident woman's words?

"Um, sure, okay."

Kiera ignored the warmth of the long, strong fingers. Well, okay, she *tried* to ignore the warmth. Instead, she found fantasies running through her mind of slipping her hand into Zarzy's, their fingers interlocking.

What the hell? Sex is one thing. Intimacy and affection is something completely different.

Zarzy pulled Kiera down the hallway. "We have to hurry."

She could focus, despite the warmth of the woman's fingers.

"What about my bag? I need to find the bag."

"This is more important. Blue has been gone a long time and I suspect he'll be back very soon to talk to you, to find out what we are all curious to know. But his methods aren't ones I enjoy."

"Are you threatening me?"

Kiera stopped in the middle of the ship's hallway, missing the warmth of Zarzy's fingers but knowing she would get over it. The fire within could warm her to uncomfortable levels. They had gone past a set of stairs, and the surrounding walls and closed doors were too close for Kiera's comfort.

Zarzy's face remained frozen.

"You wanna know why I decked Paul in Fifth Grade? Cos he was nothing more than a bully. He picked on the smallest, sweetest kid in the class, and no one stopped him. I wouldn't put up with that then. What makes you think I'll put up with it now?"

"Lucky you aren't the smallest and sweetest."

"Lucky you aren't within striking distance." Kiera's jaw ached as she held back more words, more fire begging to pour from her mouth.

A voice, both familiar and not, spoke. "I can see why she likes you."

CHAPTER 14

For a moment, warmth spread through Kiera's chest, images of Aunt Em with her half-grin and know-it-all eyes. The words surrounded them, floating in the air, and Kiera's hope grew.

Kiera's lips stretched into a wide smile. "Who is that? She sounds just like my Aunt Em?"

She hadn't known just how much she had truly missed Aunt Em until now.

And then an old woman with white-blonde hair stepped out of the doorway a few steps from where Kiera had stopped them. All of Kiera's hope deflated, her limbs feeling loose and flat.

"Grandmother."

Kiera heard the hints of that accent in Zarzy's words now. She hadn't noticed them before, only noticing how less gruff her tone was to Blue's and even Winger's. Bile touched the back of her throat at the mental images of Winger's dead body flopping back and forth in Blue's hands.

"Zarzy. We must hurry. We must get what we can now while there is time." The voice was a warm blanket, but its fabric itched uncomfortably against Kiera's skin. "I am Silana, I wish we had met with more time and far less danger. I do like getting to know a person over a nice cuppa."

"More like a glass of whiskey." Zarzy scoffed.

And hell might freeze over after all. Did the woman just make a joke?

"Hush, child, and hurry up." Silana gave Kiera a small wink before she disappeared back through the doorway.

Kiera didn't resist when Zarzy took her hand again. She wasn't sure her arm would obey the command.

They followed the older woman into a room that brought a laugh to Kiera's lips. Both women looked at her, eyebrows raised in a familial mirror to the other. She ignored them for a moment, as she took in the minutiae.

Light filtered through shelves of different-colored jars. There were a variety of sizes, making inconsistent rainbows on the deck that highlighted dust motes dancing in the air. A table pressed up against one wall was covered in a cloth of striped browns and oranges, in patterns Kiera didn't know. In the center of the table was a mortar and pestle surrounded by candles, some untouched by flames, while others dripped wax along their sides. The candles reminded her of tree trunks.

In front of the mortar and pestle lay an unsheathed shortsword, while behind it sat a photo of three females all staring out with wide, grey eyes and long, blonde hair. The youngest of the three looked little more than a child while the oldest—Silana, Kiera assumed—was much younger than the old woman standing in front of her now.

The middle woman had harder features than the other two pictured. If it weren't for the hair, shocking in its brightness, Kiera could imagine the child was Zarzy with those same grey eyes, before her mother's hardness seeped into her own features. Was the woman's hair dyed? It seemed such a strange, human thing to do. Kiera's eyes flicked to Zarzy and back again.

Her words came out on a choked laugh. "It's just like the movies."

"You have seen this room before?" the woman asked.

"Um, sure, in just about every fantasy movie I've ever seen. And a couple TV shows."

Kiera lifted her eyebrows, waiting for them to understand. The old woman looked at Zarzy, confused.

"She's talking about the Earth. About movies and television programs the humans watch. It's nothing to worry about. Perhaps her taste in entertainment is, but it's harmless enough."

Kiera seethed with the insult she was impotent to defend against, though she'd be lying if she wasn't a little entertained by the woman's snark.

"Pah." The old woman scoffed and waved her hand at Kiera. "Time to forget that garbage and remember what they have made you forget."

"What?" Kiera shuffled forward, encouraged by the waving, wrinkled hand and the warm press of Zarzy's fingers to her back.

"You have memories that are missing." Zarzy's voice was clipped and cool once more. "Blue seems to think this is a good thing. We, however, disagree. Secrets are never good things."

Zarzy's hand slid from the small of Kiera's back and up to her shoulder, giving a small squeeze.

"You've nothing to fear from us, child," Silana insisted. "You must trust us."

There were little other words that could make Kiera bristle faster. Except perhaps every other word that came out of Zarzy's mouth.

"I *must* find my bag."

"The only bag you came in with was a medical bag," Zarzy huffed.

"And that's the bag I'm looking for."

"I promise. After this, we will get your bag."

She sagged at Silana's voice. These were not the words to make her bristle. These were the words making her long for the warmth of Aunt Em's voice and arms.

Kiera nodded.

Trust them.

Make up your mind, Jiminy. Am I focusing on the egg or not? she snapped in her mind, and was not surprised when she was greeted with silence.

She was on a ship, in a land that couldn't possibly be real, though she knew without doubt that it was, and hearing a voice in her head that was definitely not her conscience. It wasn't as though she had a lot of power to deny them what they wished. But still, that snake of unease shifted in the pit of her stomach, uncoiling at things her senses were too numbed to pick up on.

"Will it hurt me?"

Kiera had a high pain threshold, but still, she didn't exactly thrive on being hurt.

"No, the memories are simply blocked. I can feel the blocks. They are crude and rudimentary. I sensed them as soon as you awoke." Silana waved her fingers toward Kiera's temple. "But I cannot promise the memories themselves will not hurt. My suspicions indicate pain will be involved."

"Great." Kiera tried to curb the sarcasm; it didn't help. "So, what are your suspicions?"

Those fingers stopped dancing around her head and lowered closer to Kiera. Slowly, as though not to frighten her, the woman pressed the palm of one hand against her forehead. She spoke foreign words on a soft breath that lulled Kiera with a beauty she did not understand. The movement of the woman's other hand pulled at her attention. She held an oblong object in her palm, too big to be completely wrapped up in her fingers. Between the pale skin, the pulse of green veins on black, shiny wet stone pulled Kiera in.

The words continued to wash around her as Kiera felt the essence inside her pulled closer and closer to the pulsing rock. No, the pulsing crystal. She knew that now.

But how did she know that?

Before Kiera could ask, the world around her shifted and she was thrown into a nightmare, both new and familiar.

Kiera's heartbeat drummed in her ears. Fast. Too fast. Fear trembled through her, while ice bit into her veins. Small arms and smaller legs, strapped to a sterile table, thrashed against cuffs keeping her in place. Steel bit into her wrists and ankles. A mirror above her reflected her red face and eyes open in terror; her trembling lips were pale as warm tears ran down the sides of her face.

She heard something. Someone shushing her. Not in any angry way; more like a parent soothing a child. A comfort, despite the horror and pain.

"It's okay."

The words caught her breath. Was it her imagination?

She ignored the heaviness in her head, turning it to the right. An empty steel table, identical to her own. Turning to the left, she found the owner of the voice. It came from a small boy. He looked young, younger than her, but he was strong. Not scared, no tears or quivering lips. He had kind eyes and a tentative smile.

"It's scary and painful, but we can get through this together." His own wrists and ankles were bound with similar cuffs to the ones she had seen in the mirror above her. Blood stained his skin around the steel. "We can be brave. We can do this."

"Okay."

The sob came out of Kiera's mouth, eyes locked on the boy as another bolt of pain seared through her chest. It was a raging fire, moving from her chest, racing up her throat and pouring out between clenched teeth, an echoing scream of what had earlier ripped at her throat.

With a gasp, Kiera came back to the quintessential witch's hut, the room with the shelves of jars and altar of herbs and candles. The first thing she saw were the three females in the frame, still staring back, frozen.

It took a few more moments, a few more large gasping breathes, to realize the hand was still pressed against her forehead. Her own hands bunched the front of her shirt in a death grip.

"What the fuck was that?" Kiera asked, her throat as dry and raw as her younger self.

The old woman's eyes bored into her as though she were able to pluck the thoughts directly from Kiera's mind. "What did you see?"

"Me. I saw myself, and a boy. We were strapped to tables. And something..." Kiera swallowed the lump in her throat. "Something horrible was happening. He told me to be brave."

"You're a child of the Infanticide Crimes?"

It was Zarzy who asked, jaw almost slack while her fingers played with those colorful squares on her wrist. Her voice was so soft, not quite gentle, but Kiera had thought even this much softness was impossible from the clinical woman she had interacted with so far.

"What?" Kiera snapped out of the memory as it tried to pull her back in again, "I'm not anything. I'm done."

Kiera turned around, unable to find the door they had stepped through. The walls were all the same. She bounced on the balls of her feet. The need to move, to run. Wanderlust, Aunt Em had always called it; liquid fire racing through her limbs, begging her to get out anyway she could.

You know the truth.

"Shut up," Kiera snapped in the silence.

Zarzy and Silana looked at her with wide eyes and pale faces. She dropped her head and watched her feet.

Zarzy stepped forward and cocked her head to look at Kiera.

Kiera shoved at Zarzy's shoulder, trying to push past. She would knock down the bloody wall if she had to. "Let me out of here."

"Hey." Zarzy's voice was gentle as her hands gently but firmly gripped Kiera's shoulders.

"I'm not..."

But Kiera had no words. The walls were too close. She met Zarzy's eyes and shook her head back and forth.

"It's okay. It was a long time ago. You're safe here." Zarzy pulled Kiera into her embrace. The warmth was unexpected. Kiera choked back another wave of tears, as Kiera's soft shushing vibrated through her chest and brought back to mind the gentle smile of the small boy. "You aren't alone, Kiera."

Kiera looked up and met the Healer's eyes. She hadn't even needed any herbs or magic to calm the roiling waves in Kiera's chest.

She wanted to slap her, or maybe kiss her.

No, definitely not.

"Fang-Ripper was the leader of a cult accused of the crimes against the children." Silana's voice was soft as she rested against the shrine. "Many of our children and grandchildren were stolen. Bodies were found days, sometimes weeks later. Never in the same order as when they went missing. Others were never found. When the cult was discovered, they pleaded their case, saying they were experimenting for the good of the Skyan race. To keep our race alive. They said they never meant to kill the children. But the Four didn't believe them. The followers were disbanded with fierce warnings and were told they would be monitored. The leaders were imprisoned. But Fang-Ripper, she was executed."

Kiera shrugged out of Zarzy's embrace, instantly missing the warmth but feeling the fire burning in her chest again. "Who is Fang-Ripper and why are you telling me about her?"

Silana twisted half around and then turned back, holding up the frame with the three blondes. "Fang-Ripper was my daughter..." A long nail tapped on the woman who stood in the middle in the photo. "...and she was Zarzy's mother."

"I am not one of those children," Kiera managed, through clenched teeth, eyes now avoiding Zarzy's gaze. "I don't know that woman. I never met her, and I wish I had never met either of you. I need to get out of here."

The walls weren't just close; they were wrapping around her like a straitjacket, pressing against her chest, making breathing a struggle.

"Just what I was thinkin.'"

The three turned and found Blue standing at the threshold of the open door. Shelves storing items, like those around the rest of the room, were solidly attached to the back of the door. Kiera would have cheered at the brilliant design of the entire room, had Blue not had his sword raised toward them, the threat apparent.

CHAPTER 15

"You knew she was one of them," Zarzy spat, as she stepped forward.

Kiera's hand reached out but didn't quite touch the slope of Zarzy's lower back.

Blue lifted the sword and tutted. Zarzy stepped back, into Kiera's hand. Zarzy's shoulders relaxed slightly as Kiera felt the warmth through her thin shirt.

"Fang-Ripper always knew some had escaped."

He stepped forward and waved the sword around, as though it were merely decorative, but Kiera had used it, had killed with it. She knew the sharpness of that steel.

"How?"

Zarzy's voice was thick. It died in the space of the large room.

"She said the count was too low."

"Count?" Kiera's breath was loud and heavy in the small room. "She talked about us..." Kiera shook her head. "...about the children as nothing more than numbers?"

No one addressed Kiera's question. She wasn't even sure they heard her. Had she said it out loud?

"You were a part of it, and you knew all along. The lies you have fed us all these years."

Zarzy's voice was quiet, but hard and sharp like glass. Kiera could feel heat wrap around her, as though a campfire was in front of her, and had been roaring away for hours.

"No," Blue snapped, but the shift in his eyes was an unmistakable softening. "I didn't know. Not until afterward. And I wasn't sure about her either. I brought her here, to you. I had to know for sure before I did anything." Blue flicked the tip of the sword toward Kiera for just a moment, before swinging it back to Zarzy's throat. "You took her blood. You know, Zarzy. But all she will do is make everyone remember what happened. And it's past time to move on. Your mother is dead, and most of the leaders in the prisons have died now as well."

No use us pleading for our life then. Jiminy's voice was as casual as though he mentioned the gentle sway of the ship's boards beneath their feet.

He's talking about killing me?

Kiera bit back asking the question aloud, fury boiling in the pit of her stomach at the most likely answer.

But she did want to understand. Her feet itched, the muscles in her legs clenching and unclenching. The memories of the torture, the experiment, rolled over in her mind, and with it the truth of what she had heard. It took over the supposed wanderlust. The warmth in her chest grew painful.

"Don't make them look at you like they used to. You have come too far for that. No one will understand that all they wanted, all *she* wanted, was to save us. To save her people. She loved being a Skyan. Nothing else mattered more to her."

"You say that like it's a good thing. She cared more about her own experiments than what she did to an entire generation of our people. Save us? She killed us."

Zarzy went to move forward again, but Kiera saw Silana's fingers wrap around Zarzy's upper arm. The first touch of the old woman's fingers on the back of her hand made Kiera jump a little.

Luckily, Blue was too occupied with his speech.

"Not all of 'em. You and yer brother survived." Blue did not look impressed as he narrowed muddy brown eyes at Zarzy. "She was a scientist; she didn't want them to die, but it is what happens with progress. A few sacrifices to save the whole. To save our people."

"*Guardians.*" Zarzy spat the word. "How can you even justify this? How can you think about forgiving her? Everything she ever did was vicious and cruel; her intent was proven."

A silence, thick and heavy like sap, rested over them.

Silana's voice was strong, though Kiera had to strain to hear her. "We always wondered if there were more in the cult than were exposed, and here you are."

"I told you," Blue snapped, "I only learned about it afterward, after her murder. I am trying to save all of you. No one needs to remember what happened."

"It was an execution, not murder," Zarzy said. "And she got off lightly. But now you want to kill a stranger, for no good reason. Is that what happened with all the Guardians that have gone missing? Did they threaten your perfect bullshit?"

"Zarzy…"

Blue's voice softened, and the tip of the sword lowered just a little.

Zarzy shook her head, a pained groan escaping her open mouth.

"I've always been in the middle of this family, between my own father and brother. I took your side. I never believed anything Jayson said, but I should have, shouldn't I?"

Jayson? No! Not that creep that sent my skin crawling. That's her brother?

Blue let out a breath and shook his head, as though he were about to explain the simplest of things to a small child. "You are not a Guardian, despite your heritage." Blue took several steps forward, let his sword rest at his side, and used his free hand to cup Zarzy's cheek. "I always loved you, my sweet one. But ever since Jayson began spending more time with your mother, you became such a jealous and distant child."

"Why did you bring her here, if you were just planning to kill her?"

"I'm not a monster. And neither was your mother. I still love you, daughter."

Wait, what?

"But if I must kill you to stop our people fighting again, to stop another war, then I will."

"Over my dead body."

I think that's the plan, K, Jiminy said.

He can try!

Silana pinched the skin on the back of Kiera's hand. She didn't jump this time, but the sting made her want to snap at the woman. Instead, she carefully looked at the woman from the corner of her eye.

Fight, Silana silently mouthed.

Kiera couldn't speak; she couldn't even mouth the question, but she felt the pull of her eyebrows as they came together.

Fight, Jiminy enforced. *It's him or us. There is no other choice.*

I don't want to kill anyone. But we can stop him. Three against one and all that.

She was clutching at straws. The energy in the room vibrated, and she knew with a certainty she hated that not all of them would leave alive. As if to confirm, Jiminy began his speech.

He won't stop. Zarzy and Silana are Healers; they have sworn the same oath as your doctors. They will not kill. If you don't kill him, you will get to watch Zarzy die, and then feel the blade within your own breast. You are the only other Guardian here.

But I'm not a Guardian.

Shut up.

Kiera closed her eyes. She had killed the dragon to save this man's life. He had brought her here instead of letting her die in that hidden forest.

Fight.

He had taught her, and he had saved her.

FIGHT!

"Fuck..."

Could she really do it?

"Get outta me way, Zarzy!" Blue snapped, his wrist moving in a circle.

The blade sliced through the flesh of Zarzy's forearm. She screamed and stepped back, her other hand slapping over the fresh cut. Beads of blood seeped through Zarzy's fingers, a red as bright as the haze that came down over Kiera's mind.

Oh, she could do it now.

She hoped.

As though she were in a movie running at half speed, she reached behind her to the short sword that lay at the front of the alter. The blade smacked against a tree trunk candle, sending it toppling to the floorboards.

Shit.

Blue's head snapped in her direction; his mouth twisted, as though he had been in the middle of saying something. She had stopped listening, the red haze of anger blocking all else out.

I can't do this, she begged, hoping Jiminy would present another solution.

You must. He will kill them both. You are their Guardian now, and his blood on your hands is better than theirs.

With a growl in her throat, she stepped forward, blade leading the way. A movement akin to a thrust, learned in her fencing classes. One she hoped Blue wouldn't predict.

The resistance was far less than the dragon's hide. The blade slid into Blue's chest until it hit something. The sword jarred with such strong vibrations, Kiera lost her grip.

Blue screamed and yanked at the sword. It pulled free with a dry scrape at first, then a sucking sound as flesh and blood released the metal of the blade.

"You idiots. I am your savior, not your enemy!"

He charged forward and swung the sword. Kiera failed to move fast enough. It sliced open her hand and she stopped, gaping at the shock and pain.

Zarzy moved to step forward.

"No!" Silana's voice was sharp and carried a power that fizzled across Kiera's bare skin.

Blue sneered, turned, and left. The door slammed behind him.

Zarzy rounded on her grandmother. "Why did you let him leave? We need to end this, before things get any worse."

"He is your father." Silana spoke with authority. "And he knows more than he has told us."

Father. That's right. What a fucking family.

"But you wanted me to kill him, didn't you?" Kiera asked.

Had Jiminy been wrong? Had she nearly killed a man in error?

"You did well. And yes, I believed fighting him to the death would be the only way any of us would survive. But did neither of you hear?"

"The scrape," Kiera said, words tumbling out as she thought them. "I felt it. It was strong and powerful. Like a zap of electricity that reached all the way to my chest."

Kiera gulped as her hands pressed against the scar beneath her shirt. She managed to shut her mouth in time before she could say just how much it had terrified her.

Those old, grey eyes turned on Kiera and the skin at the sides crinkled as Silana smiled.

"You are very perceptive. There is more yet we do not know."

Kiera might have laughed at the ominous way the woman spoke. It reminded her of a Scooby-Doo villain. But shit had gotten way too real.

"As for me, I wish I didn't know any of this." She pushed back her shoulders, wishing she could say she didn't care. At the very least, she didn't *want* to care. "You mind dropping me back on Earth before you go getting yourselves killed? Places to go, people to see."

Since when are you scared of a little mystery and adventure?

When it means my certain death, Kiera replied.

Was that really it? Did it matter? She pressed her lips tight together.

"Fine!" Zarzy snapped, and waved her hand toward the door. "Run away."

"Zarzy." Silana glared at her granddaughter. "Kiera is a part of this, you know that."

"If she's going to scamper like a scared rat, she's no good to any of us."

There was no fire in her words, just a glacial clip that could have frozen Kiera solid. The flame inside was a spark Kiera had lived by, but that had been on Earth. Surely it would be stupid to follow the fire now.

But oh, how she yearned to follow it. It had grown so much since she came to the Skyans, and she found she trusted it.

Kiera's words tasted like disgust and shame, but images of Aunt Em rose in her mind's eye. She swallowed down the sharp tang. "She's got a point."

"You're both profoundly stupid, but you are all I have to work with." Silana stepped forward and offered a hand to Kiera. "I can't promise you will survive, but if you do, I will take you home afterwards."

Kiera took the woman's fingers in her own. Silana had a mean grip, much stronger than Kiera had imagined.

With a huff, Zarzy turned and stalked to the door. It didn't move and her expletive bounced around the room, the space feeling smaller than it had. She tried several more times, but Blue had locked them inside. Zarzy turned and glared at Kiera and Silana in turn. Then she stalked past them and disappeared through a hidden doorway that made Kiera go cross-eyed when she tried to focus on it.

"Ha, it's like the Labyrinth."

Silana gave her a questioning look, but Kiera simply shrugged.

"Looks like you've made an impression on my granddaughter, Kiera."

"What do you mean?"

Silana chuckled and shook her head. "It can wait. We have far greater problems to solve just now."

Kiera quirked her eyebrows. "Like getting out of this room?"

Silana scoffed and followed Zarzy. It turned out the rows of shelves didn't quite line up, and a small doorway hid between them. Following, Kiera smiled at the setup she found. A bar to one side, with stools pressed against it. A couch beside the bar facing a small table with several chairs surrounding it. Silana took a chair and looked up at Kiera.

"Sit." It was neither a request nor a suggestion.

Kiera stepped forward but looked around. Zarzy was not here.

"Don't mind her. She needs some time to cool down. I suspect she will ignore us until the door is opened."

Cool down? She'll turn into an actual ice block if she gets much cooler.

"Will it be long? Until they find us?"

She chuckled, leaned back in her chair and closed her eyes. "No. Someone will wonder why I haven't come to yell at them."

Kiera studied her face. The eyes, so like her granddaughter's, but with more laughter lines around the edges, and far deeper shadows beneath.

Silana's eyes sparkled as she opened them again. "Have you had a good enough look?"

"I— I'm sorry."

"Guilt. Such a stupid human emotion. My daughter slaughtered children, but I take no responsibility for that. I did not teach her that it was okay. Do not take other people's anger as your fault."

"She's definitely angry at me."

Kiera hated how that idea sat uncomfortably on her shoulders. Sure, Zarzy was sexy, and there were depths under that cold exterior. A sense of humor too. But what made her care so much about her opinion?

"She's angry at the world. At *her* world. Change has never been easy for her. But she *will* calm down. My rooms have always been a second home to her, both before and after her mother... Hmm..."

Silana trailed off, and Kiera was glad not to hear again what Zarzy's mother had been responsible for. She felt the exhaustion of the week dragging on her limbs.

A week? Feels like a fucking lifetime.

"I don't want this. I have to get home. I have to see Aunt Em and let her know I'm okay."

Are you okay? Jiminy asked.

"None of us ever wanted this," Silana said. "I will take you home, but we have nowhere to go right now, so you might as well listen to an old woman and her stories."

CHAPTER 16

Kiera narrowed her eyes. Was Silana really going to take her home? When? And what happened after?

Could she trust her? Could she trust any of them? Why had she ever trusted Blue in the first place?

Prejudice. Jiminy was having far too much fun being a know-it-all.

What?

You didn't have a choice then, and you don't have one now.

There are always choices.

Yes. You can choose to listen or continue to be a stubborn mule.

Kiera sighed. She *could* listen, at least until the bloody door was opened.

The voice in her head laughed, and curiosity raised its head in Kiera's mind.

"No interrupting," Silana insisted. "Just shut up and listen."

Kiera laughed, unsure if the bubble in her chest was going to burst with mirth, hysteria or tears. Inside, Kiera crackled like a blazing fire, a snake of unease writhing faster. Would this be the closest to getting a real break anytime soon?

Her heart hurt and her eyes stung with unshed tears as she listened to the story of what led to the infanticide trials. Was this really her story? Was Zarzy's mother the one who had strapped Kiera to that table as a child? There were no sounds from wherever Zarzy had disappeared to. Kiera hoped she wasn't listening.

"He will heal. Faster than we can imagine."

"Why?"

Kiera needed to know, because the ideas her brain was throwing out... No, she couldn't entertain them.

"Why will he heal faster? What was that scrape?"

"That is a long story. There is old myth and rumor mixed up with it, but I plan to separate it from the truth."

"Not like we don't have the time."

Her legs jiggled as she thought of how she'd hung up on her Aunt. It had been days. Was she now a missing person, an old photo of her on milk cartons asking if they had seen her?

Silana said nothing. The quiet stretched out, like taffy growing translucent and thin. Unanswered questions screamed loud in Kiera's head.

Kiera braced herself for a scolding. "Did you know Winger?"

"Yes." Silana met Kiera's gaze. "I know all the Guardians. At one time or another, they all come aboard Hesperus for healing."

"But you don't know me." She had to be certain.

"No."

"So, this is your ship, not Zarzy's."

Kiera stopped herself from looking toward the small gasp that came from the other room. Zarzy was listening after all. Still, Kiera felt like fist-bumping the air. She had figured out something without having to even ask a question. She had felt nothing but stupid since she'd set foot on Blue's ship. She wasn't stupid; she could get things worked out in her head.

"What made you think it was Zarzy's?"

Kiera opened her mouth and closed it again. *Well, so much for not being stupid.*

"I guess she does carry quite the air of authority." Silana raised her voice slightly. "Zarzy, we could all use a cool drink, don't you think?"

Zarzy came into the room in cold silence and headed directly to the bar. Kiera noted the large, white bandage wrapped around her arm where Blue had sliced her. Her own father. The idea pulled at Kiera's chest, and she gently tapped the scar.

Zarzy turned her back to the two sitting women, as though their conversation meant nothing to her.

"She may inherit her one day."

"Hmm?"

Kiera's cheeks warmed as she pulled her eyes away from roaming over the curves of Zarzy's legs and butt.

"Hesperus is a Healer's ship. When I die, she may allow Zarzy to be her handler, her captain."

Kiera furrowed her brows, more questions clambering over each other, but Zarzy was standing there, offering her and Silana glass tumblers of iced water. Kiera *hoped* it was water. The confirmation of the cold liquid as she took her first welcome sip was more relieving than she could have imagined. Zarzy joined them at the table.

"Zarzy became a Healer. Her father thinks it was to follow in my footsteps, some stupid, hero worship thing, I think it was more to tell him to fuck off."

Kiera choked on the water, coughing and spluttering for a moment.

Once back in charge of her faculties, Kiera's stomach growled. How her body could even think about food while the truth of this world that shouldn't exist unfurled around her was its own mystery. She should have been more shocked, more insistent on it all being a dream, but that ship had long sailed.

"Did it never cross anyone's mind that I might actually *like* being a Healer?"

Kiera's eyes bounced back and forth between the stony gazes grandmother and granddaughter exchanged.

"Did any of them ever explain the experiments? What they were doing, how it was supposed to save Skyan? Why they killed them after it was over? Was it even over?"

There were too many questions crowded into her head and she could no longer stop them from spilling out.

Another second of icy glares before Silana turned back to her.

"No. It was never discovered, never learned. All that remained of the children were their bodies, their chest cavities hollowed out and scorch marks on their bones. A fire ritual to destroy all evidence. None in the coven ever gave up information."

Kiera sat back, her stomach heavy and her mind reeling. "Fuck..."

Silana smiled at her.

Zarzy, face impassive as though the beauty were a sculpture carved from stone, stood with a soldier's stiffness. "If you are quite finished with the history lesson, I need to check on her wounds before we get to the isles."

Silana waved her hand at Kiera, her face and movement unconcerned, as though they hadn't just been talking about Zarzy's childhood trauma. "Off you go."

"Come on."

"We're locked in." Kiera raised her eyebrows, wondering how either of them had forgotten that fact.

Silana just laughed and Zarzy raised a perfect, blonde eyebrow. When neither of them explained, all Kiera could do was follow Zarzy.

CHAPTER 17

Around another fake wall, Kiera found herself in a small medical room, both like and unlike the one where she'd first awakened aboard *Hesperus*. The sterility of it made the medical bay look downright homey. Surrounding them were silver walls with silver handles, white tiles, and cold air. The need for the iced water vanished in a moment and Kiera clamped her teeth to stop them from clacking together.

"What's wrong?"

A line appeared in the middle of Zarzy's blonde eyebrows as she looked up from poking Kiera's wounds with a cream-covered finger. Of course the woman's hair was dyed. How had she not noticed that before?

But the scolding was forgotten as she caught Zarzy's eyes. They were kind, and Kiera could see the girl from Silana's photo, hidden in the woman who stood over her still waiting for an answer.

"C-cold," Kiera chattered out.

Without a word, Zarzy opened a steel door to reveal neatly folded blankets within. She withdrew one, shook it out with a trained flick of her wrist and wrapped it around Kiera's shoulders. Pulling the edges to meet at Kiera's chest, she looked directly into her eyes.

"Better?"

Kiera's throat thickened with a lump, and she nodded.

"Good."

"I'm sorry," Kiera forced out the words. Words she wasn't used

That line reappeared between Zarzy's eyebrows. "About what?"

"About your parents. About not understanding this world."

"And you think you understand it now?" Raised eyebrows and that quirk of a smile at the corner of her lips. God, Kiera wanted to kiss that quirk.

"Oh!" Kiera laughed and shook her head. The blanket was doing its job. She certainly was not attributing the warmth spreading through her to anything else. "Not at all. I don't understand a bloody thing about it. And I don't understand how I could possibly be involved."

Silence washed over them as Zarzy gently held Kiera's hand, turning it palm up and inspecting the wound. Kiera had forgotten about the cut.

"What's your first memory?" Zarzy asked, wiping the dried blood from around the cut.

"My *first* memory?"

Kiera blinked. Of all the things Zarzy could have asked, why this?

Zarzy nodded, keeping her attention focused on her task, but Kiera got the distinct impression she was listening intently.

"I remember the farm."

Kiera hissed as Zarzy placed the now-bloodied cloth back onto a silver tray and poked gently at the edges.

"Sorry..."

If Kiera hadn't been so hyper-aware of Zarzy, she may have missed the word. She smiled and relaxed her hand to under Zarzy's administrations.

"I remember Aunt Em's arms wrapped around me after I woke from a nightmare. We were in the middle of a storm. Its why I've got to go back. I need to make sure Aunt Em is okay. My parents died in a car crash on a stormy night."

Did they? Jiminy's voice reminded Kiera of a villain twisting a greased, black moustache.

Yes. Aunt Em has nothing to do with this shit. Just shut up, Jiminy.

"Is that how you got the scar?"

"I..." Kiera took a deep breath. "You saw the scar?"

"Yes."

"I don't remember it. The night of the crash. My parents. But I guess part of me must. I still hate storms just that little bit more than I should." Why was she talking about this? She didn't talk about this to anyone. "I wish I remembered."

Zarzy's fingers finished placing a sticking patch over the cream-smeared cut, but her fingers remained resting against Kiera's palm. "I remember my mother's execution. Sometimes ignorance really is bliss."

The warmth of Zarzy's fingers against her cool skin was a balm, something Kiera wanted to lean into. But the room and its sterile, oppressive air kept her from doing just that.

Zarzy coughed, movement returning to her hands as she pulled them away. "You are fine. The wound is clean enough for your body to take over the healing unassisted."

"Thank you." Kiera knew the words weren't just for attending to the wound.

Zarzy looked up from the table, tapping nervous fingers. Their eyes met and the smile that stretched Zarzy's lips burst a light and warmth into the room Kiera thought impossible until that moment.

"Come on. She's going to get cranky if we don't get back."

Zarzy let out a small laugh and led the way out. She muttered something under her breath which Kiera thought might have been something about making out, but she had always been a hopeless optimist when it came to beautiful women.

At the table again, Kiera laughed as Zarzy pouted and occasionally blushed while Silana told stories about her willful granddaughter, the girl child who didn't let anyone tell her anything she didn't want to hear, not even her mother, especially when it came to what she could or could not do.

Silana looked at her granddaughter with such love and pride. A deep ache pulsed in Kiera's chest. "She was a mean wielder of the sword too."

"Really?"

Kiera looked over to Zarzy who stared back, eyes egging her on to argue the point. Kiera wanted to. She couldn't help enjoying, just a little, when that cool demeanor flared. What was it about seeing a put-together woman fray a little at the edges?

But of course, that was the moment the door finally opened, and a worried-looking woman, age on par with Silana, entered. She raced through to the living area, apologizing, and sniffling as she said something about being locked in the galley. Kiera flicked through her memory, mostly that of pirate movies and TV shows, and came up with 'kitchen'.

Zarzy jumped up and sprinted past the woman without so much as a 'thank you'. Meanwhile, Silana hushed, reassuring the woman that no one was angry with her.

Kiera rose slowly to her feet, eyes still watching the empty space Zarzy had left behind. She had thought the conversation, the forced proximity, had warmed Zarzy to her a little. Even that last challenge had seemed to hide some mirth. Though she was eager to also leave their temporary prison, Kiera took her time following.

A smile—not some momentary mania, but a genuine smile—danced over her lips.

CHAPTER 18

Matriol watched as the fat, old man walked again around the perimeter of the chain-link fence. The building would be big enough to cater for the cages within the overflowing hold of the ship.

He was still full from his last dozen victims, but one could always indulge in some dessert. He chuckled and the old man proved himself even more useless. His hearing didn't pick up the threat mere meters from his heavy-footed patrol.

He rose from the shadows and stopped directly in front of the 'guard', as much a stupid term on the ground as it was up in the clouds. The man screamed and clutched his chest.

Matriol laughed loud enough to echo around the abandoned buildings. It was incredible how fragile they were, how easily and in how many ways their bodies could break and die.

He reached forward, fingers elongating and sharpening into points. They pushed through the skin and then the skull of the man. Brain and blood siphoning through the digits, filling him to beyond full.

Matriol would curl up in the darkness of one of the buildings before returning to the ship where his heart still called, still begged to be returned. There was no point in letting the Guardian know the true extent of his growing power, or the fun he was having.

CHAPTER 19

A trail of blood led from the stairwell and over the railing. Just looking at it brought the taste of copper to Kiera's tongue. Blue's blood, and she was responsible for each drop and smear of it.

She leaned on the railing of Hesperus, far enough from the blood to almost forget it was there. Almost.

In front of her lay the world that shouldn't exist, the world of people's imagination. Above and below, she was entertained by the dancing light reflecting on the clouds.

Out beyond the waves of cloud, sitting on the horizon, was a cluster of dotted cities, all egg-shaped. What she wouldn't give for a map, if only to prove herself wrong, but there was a thought, a half-memory, that kept returning.

The eggs were placed over the land below. The scatter of smaller eggs corresponded to islands, while the larger bulk of land was made up of the enormous eggs, like the Guardians' headquarters. She couldn't shake the idea, or how unsettled she felt about knowing it.

If she closed her eyes, she could almost *see* a map on yellowed paper, and the silhouette of a dragon in the top-right corner.

Kiera shook her head and let out an unamused sound that might have passed for a chuckle to someone listening.

The eggs grew closer and gleamed in rainbows of bright light. The beauty took Kiera's breath away, but couldn't stop images of Winger's dead body from invading her mind again. There were already too many questions repeating over and over in her head. She didn't care to add yet another.

There were no answers, not for any of them, not even from Jiminy. With everything new she learned, more questions rose. Elbows still on the railing, she lifted her hands and rubbed small circles into her temples.

"Another headache?"

Kiera's head snapped up. She hadn't heard Zarzy approach.

"Maybe I'm just waking up?"

Kiera's smile held little humor, the corners drooping after a short moment. It didn't feel like any headache she had ever had before, a dull throb, the hum of an unknown machine, foreign but insistent. Then again, she'd never sailed on a ship between two layers of clouds. Perhaps that's all it was.

"Do you really think that?"

"No. Maybe. I don't know. None of this feels real and yet here I am."

Her thoughts suddenly shattered. If there were more words to come, she forgot them in an instant. The humming, while still low, now filled her head *and* her ears.

"Is it pain, or the overwhelming questions? I assume you have a few?"

Kiera laughed, trying to shake the humming from her head. "Oh, only a thousand or two."

Goddamn it, K. The egg!

The humming... It wasn't humming! A heartbeat? And now a cracking screech, like chalk sliding down a chalkboard. An inharmonious band.

"Where's my bag?"

"Oh, sorry. I know Grandmother said she would get it—"

"I don't care." Kiera couldn't wait any longer. The sound was too much, bringing along its friends, pressure and pain. "I just... I need the bag. I know it's here, but where?"

Sweat beaded on her forehead, and she scrubbed it roughly away with the back of her hand.

"It's in my rooms. Well, the captain's rooms, but Silana... She refuses to go along with tradition." Zarzy's words sounded almost like a ramble, and Kiera might have enjoyed it if not for the hum in her head.

Kiera grabbed Zarzy's hand in both of her own. "Please."

For a moment, the woman looked down at her fingers trapped in Kiera's hands, but then, with one sharp nod, the icy demeanor was back. She turned on her heel and led the way to the cabin on the top deck. Kiera followed, skin itching and muscles twitching.

Kiera stopped as she stepped over the threshold. It could have been her room on Earth. More accurately, the room she had in the small apartment she rented during her university days. Thin, rainbow-dyed chiffon hung decoratively over the thicker curtain between it and the window behind. Dried flowers in vases decorated half the surfaces, while the rest contained stacks of books and art supplies, ranging from pens to paint pots and brushes.

The lump in her throat thickened. She imagined Aunt Em in front of her easels, a half-filled mug of cold coffee, while a second cup swirled with the murky rinsing of brushes all standing at different angles. The paintings that filled Aunt's Em's home studio ranged from dark and chilling to bright rainbows. Kiera had always been more partial to the darkness.

She shook her head. She had to focus.

On a chair in the corner lay her clothes. The brown jacket Blue had loaned her sat on top. Even neatly folded, Kiera could see the blood and dirt smeared on them.

On top of the coat was the bag, unceremoniously dumped. Heart thudding in her ears, she stepped forward.

"It's just a Healer's bag. Every Guardian has one when they leave their ship."

"It's not just a Healer's bag," Kiera snapped, and forced herself to take a deep breath. "Can't you feel it?"

Keep it together, and for deity's sake focus, stop thinking about kissing that furrow line.

Kiera smiled, forcing her shoulders to unknit. She wanted to argue but she couldn't deny how cute that confusion, that ruffled look, really was.

"I found something in the woods, while I was following Blue. I was drawn to it. It pulled me in and I didn't know how or what that meant. I'm still not sure why it called. But as soon as I saw it, I knew I had to protect it." She wasn't certain she was talking to Zarzy or to herself, but a quick look showed Zarzy listening intently all the same. "I don't know what I'm protecting it from, but I'm pretty sure that's what I've been hearing, or sensing, or whatever."

"Hearing?"

Kiera nodded, chewing her lip as she struggled to open the knapsack with trembling fingers. "No..."

At the top of the knapsack was a wad of blood-stained gauze.

"No, no, no..."

Quickly, she pulled the gauze out, searching.

Zarzy's warmth appeared at her side and Kiera had to admit it felt good. "What's wrong?"

"It's broken. The egg, it's broken. I heard it. I *felt* it crack."

Kiera felt the pressure rising in her body, pressing against her chest.

The viscous liquid covered her hands as her fingers slipped through more cloth, ruining it's hopes of being used to help anyone or anything. She didn't care, and right now it didn't matter. Nothing else mattered. Her heart continued to pound loud enough she was certain Zarzy could hear it.

Finally, she brushed fingers against the smooth shell, but beneath her insistent touch, there was a definite wrongness. It was no longer the hard stone it had been when she had held it in her arms and cradled it to her chest.

Carefully, she extricated it from the bag and focused on the large crack that oozed fluid that was dark green, bordering on black.

"Is...? Is that...?" Zarzy's head shook and her eyes widened like a child's discovering their name on a present beneath a Christmas tree. It made Kiera smile. "You said egg, but—"

"A dragon's egg. Yes, I'm pretty sure it is."

"I thought you were just a little delusional."

"Not delusional." Kiera laughed, but the sound was choked and filled with fear. "I don't know if he's okay."

Zarzy couldn't take her eyes off the egg. "But you can hear it?"

"I can hear him humming, a low throb. I think it might be his heartbeat. But there's pain with it as well, not just pressure. I don't know what it means."

She looked up at Zarzy. She knew the panic that swirled around must be evident in her face because Zarzy straightened.

"Okay." Zarzy nodded and stepped up to the desk. Quickly, she stacked away books and papers, pencils and pieces of thick leather from the much-used desk. Or maybe it had never been used for much other than a dumping ground. "Bring him over here."

The authority was a calming wave over Kiera. The doctor—the Healer—was back, and she was in charge. As much as Kiera wanted to be the one in control, she knew her expertise paled in comparison to an actual Skyan who hadn't just *believed* in dragons but *known* the truth of their existence her entire life.

Kiera gently let go of the egg, though the minute the connection was lost, the throb in the back of her head resumed. There was no longer pain and relief washed over her, bringing tears to her eyes.

Kiera hovered, but after a moment she forced herself to step back. She mentally patted herself on the back for not flinching too much, as Zarzy wiped the egg down.

"Is it okay?" Kiera asked, searching the other woman for any sign of hope.

"I have no idea." But there was a smile on her lips as she looked at Kiera. "I've never seen a dragon this close before, let alone an egg." There was a softness in her that Kiera hadn't thought she'd be capable of until now. "But I don't think it's broken."

Kiera waved her hand at the egg. "But the crack? The ooze?"

"Dragons were thought to birth only one egg every ten years. Some dragons only have one egg their entire lives, or so the history books say. They are also very careful with where they make their nests. But from what I remember, this is how they hatch."

"Hatch?"

"Yes." The warmth in Zarzy turned cool once more. "How did you get it?"

"I found it," Kiera said quickly. She wasn't stupid. She knew where Zarzy was going with this.

"Before or after you killed its mother?"

The walls closed in. Even though it was true, the accusation hurt. Zarzy wasn't wrong. Kiera *had* killed its mother. She had driven Blue's sword down into the back of the creature's neck. Bile rose to the back of her throat.

Her fingers burned. Memory of the vibration from that killing strike fizzed through her skin. She looked down, expecting to see evidence of it, some kind of scarring or burned flesh. Her hands gave no clue to their crime. The bandage across her palm seemed more like a mockery.

"Before," she forced out between clenched teeth. Her breath came fast and hard. Her nostrils flared as memories of the smell of rotting vegetation washed over and took her back.

"You weren't to know." But Zarzy's cold words gave no comfort.

"I wasn't to know that stealing an egg was wrong?" Kiera laughed, hard and sharp, as the words came out a little too fast, her eyes staring at the crack. It continued to leak a thick, clear membrane of life.

When had the red disappeared?

"That's weirdly kind of you to say, being you. But I knew. I did. Jiminy told me it was wrong; he told me to leave it alone, to put it back down. But I didn't. I couldn't. Once I saw it, I had to have it."

And now you do. The first hands to touch it. You are it's Guardian, moron.

"The dragon hatchling spoke to you before? And you called it Jiminy?"

That raised eyebrow. Another stab in her chest. Kiera would never be good enough for this woman.

"What?" Kiera's attention snapped away from the egg. "No, not the hatchling. How would I have spoken to the dragon? It's not even born yet."

"Dragons have telepathic abilities."

Kiera's head was ready to explode with all the things she still didn't know about this world. "Of course they do."

"So, who is Jiminy?"

"Doesn't matter. Is the dragon still alive?"

"Yes, it's moving."

Zarzy smiled, but it wasn't to Kiera. It was a smile for the hatching egg in front of her.

I can't look after a dragon.

It's your responsibility now. He needs you, K.

"Good." Kiera felt like a robot as she said the words, all emotion draining from her, a coldness washing through her. "For what it's worth, I'm sorry."

"What are you apologizing for?" Zarzy's voice hinted again at that challenge.

"Does it even matter?"

Kiera turned toward the door, the egg left under the care of the Healer. It would be safer there.

She had never wanted children because that was not who she was. As for being a dragon's mother? Definitely not.

CHAPTER 20

The harsh screech stopped Kiera in her tracks. She turned and looked at Zarzy. Her eyes were still riveted to the egg, but the smile had disappeared. The egg shook on the table.

No, not shaking. It trembled and rolled in a perverse mockery of somersaults.

Kiera stepped forward. Without conscious thought, she shifted closer to Zarzy, pulled by the self-preservation of safety in numbers as the danger truly hit her. Dragons were dangerous, and this egg would birth another one.

Dragons aren't the problem, K!

Sure, let me just check with Winger about that. Oh wait!

Stop listening to these bloody Skyans and listen to me for once.

If you decided to offer any insight besides sarcastic insults, I might. The dragon killed those Guardians. She would have killed Blue.

And what a shame that would have been. But instead you killed that dragon. In her own nest!

The lump caught Kiera's breath in her throat. Yes, she had killed the dragon. But it was self-defense. It *was,* damn it. She huffed and flicked a look from the egg to Zarzy. Zarzy's eyes were wider than Kiera thought possible, her soft-looking lips frozen in a small O.

"I'm guessing you haven't seen a dragon hatch before either?" Kiera asked, returning her attention to the egg.

"Of course not," Zarzy snapped. "Dragons were thought to be extinct for over a hundred years, until about fifteen years ago."

"What happened?" Kiera asked.

The egg had stopped thrashing about. Thin fissures were spreading across its surface.

"They reappeared. And the world turned to shit once more."

"Okay. Well, that's helpful."

"What can *you* tell me about them?" Zarzy shot back.

The cracks in the egg grew wider, breaking apart under some inside force.

"Oh..." Zarzy's voice came out on a reverent breath.

Kiera nodded, smiling in agreement. "Yeah."

Between the widening cracks, bright green scales peeked through a thin, translucent membrane.

"It's beautiful," Zarzy said, no doubt or hesitation in her words.

"Yeah. It really is."

Kiera couldn't imagine even the most jaded of souls being unmoved by the beauty revealed before them. They stood and watched, neither moving nor breathing too hard. The hatchling pushed and turned, mewling now and then as he broke through the last of his protective cocoon and into a room entirely unequipped for him.

Kiera's shoulders and necked ached; her muscles were tense and had been still for far too long. Time slid past as they continued to watch the dragon. She nodded. Inaction itched her skin into a buzz. She rolled her neck, unable to take her eyes away, and was rewarded with a gratifying pop in her spine.

The hatchling turned and looked at her.

"Oh..."

This time it was Kiera's turn to be entirely inarticulate. Her eyes met large, black pupils, inky rainbows dancing over them. They were beautiful, hypnotic and...scared? Fear, was that what she could see?

Slowly, she raised her hand. An intake of breath echoed in her ear—was it Zarzy or Jiminy—and then silence.

One small step closer.

"Hey, little guy."

On bare feet, she shuffled forward another step.

"You're not dangerous, are you?"

The hatchling tilted his head to one side, as though trying to understand her words, or at least her intentions. Kiera let out a small laugh, amusement and nerves sounding too loud in the room. As though satisfied with what he found, he pushed wings out from either side of his body. Kiera jumped and, from the corner of her eye, Zarzy did the same. The wings were smaller versions of his mother's, and while the burn of bile rose to the back of Kiera's throat, she couldn't turn or walk away.

Damn it!

You're his Guardian. A real Guardian, not these Skyans perversion of our name.

The original Guardians. They weren't protecting the people but the beasties?

Dragons are not beasties, K.

Oh...

If only she had gotten out before she looked at those eyes. If only she could unhear the shit Jiminy said to her. But now, those eyes were all she wanted to see. Those, and perhaps another pair, pewter grey. She blinked quickly, not wanting to miss a moment, while simultaneously trying her best to shut off all the other thoughts.

"You are beautiful, little man. So incredibly beautiful."

He mewled and Kiera took a solid step forward. No more shuffling. She heard another sharp intake of breath from Zarzy. The previous gasp had been hers as well. Kiera was certain of it now. Jiminy's encouragement was silent, though she gleaned a nod in her mind.

The hatchling stretched his neck forward and nudged Kiera's open palm with the horn at the tip of his nose. It was soft, and bile rose in Kiera's throat as she was reminded too clearly of Blue and the dragon's mother. She gulped a few mouthfuls of the cold air and pushed down the bile.

"Hi." She blinked back tears. "I'm so sorry. I didn't know, I didn't remember. But I'm your guardian now, and I will do everything I can to protect you. I promise."

The nose pressed harder, and before she knew what was happening, the hatchling had jumped off the table and wrapped his wings around her arm, head moving into her hand. It reminded Kiera of a cat one of her ex's had. The feline's insistent demands for pets had always brought a smile to her face.

Her other arm came up and wrapped around the dragon's back, holding him up. The pulse beneath his scales was warm and rhythmic.

She smiled and turned around. "He's not dangerous."

The room was now empty, but Kiera didn't have to wait long to find out where Zarzy had gone. Zarzy rushed back into the cabin, this time followed by Silana. The older woman stopped on the threshold; her hand fluttered to her chest as though she might be preparing to have a heart attack.

"It's true," she whispered.

"Yes." Zarzy nodded. "They're breeding, Grandmother. This could help."

Silana managed to gather her wits once more and stepped closer to Kiera and the dragon. "Help with what exactly, child?"

"With the threats of the Void. It might know. We can hook it up with one of the telepaths in the Onyx city."

"He's just a baby." Kiera pulled the dragon closer. He wiggled and twisted so he could relax into the warmth of her body and still look at the two other women in the room. "You aren't taking him anywhere, especially sprouting words like 'hook him up'. Jesus Christ."

"He's a *dragon* baby, a hatchling." Zarzy's words were cold and hard. "He can help our people fight back. Our Guardians are going missing, and no one knows where the Void are being kept."

"And what makes you think he does?"

"Because the telepathy of the dragons comes with a certain level of genetic memory."

Kiera shook her head. "I don't care. He's not a tool."

"He has done nothing wrong, and we do not wish to hurt him, Kiera." Silana spoke with authority, a reminder that she was in charge. "But Zarzy speaks the truth. Our world has become unsettled. The Void returned many years ago and we are no closer to ridding ourselves of them than we were fifteen years ago. I fear a war is creeping over our horizon. But we will not experiment on the creature."

She looked at Zarzy with raised eyebrows. Kiera's breath caught in her throat. The women looked at each other, shoulders stiff and teeth clenched.

"Fine. But keep it away from—"

The walls vibrated around them, the boards beneath their feet starting to bump rhythmically.

"We have a boarder!"

The same woman who had been locked in the galley when Blue escaped pushed through the open door of the cabin, red-faced. Her mouth dropped open when she saw what Kiera held in her arms.

"Thank you, Mila." Silana's calmness washed over the room. "We must hide you and the hatchling, Kiera."

"Why me?"

Before she could get an answer, Kiera felt a sharp prick at her chest, and stumbled back slightly as the hatchling broke free of her embrace. A flap of wings, a gentle breeze against Kiera's cheeks, and then a flurry of papers fluttered around the room. Kiera watched, stunned, as her dragon flew out of the cabin's open door. Outside, there were no sounds except the fading sound of wings flapping.

"Shit," Zarzy spat, closer to Kiera than expected. "There goes the element of surprise."

"Surprise? How long could it really be a surprise? We're in the Captain's cabin. Pirate rules one-oh-one says this would be the first place boarders would look, right?"

"Not on this ship." Zarzy smiled at her grandmother, who returned the smile with her own conspiratorial look.

"And you assume whoever has boarded us knows this about Hesperus?"

Zarzy opened her mouth, snapped it shut and turned again to Silana.

"She has a point." Silana shrugged. "But we must deal with the new threat."

"Why are you being boarded? Aren't you a Healer's ship?"

Kiera bounced on the balls of her feet. She wanted out of this room, and she wanted to find her hatchling. The moment it had pushed away from her, the low thrum in the back of her head had returned. It no longer hurt, but it was there.

"Yes, we are. But being a Healer's ship does not make us untouchable. We must stop them going below. We need to protect them."

Silana rifled through the desk, pulling out a small box. Kiera caught flashes of colorful gems glowing within, before the older woman snapped the lid closed again. She tucked the box inside her vest and nodded toward the door. The crystals raised Jiminy's head, and that got Kiera to make a mental note for later. She put a pin in it, so to speak.

"Protect who? Who's downstairs?"

Surely now wasn't the right time for questions, but hell, she was on a pirate ship in the sky, being boarded by God-only-knew-who, and had a telepathic link of sorts to a dragon she was now the guardian of. Was there really any better time?

Warm fingers wrapped around her own. Kiera snapped her head around to meet Zarzy's eyes.

"Guardians," Zarzy said.

All Kiera could do was stare.

"Safety in numbers." Silana nudged her way between them, leading them out of the cabin. "We deal with the boarders first, and then we find that hatchling of yours."

CHAPTER 21

The deck appeared empty, but for a lone figure who stood with his back turned toward the three women as they stepped out of the cabin.

Kiera recognized the clothes, but the beauty of the flight pillar distracted her. As she stared, it shifted colors like one of those cyclic lamps sold in old cigarette shops, but were now called the politically correct 'knickknack store'. She'd once had a lamp like that. It'd cycled through more than a dozen different shades of color. It didn't have anything on the beauty of this pillar.

They crept forward. Kiera felt a warmth shudder through the soles of her feet. The deck smelled of beeswax and care. She hadn't noticed it before, but the stillness in the air, a stillness she hadn't felt up here before, made everything else come alive. All three of them moved forward together, a synchronicity Kiera had not experienced before. They stood halfway between the cabin's door and the helm when they stopped in their tracks.

The man they approached stiffened, and called out, "Where is it?"

Silana stepped forward, making a triangle out of their formation. Kiera leaned in closer to Zarzy. "Where is what, Jayson?"

"The dragon egg, Grandmother. And if you want to hand over that good-for-nothing scoundrel, Blue, while you are at it, I'd be much obliged." Jayson turned and bowed deeply with his last few words.

Kiera would have smiled at the over-the-top gesture, but the electricity in the air was volatile.

"The dragon egg is no more, and as for your father, he left once he received a few new holes." Silana nodded to the stains still smeared over the deck.

"He is not my father," Jayson spat between clenched teeth, as he turned away from the pillar. The blade of a sword glinted in his hand. "He disowned me, but I should have disowned him long before."

For a moment, Kiera looked at this dangerous person and saw nothing more than a petulant child rebelling against his daddy. But then the look solidified into something far more sinister, sending a shiver down Kiera's spine.

"Long before you started stealing and selling pieces of beasties on the black market, Jayson?" Zarzy asked, as she stepped up beside her grandmother. "Long before you backhanded me for telling you to stop? Do you even know that you broke three of my ribs that day? Or maybe, before that." There was fire in her words and a hint of things Kiera didn't understand. "You are just as bad as each other. I would be better off having no family at all."

Jayson's laugh was high-pitched, and he shook his head. "So, what could possibly, finally come between daddy and daughter?"

The silence crackled. Kiera couldn't look at him. Was the value of her life really the cause of the rift between father and daughter? It had seemed to her that Zarzy had little love for her father, from the very first moment they had spoken. Perhaps Kiera really had dodged some bullets with the death of her parents, if this was what happened with immediate family.

"Enough, Jayson." Zarzy spoke without a tremble or rise of her voice. "We have had no part in whatever Blue is up to. You know this. Take your daddy issues out on him and get off our ship."

Kiera stood slightly behind the two women. She glanced down at Zarzy's pale fingers, trembling slightly. Perhaps she wasn't the unflappable ice queen Kiera thought.

"Yeah, right," Jayson sneered. "You're all as corrupt as each other. And you, of all people, Zar. You..."

He waved the sword around, causing both women in front of Kiera to stiffen.

"Me, what?" The voice that snarled out of Zarzy sent fingertips of fear skittering over Kiera's skin.

"You should know better. Proof." He scoffed and spat on the deck. "I felt the truth, Zar. I know. Every single person who was in that room, who my mother *touched* with her experiments, knows. We hear the truth. If we can hear it, how can our Guardians not? They have all heard the call, the plea to fix a past that drags them into the now, a now they no longer want. You can't protect them anymore."

"Stop."

Zarzy spoke with an authority that made Kiera's chest liquefy. The only impact it appeared to have on Jayson, was to make him narrow his eyes and keep waving his sword.

"You aren't making any sense, Jayson. You were never in that room, you know that. When did you stop taking the herbs? They were helping. I've done everything I can to help you. Mother never experimented on us. Not on either of us. The voices are only in your head."

In front of her, Silana's head snapped to look at Zarzy as she spoke. Kiera's Spidey senses tingled up the back of her spine, snapping the fine hairs to attention.

"Before this is over, you'll get your proof." Jayson sneered, and then let out a loud laugh. "Come on out, boys."

Kiera turned first and saw three men step out from behind the captain's cabin.

Shit, why didn't we check?

"You bastard," Zarzy muttered behind her. The words were unsurprised, and Kiera wondered what else had happened between the siblings.

"I am only what they made me."

Jayson's voice was too close. Kiera turned around, just as his sword smashed against a small blade Zarzy held between her brother and grandmother.

Where had she been hiding that?

"And what makes you think that what they put us through gives you an excuse to hurt others?" Zarzy pushed Jayson back, sending him staggering away. The way he stumbled made Kiera notice the depth of the hollow in his cheeks and the way his clothing seemed to hang from his frame, like a drug addict's. "I was there as well, Jayson, and grandmother was the only one who ever tried to protect us."

"Us?" Jayson scoffed. "You have no idea what really happened, Zarzy. You were the golden child, protected from the truth. I was the one she took into that room. I was the one she used as though I weren't her own flesh and blood."

Kiera let out a guttural yelp as an arm grabbed her from behind and threaded itself around the neck. A prick of pain in the side of her neck made her hiss an intake of breath. Her back was pressed against a wall of muscle—the man's chest, she assumed. His odor, a mix of sweat and beer, filled her nostrils and made queasiness swim in her guts.

"I wouldn't be trying anything funny if I were you." The man's voice was rough and mixed a vile stench of gum disease and rotten fish.

Sure, they were pirates, but hadn't they heard of toothpaste?

Jayson smiled, the kind of grin that slipped beneath Kiera's skin and made her want nothing more than a scolding hot bath. "Looks like you and Silana are all out of tricks."

Before Zarzy could respond, her mouth open in readiness, a screech filled the air and the dragon hatchling whipped past them. He was already bigger, his silhouette on the deck filling the space between Kiera and her companions. The dragon flew above them with a grace obviously innate to his kind. Light winked from his green scales, while leaf-looking tendrils on his wings fluttered in the air he created, as he twisted and turned above them. Two short stumps sprouted from his forehead.

Without any audible warning, he swept down, all eyes mesmerized by his acrobatics. With a squawk, he sped up and darted toward Jayson.

Before Jayson, or anyone else, could react, a talon cut him across the cheek as the dragon flew past. The hatchling turned, a somersault in mid-air, and sped back toward Kiera. She tensed, holding her breath.

She needn't have worried. He flew past her head with a close rush of air. She felt the brush of a wing against her cheek but there was no pain. The dagger at the side of her neck dropped with a heavy thunk to the deck and the arm around her throat loosened its hold. Without hesitation, she stepped forward and turned, pivoting on the balls of her feet. What she saw froze her in place.

The hatchling sat on the pirate's head. His claws dug deep into the eyes, blood seeping down the man's face while his arms flailed and his mouth gibbered unintelligible words amongst pained screaming. The other two men, who had once flanked the one being feasted upon, cowered at the railing of the ship.

"Back!" Zarzy snapped, an arm coming across Kiera's chest and pushing her away.

"Not a Guardian, hey, sis?" But the fire in Jayson's voice was gone.

Kiera flicked a look over her shoulder. His sword was back in his scabbard, a dirty cloth pressed to his cheek as he shuffled backwards, unable or unwilling to take his eyes off the dragon now feasting on one of his men.

"Shut up, Jay," Zarzy spat. "I may not be able to kill you now, but just give me time."

"Right back atcha, baby sister."

Kiera vaguely registered the conversation going on around her. Her eyes were once again glued to the hatchling, so she saw when it lifted its horns and locked eyes with her. For a moment, they stared at one another, before the dragon slammed his beak down into the top of the man's head, cutting off the last of his screams. His body collapsed to his knees, and stopped for a moment, before crumpling the rest of the way to the deck. The hatchling remained on his head, cracking his skull with repeated blows from his beak.

Levison, Jiminy's voice said, the word urgent in a way Kiera had not felt from him before.

"Levison?"

Kiera hadn't realized the word had slipped from her mouth until the hatchling, Levison, looked up and met her eyes once more. Gristle from the man's head hung from the blood-spattered silver beak.

Levison cocked his head again. No laugh came from Kiera this time. In fact, no idea of laughter even entered her thoughts. Would she ever be able to laugh again? Would her ability to make a joke out of the direst of situations be available after this? Was this one of those turning points in a person's life? She could see that potential.

Levison swallowed the piece of meat dangling from his beak and cocked his head the other way as Kiera's mind raced with questions and fears. The curious gesture's innocence was lost as Levison lowered his beak once more and with a jerk of his head, pulled the next morsel from the man's head with a squelching snap and swallowed it with a slurping twitter. It was a sound Kiera hoped never to hear again.

Nausea rolled inside Kiera's stomach.

"Back." Zarzy's voice was low and thunderous. She put her hand flat against Kiera's shoulder and pushed. When had she moved to Kiera's side?

Levison screeched and glared at Zarzy. Black liquid eyes narrowed on the Healer.

"Zarziana…" Silana's voice was low, somewhere still behind Kiera. There was a forced calm that did not permeate the panic that rippled over the deck of the ship. "I would suggest not pushing or touching Kiera like that again."

Zarzy's nod was barely perceptible from the corner of Kiera's eyes as a small gust of warm air brushed against Kiera's cheek.

Zarzy pulled both hands back to her own chest, palms open and out. "I'm not hurting her, Levison."

"The dragon has chosen it's guardian." Silana's words were filled with a smile Kiera couldn't even begin to understand.

"Huh?" Kiera asked, eyebrows almost reaching her hairline as she finally pulled her eyes from Levison and his meal.

How very articulate.

Silana chuckled, and Zarzy and Kiera turned to stare at the older woman.

"You're up, Kiera."

"Okay?" Kiera asked, with a shrug.

Silana nodded.

Kiera took a deep breath, "Now what?"

They turned to see Levison pull another piece of meat out of the dead man's skull, before he took off into the sky. A blast of air pressed the man's corpse harder into Hesperus's deck, while the two who had been clinging to the railing dove overboard.

Jayson laughed. "Until next time, little sis."

Kiera spun around yet again, to see Jayson jump over the railing near Hesperus's flight pillar.

"The dragon will now obey you," Silana said, amused in a way that Kiera found not just baffling but downright terrifying.

"Well, he's all grown up and eating people. What a good mum I must be. Should I thank him or barf?"

Nice. Her ability to save her sanity through humor was not yet lost.

"Do you think this is a joke?" Zarzy's voice was still low, a glacial sword, as she rounded on Kiera, eyes blazing as her hands balled into fists and jammed onto her hips.

"No, I don't." All amusement was gone, the fire inside, the one that seemed to flame furiously every time Zarzy opened her mouth, threatened to pour out. "But what would you have me do? I get fed bits of information as though I'm an idiot who couldn't possibly understand what's going on up here. I am *not* stupid. I may not be a Healer, or a damned Guardian, but I can figure some shit out all on my own. Your brother is the black sheep, breaking all the rules of your people. That much I get, but there is more you're holding to your chest as though secrets will protect you. I saw the look Silana gave you when you asked about the herbs? How long have you been drugging your brother? Hiding the truth of his condition? What is he, schizophrenic?"

"No." Zarzy's pale face had somehow gotten even whiter. "He's just sick, and he gets confused."

"Did your mother experiment on him?"

Zarzy shook her head but she wouldn't meet either Kiera's or Silana's eyes.

"Well, you need to tell me what the fuck you've put me in the middle of..." Kiera gestured around, taking in the mess that Levison had made of the man he'd feasted on. "...or there is going to be more of this. How can I tell Levison to stop when I don't know who the real bad guys are?"

The two stood toe-to-toe, glaring at each other. Kiera wore

everything on her face, the fury and anger hot and raging, while Zarzy's face wore the icy, chiseled expression of a vengeful goddess.

"Jayson isn't the bad guy. He's lost his way. But we need to focus on the real threat to our people."

"And what's the real threat?" Kiera asked, with a loud sigh, her shoulders dropping as though more weight had just been pressed upon them.

"The Void," Zarzy muttered, eyes looking up now, and boring into Kiera's.

"Tell me."

"We need to get out of here first. We need to get Hesperus moving."

Kiera lifted her hands up and shook her head. "I'm done."

She'd had enough. Enough of it all. Enough of the barbs, and snide comments, enough of being left out of the conversation. And most of all, enough of feeling like these fights with a near-stranger were the most exciting thing she'd ever felt. Too much roiled inside of her, and the sense that she controlled none of it was exhausting.

She walked to the railing, skin tingling and mind reeling. There was no safety in this land. No farm, no Aunt Em. No place to rest. As soon as her hands rested on the smooth wood, she gasped and realized her error.

She hadn't just been tired. She hadn't just been sick of this drama-filled bullshit. Something inside of her had been able to sense a darkness, but she had no way of knowing or naming it.

But she *did* have a name.

"Void."

She managed to whisper it, before the darkness she had mistaken for a shadow spread over her hands. Sharp needles pierced her skin and tugged her over the railing.

Noise from behind her was drowned out by her own screams and the loud pounding of her heart in her ears.

Don't fight it, Jiminy said. *I will keep you safe.*

She couldn't answer, but like hell was she able to relax. The touch of darkness continued to pierce every pore of her skin with its needles.

Relief came only when blackness overtook her.

CHAPTER 22

"**S**he doesn't belong here, Jay. Just remove the shard and get it over with. She's just another Guardian."

A nasal voice pierced through Kiera's skull like a rusty saw being forced back and forth, back and forth. She wanted to snap the fucking thing in half.

"She's not a Guardian. She's something else. Something I might be able to use."

"Something else?" The other voice was harder than Jayson's, without the small traces of Silana's influence. "What else is there?"

"There's something different about her. Trust me or don't step back on my ship."

There was a gruff humph, the whir of a door, and the wheeze of a laugh.

"You can stop pretending to be asleep now."

Jayson's laugh drew closer, and Kiera fluttered open her eyes. The light wasn't as bright as she feared, nor as unfamiliar. There was a dull glow to her right. Tentatively, she turned her head toward the light, fearing pain. No pain came. Instead, a horror far heavier laid over her chest like a hand squeezing down on her heart.

"Upfall..."

Her voice trembled and her teeth clacked together with the cold.

"Yes. It's the same one I found Winger next to."

"Why am I here?" She sat up too quickly and gulped back a sob. It was like a bubble forcing its way down too small a tube. Her breath caught and her chest ached.

"It's okay."

Jayson was beside her in a rush, a warm hand rubbing circles on her back. The bubble popped and Kiera sucked in air and thrust her shoulders forward to get away from the man's touch. How could he be so gentle after he had held them all at sword-point?

"Somehow you have found a way to be important to my sister. I thought if I convinced you, she might finally listen. Really listen, and not just give me more herbs." Jayson let out a sigh. "But then I felt the beat in your chest. It took me a little time to place you, but I remember now."

His voice was soft, his eyes staring at the upfall. Or perhaps staring through it.

"I've not grown up so together as you, but I do remember you, K."

He turned and smiled self-deprecatingly, twirling a finger in a circle near his temple, so very human an action Kiera wanted to slap his hand away.

"Don't call me that. You don't know me."

"Don't I?"

He snapped back to attention and looked at her chest. She looked down to see her shirt had been torn down the center, the scar from her parents' fatal car crash, a wide, twisted rope of pink tissue, in stark relief to the pale skin surrounding it.

She pulled the tattered remains of her shirt closed as best she could. "Fuck you. I don't care what you're up to. I don't care what you and Blue have planned. As soon as I get out of here, I'm going back to Earth and lighting up the sky, you fucking pervert."

He laughed, but not before she saw that glimpse of doubt in his eyes. "You think Blue and I are in cahoots? I cannot stand the man. He is everything that is wrong with this world." He smiled and the familiarity was a clenched fist in Kiera's chest. "That's a new one. He is nothing but a Guardian, a defiler and a murderer. And he is far worse than most."

"So, what does that make you?" Kiera spat.

"The one to put it back to rights. I'm the one to save this world."

Stall, Jiminy ordered. *Use that incessant babbling brain of yours and goddamn stall.*

"Funny. Blue called himself the savior of his people as well."

"I am not like him." He turned his back on her and she felt the anger rising inside, mixing and combining with another's.

"You kidnapped me. Just like your *father* did."

"I *saved* you!" His voice was a roar, unrecognizable.

Well, that's a nice little trigger to know about.

"It was only there to keep an eye on you and your little pet. The Void are mindless, bloodthirsty creatures, yes, but they have their uses. Unfortunately, when you touched it, it got a little excited."

"Excited? It pulled me off the side of the fucking ship."

The words didn't convey the true horror of that touch. The mere memory sent Kiera's body into a trembling mess. The moment that creature, the Void, had touched her, light disappeared and there was nothing but true darkness, sharp and hard and painful, so very painful.

"I know. And I'm sorry, but now you know not to touch them."

"What are they?"

Jayson ignored her question. "If it weren't for me, the Void would have overtaken the world between the skies. They would have killed every Skyan they touched. And then they would have started on your precious Earth and the humans.

"I didn't know we created them. I didn't know what I had to do would only make them stronger. But it doesn't change what has to be done. It's a consequence, a punishment for all the years of pain and anguish. It is their last 'fuck you' to the rest of us, and I can't say I blame them."

"You really are crazy."

He laughed again.

"You would know all about that. Tell me, what is the name of your crystal?"

"My *what*?" Kiera asked.

"That voice in your head. The one that is not your own."

Kiera's breath caught in her chest.

"What, no strong words and vicious threats now?"

Keep talking. Help is on the way.

How do you know that?

Look.

Kiera over Jayson's shoulder and saw the shadow. The door was open, but she had heard it close, hadn't she?

It took all her energy to school her features and remain neutral as the shadow passed again. A shadow of hope, a shadow she was already surprisingly familiar with.

Kiera's head throbbed. Her body ached. Help was moments away, just beyond the doorway. "I don't care."

"I think you just might," Jayson said, but then all Hell broke loose in the room.

Levison barged through the doorway with a screech. Jayson turned to see the dragon charging with jaws open. His hands clamped over his ears and he fell to his knees. Kiera winced at the sound, but it didn't paralyze her, or even ring pain in her ears like his mother's had.

Stepping forward, she wrapped her fingers around the handle of the sword sticking out of Jayson's sheath and slid it free before he had a chance to register.

"Let me make that even for you."

Kiera smiled. The snake in her stomach had uncurled and was now poised to strike. Her arm curved backward, a target on Jayson's cheek.

Yes. We will run free once again.

At the sound of the dripping darkness of Jiminy's voice, Kiera flinched. Jayson saw the hesitation and moved, just in time. He rocked backwards and onto his feet. The tip of the sword sliced open his shirt instead of his cheek.

Kiera stared, her eyes begging to be closed, but her mind couldn't let the sight disappear. Jayson's shirt had dropped open, revealing a mirror image to Kiera's own scar.

"You fool!" he screamed, thick liquid dripping from his ears.

He ran from the room. Kiera's winged defender wriggled his tail, as though this chase was nothing but a game, like a cat pouncing on a speck of light.

"Levison, no!"

Levison's head snapped around and the wiggle in his tail stopped.

Well, I'll be. Silana was right.

"It's okay." She reached out a hand willed her fingers to stop trembling. Levison nuzzled into them instantly.

For a moment, she stood, unable to think. She'd been kidnapped to be used as a pawn, for Jayson to convince Zarzy of his truth, but she was no closer to knowing what that truth really was. Some things were starting to fall into place, albeit uncomfortable, and more than a little unsettling. He had been gentle with her, and that spoke volumes.

"How the Hell did I get wrapped up with this psycho family?"

Levison cocked his head.

She was too exhausted to even huff out a sarcastic laugh. "Let's get out of here, boy."

Levison moved and took the lead. She hesitated just the once. The pull at the end of the hall was just as strong, if not stronger, but she shook her head, glad she had Levison to follow.

Her mind raced. Jiminy was lost in the swirl of darkness, or maybe he *was* the swirl of darkness? Either way, Kiera had never felt more alone in her entire life. Thoughts and memories whirled through her mind, like hale hitting against a window pane—plink, plink, plink. Loud and jarring, unable to be ignored, though not quite fitting together as puzzle pieces should.

The scar was a sticking point. A point Kiera couldn't deny. She had never felt comfortable with the story of her parents' death, the car accident or the scar that split her chest in half. If she was a Skyan, and an experiment of Fang-Ripper, that answered some questions, and formed new ones that made her pulse race.

Who was she? And how had she escaped that room?

It didn't take long before Levison led her out of the building. From where she stood at the entrance threshold, she saw a ship in the distance. There was no real way she could know, but she did—it was Blue's ship, Zephyrus. That's what Zarzy had called it. The first ship she had seen, the moment that started her down this path of chaos.

Why hadn't she listened to Aunt Em?

Oh no, she couldn't even begin to go down that path. Not yet.

The ship was docked just inside the egg city, a mere foot away from the transparent shell.

"Fuck me. Are they really working together after all?"

Fingers wrapped around her ankle and Kiera screamed as she turned. Levison was at her side, hissing down at a bloody faced, broken-nosed Blue.

"He's going to destroy it all. The Guardians, our world, our way of life."

"Why?"

Kiera clenched her teeth against the warring feelings bashing each other up inside of her. Blue had trusted her with a sword, shown her how to guide the ship, albeit more in theory than application. And then he had betrayed her, tried to kill her, thought her death would be better for his world.

Blue coughed and blood splattered from his lips onto the deck. "He thinks the past needs to be rectified."

Jiminy's laughter echoed through the swirling in her mind.

"What past?" Kiera's hand fluttered to her chest. The sensation of her fingers as they touched bare skin made her pull uselessly at her torn shirt. "Do you mean your wife's experiments?" She spat the last two words, but her movements had caught Blue's attention.

His eyes were wide, and behind them she saw so many thoughts flashing with lightning speed. "It really is you."

"What is me?"

She would have done anything not to have that desperation in her voice, but she wanted to know, more than anything.

"It's too late. The past can't be changed, and trying to do it now is only going to destroy everything. Bringing you aboard was a mistake, but I had to know."

His words hurt more than Kiera thought possible. The first time she had felt at home, away from the farm, and it was a mistake.

Blue's hold on Kiera's ankle loosened and he slumped back down. Jayson—she assumed it had been Jayson—had created a macabre artwork out of Blue's chest. It was covered in blood, flayed from what looked like a frenzied blade thrusting again and again, taking chunks of flesh and skin.

"What do I do?" Kiera asked, over the lump in her throat.

"You have to stop him," Blue replied.

"Why should I trust you? You tried to kill me."

"Better one to die, than an entire way of life."

"Seeing as I'm the one, I find myself disagreeing."

"He is the one who needs to die. With his death, it could all be forgotten, moved on from."

"They were children, Blue. Tortured and massacred. Maybe no one should be allowed to move on from that."

"Not the experiments."

"Then what?"

Blue coughed, blood and spit sticking to his chin. "Kill the dragons."

Levison screeched, and before Kiera could stop him, he slashed his claws across Blue's throat. His head fell forward. Jayson had been the one to kill him. What Levison had done was closer to mercy.

"Fuck!"

Kiera screamed into the clouds above. She turned and looked around. She was alone again, except for a dragon she couldn't communicate with.

Have you tried? Dragons are telepathic, K. Or did you forget that?

"Maybe, but I don't care right now," she hissed, between clenched teeth.

She didn't want to touch that damned pillar on Blue's ship again, not after the migraine from last time. But standing still had never been part of her makeup. The headquarters were dead. It was time to get the hell out of there.

Something pulled at the back of her mind, but she was so tired.

She stepped over Blue's still body and moved into the egg city. Levison alternated between waddling beside her and hovering a few feet off the ground.

Everything was as dulled and muted as she remembered from her first visit. She lightened her steps as best she could as she moved toward Zephyrus. The ground lulled gently beneath her, as though it was breathing a slow and steady rhythm, just waiting. For what, she was still trying to grasp.

The walk through the abandoned city would have benefitted from the gentle clink of spurs on booted heels and the occasional tumbleweed blowing past. At least then she could be almost convinced this whole thing was a prolonged and twisted dream. But even as she thought it, she knew it was wishful thinking.

The ground breathed beneath her, and the ship seemed to stay forever the same size, until suddenly she was beside it. Her hand trembled as she reached out and placed a flat palm on Zephyrus's hull. The urge to say something to the ship was almost overwhelming. Instead, she turned to her companion.

"What do we do, Levison? Go home and leave it up to the psycho pirates?"

His caw was low and soothing. Kiera felt her shoulders drop marginally. She had never been okay with mysteries left unsolved. They worried at the back of her mind, like an itch she couldn't quite scratch.

She'd had enough of conversations she didn't understand. And really, what was she hurrying back to Earth for?

"What was it Aunt Em used to say? In for a penny, in for a pound?"

Levison rubbed his head against her side. She made her decision.

"Screw it!"

CHAPTER 23

She walked with confidence back toward the building. If she'd been tracking her steps, this would have scored her big points.

When they reached the door, Blue's body remained inert. Levison screeched and she pulled her eyes away. The dragon screeched again and flapped its wings, staring at Blue's body.

"Hey, don't blame me. You're the one who lost your temper."

Levison let out a puff of smoke from his nose.

"Fine, stay out here. Guard the doors for me. And if Blue becomes a zombie, eat his brain before he can eat yours."

Was she really joking about that?

Another puff of smoke came out of Levison's nose, but he circled, much like a cat might, before laying down across the threshold of the door and raising his wings. The sun became green-tinged light that dappled color along the hallway. Each step, the light tickled across Kiera's skin and she shivered.

"Okay then."

Why are we back inside?

"Hello, shithead. Where have you been?"

Fucking your mother.

Kiera laughed out loud. The surprise stopped her in mid-stride.

"What the Hell?"

It was in one of those terrible movies you watch. Though I did always like that line.

"You watched movies through me?"

Sometimes, when the weather was clear. So, why are we here?

"When you are lost, go back to where the trouble began." How she missed Aunt Em and her advice. This one had been given over a nighttime meal of cereal and ice-cold milk, a summer's night that was too hot to even consider turning on the oven or heating anything on the stove. And neither of them felt like sandwiches again.

And where did the trouble begin, oh wise one?

"At the waterfall."

Oh, trouble began long before that.

"Yeah, but there's something else there. Something I can feel, but I shouldn't be able to. Theme of my life, really. All the things I know that I shouldn't. So, how do I keep knowing these things?"

The smirk was damn near visible in Kiera's mind.

"I'm missing something, aren't I?"

No shit, Sherlock.

"Damn it, Jiminy. How many movies did you watch?"

Too many. And its Tamin.

"Tamin?"

My name. There was no arrogance or jest in the voice now. *I'm sick of waiting for you to ask.*

"Okay, so what am I missing?"

And just like that, Tamin's cockiness leaked through again. Kiera could all-but-imagine him blowing on curved fingers and polishing his nails on a piece of cloth. But, for some reason, not a piece of clothing. Bloody nudist.

She laughed and shook her head.

"Yeah, there's still a pretty good chance you are just a tumor or something." She looked at the dappled green light around her. "But at least Levison isn't a figment of my imagination."

No, he's just a dragon.

Was it weird she found the running snark a comfort? Kiera couldn't keep the smile from pulling up the corners of her mouth.

"Tamin?"

I cannot follow you in there. It holds too much pain.

"I'm sorry."

Heavy and loud, her heart thundered in her chest and pulled at her, as though an invisible string had lassoed her and was dragging her in. She knew exactly where she had to go. Even alone, there was no turning back. She stepped past the room where Winger died, forcing her head still, so she didn't look as she walked through.

She understood Tamin's hesitation to hide from the building, but not the depth of the fear that radiated from that corner of her mind. He had not been so worried when they had gone in the first time. Had Winger's death made such a heavy stamp? Or was it something beyond Winger?

She continued past other closed doors, her usual curiosity ignoring what was behind each one of them. As she got closer, her breath came out cold. Dragon's breath she had called it, as a child in the playground. The boys had laughed and joined in. The girls had scoffed and ridiculed. Most of them at least.

Shaking her head, dislodging that train of thought as much as possible, Kiera forced herself to continue down the hallway. Her puffs of cold, white air led the way. Her eyes remained focused on the floor-to-ceiling double doors at the end of the hallway. She didn't turn to look at the other doors. She wasn't entirely certain she would be able to, even had the desire crawled up the back of her neck and begged.

The cold seeped beneath her skin and threatened to solidify her blood. Still, she walked onward, fear and doubt warring with the knowledge, ancient and unknown, that this was exactly where she needed to be. Wanting had absolutely nothing to do with it.

At the doors, she lay her hands flat against the dusty wood. The metallic impressions were nothing more than fading facade and chipped paint. Heat radiated through the door and the reawakening of her fingers tingled and stung. The 'dragon's breath' was all-but-gone.

Kiera put her shoulders into it and opened the doors. They groaned, but she pushed through their resistance.

Noise of voices, hundreds of murmuring conversations, flooded her ears. She stopped still, eyes flying around the room. Her mind took longer to register all that she was seeing. Quickly, she turned on her heel, but the doors were already closed behind her. They were strong, with undamaged paint and tall, square-shouldered guards standing sentry on either side.

A crack of noise had her spinning on her heels again, back to face the front of the room. It reminded her of a court room in that TV show she loved to watch. The one with the tall, dark and handsome, dyke-in-her-fantasies cop and the lanky, blonde lawyer. But it wasn't the same.

At the front, there wasn't a judge in his throne. Instead, a tall, rectangular cage took center stage. The rows of seats curved around, stopping on one side for a large bench where several grim-faced people sat. Four stern-looking faces.

The roof was a dome of glass atop high walls, like she was inside a demented ice cream cone. All the seats were taken, and everyone was leaning over, talking to those sitting in front, behind, or several seats over. It was almost comical, until the statuesque figures of three drew her attention—the back of a tall man's head flanked by children, one on each side, a long-haired blonde to his left and a short-haired, scruffy mop of hair to his right.

Kiera stepped forward, but was stopped by words spoken a louder than the rest of the surrounding din. "What do you mean the seer is gone?"

"No one can find her," a younger voice replied. "Her ship is exactly where it should be, but she is not on board."

"Her supplies?"

"All gone."

The silence stretched and Kiera spun, desperately searching for the speakers. She excused herself as she passed by people, brushing their sleeves, or bumping a knee, but no one seemed to hear her or pay her any mind. She would have laughed, had her spider senses not been tingling since the moment she awoke in this building.

"Has anyone asked about her children?"

"Do we know a final count?"

"What if she has more no one knows about?"

"They aren't her victims."

"He can't have known."

"How can this even happen?"

"Why else would they remove him as one of the Four?"

Snippets and more flooded her ears as she pushed her way to the front, no longer caring to apologize when she pushed a random limb out of her way. No one screamed out or yelled. They were solid to her touch, and yet she was growing more certain that they could not feel her.

Standing beside the front row of chairs, she sensed the three statue-still figures as they continued to stare at the empty cage. She sensed them, but she couldn't quite bring herself to look. She was certain she would see a younger version of Blue sitting with his children. The idea was macabre beyond even her ken.

A woman was brought out and words were spoken. A hush fell over the crowd. Kiera heard the charges as she stared at the woman. There was no doubt she was the same woman in the photo in Silana's rooms, though a lot worse for wear.

She was more familiar than she should have been.

The woman's eyes were hard as they looked past Kiera. The movement shifted, and for a moment, Kiera's heart stopped. She was certain the prisoner looked *at* her and not through her. Kiera shivered, an uncontrollable sensation up her spine.

The silence built like pressure before a storm. A man stepped forward, and Kiera saw the glint of obsidian in his hand. She couldn't hold back the gasp as he drew the weapon across the woman's throat, across Zarzy's mother's throat.

Across the throat of the woman who had cut her open.

She slammed hands over her mouth, holding back a sob, and looked away as the first beads of blood seeped through the clean cut that glided open Fang-Ripper's throat. In her shock and distress, she had forgotten that beside her, in the direction she had turned her head, was the family she would meet so many years later.

None of them had gasped or let out a sob of their own. The children huddled closer to their father, but their eyes were wide open, still staring, as their mother choked and bled to death through sanctioned murder in front of their eyes.

Kiera closed her eyes and collapsed to the floor. She leaned forward with her arms locked and palms pressed to the ground, holding her upright. She forced deep, slow breaths in and out. The pounding in her chest lessened as her skin prickled, and she opened her eyes on the next slow breath out.

The white mist floated in front of her, coiling over the thick dust that coated the floor between her hands. She was alone in the room. No more ghosts.

Goosepimples rose on her arms and tears she hadn't noticed shedding froze on her cheeks.

CHAPTER 24

"This is where it all began," a soft voice said into the silence. Kiera looked up and saw Winger standing in front of her, a younger version than the one Kiera had met. Kiera stood and stepped forward, stopping when another voice spoke behind her.

"No, it's not where it began. It began so much earlier."

Kiera turned to see the boy from her vision as he aged and turned into a young adult. A familiar young adult. This version of Jayson looked down at his feet while his hands fumbled at the buttons of his shirt. Down the middle of his chest was a thick rope of scarring, a familiar sight Kiera had been forced to see too many times in the mirror.

"He's the boy." She shook her head and stepped back a little further as the memory, not her own, played out in front of her. "He *can't* be the boy."

Winger's fingers gently touched the scar. Kiera could almost feel it. That strange not-quite-there sensation. "I thought you and Zarziana were both examined. Why didn't you tell anyone?"

"We were never examined. The Four only wanted to placate the Skyans. They took, *him*..." Jayson spat the word. "...off the council and they killed her. But I did tell someone. I told Blue. I told my father."

Kiera felt the tears prick at her eyes.

"And?" Winger's voice was close.

There was another noise. It was even closer, the scrape of soft shoes drawing nearer.

Jayson looked up, eyes filled with confusion, more confusion than Kiera could stand. Her own chest ached as her fingers bunched in the tattered front of her shirt, clutching at her mirror scar.

"He told me not to tell anyone, or I would be taken away. He told me it didn't matter. She was crazy, and to forget about it. So, I stayed quiet, until recently."

Jayson's voice was hard and brittle as he laughed the kind of laugh that held pain instead of humor.

"He told Zarzy I was crazy. That he should never have allowed us to see her death. Zarzy's been giving me herbs to dull everything, to make it all quiet, but I can't take it anymore. It all hurts too much."

"What happened, Jay? What needed quieting?"

Winger's hands were now flat on his chest. Jayson pushed her away and turned his back. Furious hands buttoned his shirt hurriedly.

"It started talking to me," he said, with a sniff.

"What did?" Winger asked.

"The thing she put inside me. The same thing every Guardian has inside them."

"Her experiments were trying to create younger Guardians?"

Jayson's laugh was too high, and the hardness of it set Kiera on edge.

She reached for the sword that wasn't there, as though somehow she could defend herself from the memory playing out in front of her.

"Jay?" Winger asked.

"She wasn't turning us into Guardians. She was turning us into soldiers, but it backfired. They died screaming. So many of them. I hear them every time I close my eyes. I thought when she died, it would finally be over. But Blue found her books. He started buying into her bullshit. He..." He threw up his hands and turned back to Winger, shaking his head, tears streaking down his face. "What kind of people are able to justify the murder of children?"

Winger's mouth opened and closed.

"My parents. That's who. What chance did I have, Winger? But I *will* end it. This will not go on."

"The experiments have stopped."

"But the lingering death of the Guardians, the real Guardians, keeps going. Do you know how Guardians are actually created? Do you know where our people get the magic from? Do you have any idea what they put inside your chest?"

"It's a crystal." Winger shook her head, her face confused as she gave knowledge every Skyan knew, from child to elder, common knowledge of their people. "A shard."

"No. It's so much more than that. It's so much worse."

The world shifted to darkness and dust. The memories, the visions of the past, whatever the fuck they were, vanished. But the answers only raised more questions.

Kiera looked around, turning a circle, desperate to see more, to *find* more. She knew Jayson, she knew those eyes. She knew without a doubt he was the boy from the room, and she was nothing more than an experiment. It was all true. Everything she saw. She felt it. She knew it.

She got to her feet, rage keeping her warm, and stormed out of the room, out of the building. Her heavy footfalls echoed in the emptiness. Her head shook back and forth, imaginary conversations playing out in her head. She got to the ship, only to find the revulsion of getting back on board too much for her to fight against.

Fuck. Should have grabbed that bloody sword.

She laughed and the sound was disturbing as it filled the abandonment. Disturbing and uncontrolled, like a bad guy in a corny B- movie, all hysteria.

"Do you have your answers now?"

Kiera spun and came face-to-face with Jayson. He leaned on his sword as though it were a cane. Kiera wasn't fooled. The thick sinew of his forearms bulged, his hand itching for an excuse to wrap his fingers around the handle of the sword.

"Some." Kiera tried not to step back. "How about you?"

"All but what I most want to know."

"Which is what?"

"How did you get away? How did you escape this land? You were just a child, locked up tight like the rest of us."

"I don't know."

Maybe I'm just the bad guy.

Kiera kept that thought to herself as her mouth ran on without her permission.

"You can ask all you want. But I've got less answers than you might imagine. Hell, I didn't even know I wasn't human. I didn't know there was something shoved in my chest."

"When did it start talking to you?"

The man that stood in front of her looked more like that boy, calm but shy, sheepish hope in his eyes.

"It's always talked to me." Kiera couldn't imagine that holding back Jiminy's truth mattered now. No, not Jiminy. Tamin. His name was Tamin. "I just thought I was, you know, crazy."

Jayson laughed and Kiera ached for the trust she had felt in that revelatory vision in Silana's rooms. She might have trusted that boy; she might have even followed him, but that innocence slipped as anger and a dark sickness thickened the air between them. Kiera could almost see it, like electrically charged wavelengths.

"We are crazy. But that doesn't mean the voices aren't real. Has it told you what it is yet?"

"No. What is it?"

Kiera had a feeling—a deep, rotten root twisting down to her toes kind of feeling—but she really wanted to be wrong.

Jayson smirked. "Oh, I wouldn't want to ruin the surprise."

"Did you take the Guardians? Did you kill them?"

"Oh yes." He smiled. "Wait, no. Oh yes. They deserve what they get. In fact, they deserve much worse than what I have and will do to them."

"And what is that? What are you planning to do to them?"

"I plan only to take back what they stole."

His voice was hard, spoken between clenched teeth. He stepped forward, into Kiera's personal space.

"What did they steal?"

"You really are lost in the dark, aren't you?"

"Urgh, just answer a damn question."

Jayson raised his eyebrows as though bored with the entire interaction. "I'll start answering questions when you ask the ones worth answering."

"The crystals. That's what they stole, isn't it? The original Guardians never gave them to the Skyans. Why did they steal them? Just for power?"

His smile was wide. Too wide. "We were given the crystals, but that was not enough for them. The crystals provided us all the magic we needed to defend our people. But they still wanted more."

"So, it's all about trying to correct their greed?" Kiera scoffed and lifted her arms, taking in the city surrounding her. "Welcome to the world."

Only she didn't think that *was* what it was all about. A new question formed in her mind.

"Who were the original Guardians?"

He stepped back, a smile she didn't like spreading over his face. It was too sweet, dark and sickly, like molasses.

"Finally, you are asking the right questions."

"And you think they all know? The Skyans? The Guardians?"

"Of course they all know."

"Winger didn't. Not before you told her, so how can you be sure?"

That stopped Jayson from his peacock pacing.

"Winger is dead," Jayson spat.

"I know." Kiera's voice was soft, a whisper. "I was with her when she died."

Rage transformed his features. "You killed her?"

"No," Kiera insisted.

After a few moments, Jayson took a deep breath and growled. "How did you get away from this place? How did you recover?"

"I honestly don't know. I didn't remember this place. I thought I was human, until I saw Blue."

"Ah, Blue, and how is he?" That smile, too wide, with the deep-sunken eyes bulging above. "In agony, I hope."

"He's dead. You killed him."

"Did I?" He chuckled "He was one of the first, you know?"

"One of the first?" Kiera asked.

"One of the first to harness 'the power of the crystals.'"

He made air quotes around the words. Kiera almost burst out laughing. Such human gestures from such a monster.

Kiera shook her head. She was so sick of having to mine for answers. "How? How did they harness the crystals? And how the hell can Blue be one of them? You're talking about the history of your people; I'm guessing it wasn't just twenty years ago."

"Guardians don't age like humans, or Skyans. The crystals slow the aging process. And how?" Jason's laugh was brittle, and stuck in Kiera's ears like overcooked toffee. "They murdered the original Guardians. Well, they did worse than that."

His anger was replaced with a sadness that gripped Kiera's heart. What she wouldn't give to have the anger back.

Kiera raised her eyebrows and cocked her head. "So, you're trying to tell me you're actually the good guy and they are the big bad evil?"

"Not at all." The sadness washed away like a sandcastle made too close to the water. "But who says there has to be a good guy? Oh, and by the way, your dragon might need some help. Last I saw him, he was having a very rough day."

"Levison." Kiera's heart sped in her chest. She stepped forward, but Jayson raised his sword, point nearly touching Kiera's throat. "What is wrong with you? I got a crystal as well. I had that psycho bitch of a mother of yours experiment on me too. You don't see me turning into a vicious son of a bitch."

Jayson laughed and the sound sent hot pokers into Kiera's skin. "Because you aren't the son. Of. The. Bitch. And just wait. We are all just one push away."

Kiera didn't care about what had happened to the boy, not anymore. "What did you do to Levison?"

"What I had to." He waved his fingers and turned, running faster than his drawn features implied possible. "It was me or him."

She had been too distracted to notice the throbbing at the back of her head. But now it pounded with each moment she couldn't find him. His mewling grew louder in response to her calls, echoing around the quiet world like a twisted version of Marco Polo.

"Oh."

Kiera raced toward Levison, where he was trapped beneath a net. Weights pressed down at each intersection of crossed wire. It cut bloody lines through his back and tore at his wings.

His eyes locked on hers and she pulled at the net. He screeched and pushed against it, only succeeding in digging the wires deeper into his flesh.

"No, Levison. It's okay. I'll get you out, but you have to stop thrashing."

But Kiera's words were choked, tears brimming in her eyes, pouring down her cheeks with the fear and panic.

Levison panted heavily as he collapsed to the ground, body bleeding and wings torn.

"Come on," Kiera said through gritted teeth, as she pulled at the weights. They were even heavier than they looked, each disk an inch thick at least. "Come on, you sons of bitches!"

Kiera pulled and yanked, and a sound behind her made her yank harder still. Were they footsteps? Was Jayson watching, a twinkle in the bastard's glistening eyes as she failed to free her dragon? As she failed to be the Guardian she never knew she was supposed to be?

"This might help."

Kiera gasped, jerking her head up to see Zarzy standing over her, hand wrapped around a pair of wire cutters.

"Thanks."

It still took Kiera too long to snap enough of the wires to let Levison free. Far too long. With the removal of each weight, Levison wriggled and fought and the beat in Kiera's chest thumped along to his thrashings.

"Hush. Levison, you need to stop, or I'll end up hurting you more."

"Does it answer you?" Zarzy whispered, as though they were in the middle of a church during a moment of silence.

"Of course he does," Kiera snapped as Zarzy remained back a few paces, simply watching. "He's telling me now to get him the hell out of this fucking cage."

For a Healer, she seemed far too squeamish about the damaged dragon hatchling, or maybe she was just like her brother. Uncaring about what happened to an innocent.

"Not what I meant."

Zarzy didn't allow her voice to rise to Kiera's annoyance. But, when Kiera looked up and met Zarzy's eyes, she saw storm clouds in those pewter-gray eyes.

"Well, Jiminy doesn't exactly answer many of my questions. He snarks and insults me more often than not."

Levison nudged his nose free and headbutted Kiera on the arm, knocking her off-balance from her crouch.

"Oi!"

She pulled herself back up and caught Zarzy running fingers over her cheeks, beneath her eyes. Did the woman have a heart after all? Kiera knew she wasn't really being fair, but she had never been good with fear. Adrenaline, sure, but not fear.

Zarzy's hands dropped to her hips and her face hardened once more. "What happened?"

"Your brother is a god-damned psycho, that's what happened. Why didn't you and your dad stop him?"

Kiera returned to snip the last of the wires that held Levison grounded, more vigor in her movements, a mix of anger and frustration.

"Stop him?" Zarzy let out a sharp bark, which Kiera assumed was Zarzy's version of a sarcastic laugh. "You and your assumptions. Do you think we knew what was really going on? You think we know it all now? Do you really think, as a Healer, I would just sit back and let him kill Guardians, no matter what I think of them?"

"So, you had no idea?"

Kiera shook her head as she asked, cutting the last wire, deeply embedded into Levison's skin, and muttered a quick apology to the dragon. He rubbed his cheek against her shoulder and slumped back down to the ground with a long puff of air. Kiera ran her palm over his head before standing back up to face Zarzy.

Zarzy's pale cheeks had taken on a pink tinge. "I've never had any proof." She let out a heavy breath. "But I did suspect, yes."

"You and your fucking proof."

Anger toward this whole mess lashed out, like an exploding flame, threatening to engulf Zarzy for the mere crime of standing too close.

"Guardians think themselves immortal. How could I believe that my own brother was able to kill them?"

"Oh, great. So, is it just daddy issues, or are you one snap away from being just as psycho as your brother with your Guardian issues?"

"What would you know about it?"

Kiera sucked in her breath and clenched in anticipation of the physical impact her words might have, the impact that happened every time mention of her being an orphan was made on Earth. But nothing happened. It seemed the least of her problems now, and her flames petered out further.

"I saw what happened to your mother."

Kiera's voice was gentle. Perhaps she and Zarzy had more in common than she's realized.

"And? She killed children out of her need to be king of the skies. To save a race that wasn't dying."

"But..." Kiera lost all words.

"But, what?" Zarzy asked, the coldness in her tone warming slightly.

"But surely that explains why you don't like getting close to people?"

"You don't know a thing about me. You think I am just a product of my parents? Just like everyone else, assuming you know me because you discovered my childhood trauma? I thought you would know better. Now, Hesperus is willing to take you and the hatchling back on board, but I'm not staying any longer. You can come or not. I don't care."

"Jayson's still here."

Kiera looked around. Why hadn't he come after her while Levison was still trapped?

"No, he's not. He took Zephyrus and left."

Kiera's cheeks warmed; she had no words as she watched Zarzy storm away. She had done exactly what Zarzy had accused her of. And was the Healer really so distant? She had smiled when Kiera had awoken; she had been gentle and kind on occasion.

"Kindness only until I was better and no longer a wounded bird," Kiera muttered, before helping Levison back to his feet and following slowly behind.

CHAPTER 25

The ship shuddered down against the dry-packed field behind the warehouse.

Matriol had chosen well, Jayson would give the creature that. But he was only a means to an end. All the Void were. When the world was set to rights, the original Guardians would take care of the detritus left from their torture. But for now, he would do what was needed, and use whatever he needed to get it done.

The crisp, dead grass crunched beneath the stomp of his thick-soled boots as he dropped from Zephyrus. The hardness sent jarring shockwaves up through his legs. Growling slightly, he strode toward the back door of the warehouse.

"Matriol!" The word snapped out as he stomped into the dark, cavernous space.

Yes, it would serve his needs perfectly.

The slimy beast detached from the shadowy corner. It had grown. It had feasted a lot. Jayson forced down the disgust and anger as the creature slithered closer.

"Unpack the hold."

Matriol said nothing as it brushed past Jayson on its way outside, sending a thick coil of darkness to spread from Jayson's chest out through his limbs.

CHAPTER 26

Hesperus's deck rumbled gently beneath Kiera's shoes as she stepped back on board. She headed to the medical bay, hoping that Zarzy wouldn't be there as much as she hoped she would. The door opened to silence.

Concentrating on helping Levison allowed Kiera's mind to focus on the teeming questions as the heat in her cheeks cooled.

"Did you truly never ask it what it was?" Silana asked, her voice making Kiera jump.

She hadn't heard the older woman slip into the medical bay. Kiera closed her eyes against the longing for hot chocolate, lumpy knitted blankets, and open fires on a winter's night. Who was Aunt Em and why did she sound so much like these Skyans, these strangers living in the clouds?

"It was never so strong down there. I mean, I heard him still, but it was like bad reception compared to what it's like up here. And what was I supposed to do? Everyone just told me it was my conscience. Hence, Jiminy."

Silana's eyebrows knitted in confusion for a moment before she spoke again. "Well, perhaps now would be a good time to find out, hmm?"

"Why?" Kiera snapped, and a low rumble came from Levison before he jumped off the medical bed and landed on the floor between Kiera and Silana. His wings, ripped and torn in various spots were still magnificent as they half-stretched out.

"Your grandson has gone batshit crazy because he's been talking to whatever it is in his chest. I've been carrying a living creature around inside of me and you think talking to it *isn't* going to send me into the same spiral? Even your granddaughter's a cold-hearted bitch because of all of this. I get it. I was a victim of Fang-Ripper's experiments, but guess what, I don't care. I want to get the hell out of this place and go back home. I'm done with every single one of you figments of my imagination."

"You think we don't exist?" Silana asked.

"Oh, you exist. Every single one of you bastards exists. But it's going to be easier to sleep at night if I start convincing myself you don't."

"Well then, I guess Zarzy was right. You are of no use to us if you refuse to connect with your heart."

Silana nodded, and the disapproval on her face twisted uncomfortably inside of Kiera.

Only Aunt Em had ever made her feel so shamed. But what did they really expect from her? She was an escaped experiment. One with no memory. It had all been kept from her, and now she was just supposed to be this tool for them? To what end?

She had escaped, but it didn't give her any special skills. She was behind all of them, racing catch up with things they still kept secret. But Kiera's mouth had dried, her tongue sticking to the roof of her mouth. There were no words.

Silana left and Kiera slid down to the floor.

Exhaustion washed over her like a spray of snow, or at least what she imagined snow would feel like. It seeped through her clothes and skin, chilling her to her bones.

"I'm not a cold-hearted bitch," Zarzy said from the doorway, as though scared to step into her own medical bay.

"Sure. You're just a big, cuddly teddy bear."

Zarzy laughed a little, a small smile dancing on her lips, as she stepped into the room. The door swooshed closed behind her. It had never swooshed before, and Kiera realized it was because the door had never actually been closed before.

"I wouldn't go that far."

"So, are you going to tell me I can't go home?" Kiera asked.

"I don't tell anyone what they can and cannot do. My role is to be a neutral Healer. I came in to see if I can be of assistance..." She jerked her head toward Levison. "...with it."

"*He*. He is a dragon hatchling, not a monster. And his name is Levison."

Zarzy ignored Kiera's reprimand. "I thought you might also like some new clothes."

"Yes please."

The torn shirt that struggled to cover Kiera's chest was matched by the shorts that made her feel more exposed than nakedness might.

Zarzy tilted her head, that line creasing down between her eyes. Kiera waited for some explanation, but of course the line flattened back out and no answers were given. Zarzy opened one of the cupboards, two over from the one she had once pulled a blanket from, and handed over a pile of clothes. Healer's clothes.

Beggars can't be choosers.

"Thank you."

Zarzy nodded and turned her back. Kiera was only half-dressed when Zarzy spoke.

"My grandmother is right. Unless you are willing to accept that there is a sentient being fused into your chest, you may as well be just another Guardian."

Kiera finished dressing and sat on the end of the medical bed where Levison had previously been her patient. "Why do you hate the Guardians so much?"

"Didn't you already decide it was because of my mother's execution?"

"I'm sorry." And Kiera was, more than she'd realized. "You can turn around now."

"When we were younger, my brother and I were extremely close. It's hard not to be close when you are twins."

"Twins?"

Kiera looked harder at Zarzy, studying the porcelain skin, grey eyes and thick lips. She saw nothing of Jayson in her angelic face.

"Yes." That laugh, melodic and tinkling on a non-existent breeze.

"But things changed when my mother and him started spending a lot more time together, alone in her rooms. I was welcome there too once. She would tell me stories of the great past. She was my friend. And then it all changed. I was so jealous. Even after we discovered the experiments, I found I was still jealous of the time he had gotten with her, where I didn't. After that, it was Blue who spent all *his* time in her rooms, apparently trying to work out why his beloved had turned against their own kind. He seemed like he wanted to follow in her footsteps. I don't know exactly what he's been doing but it isn't good. None of our family are. We are a danger to our people. So, I have tried to balance that out as best as I can."

Zarzy danced her fingers along the top of the cupboards that ran along one wall before hitching herself up on to the other end of the medical bed.

"We didn't talk about it. The experiments. I was left alone while my father and brother hid their pain. I wanted to heal my family. It's not so surprising."

"No, it's not." Kiera could follow Zarzy's thinking, and guilt at judging her solidified into stone. "I'm sorry."

Zarzy shrugged and gave Kiera a small smile. "After I had taken my oath as a Healer, Jayson came to me and told me what was inside of him. What our mother had done to him, and what was actually inside of every Guardian."

"What are they?" Kiera tapped her chest, feeling the scar tissue under her fingers. "What do I have inside of me?"

Though the well-known numbness continued, her chest registered the pressure. The nerve endings never worked the same as the unscarred skin on the rest of her body.

Zarzy responded with her own question. "It does speak to you, doesn't it?"

"Yes," Kiera answered, with a resigned sigh.

"And you have really never asked?" Zarzy's eyes were wide.

"No." Kiera shook her head. "Who wants to be proven correct about their own insanity?"

"I can't tell you. I wish I had never known, that I'd never been told. I could not ever give that information, that burden to someone else. Until today, I believed he had lied."

Zarzy left, without another word, without a look or a gesture. She simply hopped back off the bed and left the room.

"What are you?" Kiera asked, addressing Jiminy. The silence in Kiera's mind remained.

It couldn't be because she'd asked too quietly. Volume shouldn't matter. Slowly, she slipped her hand under her new shirt and lay her open palm against the twisted rope of scar tissue. A lifetime of fear fought her fingers, begged her to pull them away. She warred inside herself.

She had to stop being such a coward.

"Please?"

I can show you.

Her nod was hesitant, but it was enough. Her body fell back on to the bed, and the world she knew disappeared in the darkness that overtook her.

CHAPTER 27

The sky was perfect. A deep azure streaked with fluffy, white clouds. On the ground, the river bubbled slowly, flowing down through mountains and forest, splitting their part of the world. They could leave this mass of land anytime they wanted—the sky was their true home—but they had learned to love the other creatures who lived here. There was pleasure in visiting friends and feeling the earth beneath their claws.

Their friends were landbound, like so many of the creatures here. They revered the larger, winged beasts, and many understood the privilege of riding on the backs of them. Demiarus had allowed only two to ride on their back. The weight and feel of them against their hide had been surprisingly comforting.

But the rumbling among the trees, and the shudder of the mountains themselves, had grown and even the dragons began to feel the discomfort in the air.

Demiarus, the oldest of the dragons, had to find the cause and stop it. Nostrils flaring, they took a deep whiff of the air. It had been too long, this discomfort. Why had they left it so long to ask Demiarus for assistance?

Their descendants covered the Earth. All land masses had dragon nests and forests. Many had become inhabitants more of the earth than the sky, and Demiarus loved all of them.

The rumbling continued and their back soaked in the heat of the sun while their shadow played games on the ground far below. They could not deny the whispering rumbles any longer. Flying low, they rested their talons in the cool touch of the river's water, disrupting the flow of the stream as little as possible. The water brushed against their scales and a light rumble of pleasure started in their rounded belly and bubbled up over sharp teeth and thick tongue.

"Demiarus..."

The tree sprite glided out from behind the thick trunk of a paperbark. The sprite bent forward, arms following up behind their prostrate form, to point stiff hands to the sky. The traditional greeting to a respected elder.

"Hello, Liatha. I have heard the rumblings. There is much to concern myself about, if what I hear it correct. Is it true? Have my kin gone missing?"

Liatha unfolded themselves and looked Demiarus in the eye, leader to leader. "Yes."

"Is it the ones we shared with?"

"Yes, Demiarus. More from across the seas have come, and the ones you made peace with now teach them how to steal the magic as though they still feel none of it. Are they truly still ignorant? Have the hearts not beat enough for them to feel us, or are they merely evil?"

"I do not know," Demiarus rumbled.

Anger puffed out in white-hot jets from their nostrils. They had hoped, however vainly, that the rumors were exaggerated or, better yet, entirely false.

The confirmation flamed the fire in their belly.

With a surge of water, they pushed strong legs against the floor of the river, and raced upward into the sky. With wings pressed against their body, they continued up until clouds surrounded them. Demiarus called on the clouds and they came without hesitation. Building and darkening, they surrounded Demiarus as they sent their thoughts out to their kind. All of their kind. Any creature with a drop of dragon's blood and lifeforce would hear the words in their mind and in their blood.

The rustlings and rumblings are true. The truce, the time of peace has passed. They are killing the magic; they are stealing the living. They must be stopped.

A war of blood and fire overtook the world. Rivers overflowed with blood. Demiarus saw their life mate die. And, after that destruction to their heart and soul, three of the fiercest soldiers went missing. They sought to end the war. They sought to end their own pain, once and for all. Demiarus's own life, forfeit, in the hopes of saving their kind, saving the world and the magic.

They had learned enough of this race to understand one thing. The humans would never be satisfied.

It took too long, but finally Demiarus tracked down their missing kin. There was a cave, built bigger than nature would have allowed, carved into the side of the mountains. The air that blew out from the depths of the darkness was stale and putrid. It cooled their blood and worried at their magic; it begged them to return to the light, to the fresh air.

But blood had been spilled for too long, and only they, the master of the skies and the dragons, had the power to truly end this war.

"Hello, beasty."

The human stood with a sword in his hand. Over time, Demiarus had learned all they could about this enemy, and they knew what they called themselves. They had watched many of their kind. They seemed so different and familiar all at once. There were ones that Demiarus could imagine befriending, but the ones in power were ignorant, and willfully so. They did not try to listen to the world they invaded, and they hurt others before they allowed thought or communication.

Demiarus stepped forward, wings opened and up, ready for a battle. Until they focused on the sword in the man's hand.

It was not made of a material he had seen in the hands of the humans. It was the massacred remains of one of their soldier's hearts. One of their Guardians.

"No!"

They roared and pulled on every ounce of magic and anger they could reach. They yanked the sword from the man's grip. The man held on as long as he could, but he was no match for the leader of the dragons.

With swift movements, Demiarus thrust the blade, the obsidian heart of their lost friend and kin, into the soft, pulpy body of the human.

The human's scream was a newfound nourishment and joy to their mind, body and heart.

But it did not last.

Demiarus stepped over the crumbled meat sack of human and followed the light further back in the cave. The light was not natural. It was an eerie sickness that turned their insides aflame. The magics that coursed through their blood continued to beg them, sobbing in their mind, to turn back, to leave the cave of death and horror.

But they had never run away like a coward. They had never backed down, and today was not the day to begin.

Because why should they? They were the master of the skies. They were the only one able to call the clouds to their side, to communicate with the waters. The magic flowing in them was energy and life itself.

The rumble in their chest shook the walls around them as they stepped into the first fingers of electric light. Debris fell from the roof as the roar exploded from their jaw. Around them, were the missing kin. They were splayed and pegged to the walls with the poisonous bones of their own wingtips, snapped off and turned into weapons. Their bodies, once beautiful and majestic, were eviscerated, empty cavities in their chests where their hearts had been. Lifeblood had dripped and dried on the floor beneath broken feet and claws.

Beneath some were rusted, metallic containers, catching the falling blood.

They passed them, anger filling Demiarus with a fire hotter than they had ever felt. Hot enough to burn them and the entire world along with them.

They named each dragon as they passed, sending condolences to their kin through the mental connection of their kind, before moving on to the next. They were near the end of the field of light when one dragon, eviscerated and heart removed, lifted her head, blood dripping and splashing into one of those containers, slow but constant from her opened body.

Hope flamed in Demiarus's chest. "You are alive."

"Demiarus..." The name rasped out. "Kill me... They keep me suspended, undying but not living. They continue to feed from the magic in my blood. My heart, I can still feel it. It now resides in another, but this other does not hear me. Please! Please kill me, my liege."

Demiarus could not bear to allow another of their kin to die. "I will retrieve your heart."

"No. I do not know what will become of the other should the heart be removed now. Please, put me out of my misery. I cannot continue like this. The magic continues to heal me, and I continue to live. I just want death. Please?"

Demiarus roared. The walls trembled, and rocks fell. Large chunks of earth and stone tumbled from the roof. They continued to roar until the pain inside was distracted by a far more physical sensation.

They turned to see the human, dismissed as dead when they had stepped over it, holding the same obsidian sword. It had cut through the sinew of Demiarus's wings. They opened them to attack, and agony rippled through their body. While Demiarus measured the extent of the damage, the human took the opportunity and swung the sword again. It sliced and cut through the right wing, the wielder far more agile than Demiarus gave him credit for being.

Their pride would be dragon-kind's undoing, but not before the humans received their own, long-overdue reckoning.

Their breath was heavy and hot, flames absent as all energy and healing focused on saving them from the onslaught. Three more humans, all wielding swords forged from dragon's hearts, joined in. Soon, Demiarus saw their own fate clearly.

With their last strength, Demiarus sent the force of their magic to every dragon that inhabited their world, because what was the magic but energy, and energy could be channeled.

No single dragon would ever possess the sole power over nature again. Demiarus would be the last to hold single rule over the clouds and the trees, over the water and the skies.

The risk was far too great, a risk their pride and arrogance had never allowed them to see, until it was too late.

Kiera gasped. A broken scream blistered her lips as she came out of the memory. Tears streamed down her temples, and she shoved the edge of her palm into her mouth as far as it would go in a vain attempt to squash down the horrors she had seen. Her teeth bit into the flesh and the pain helped ground her. She had felt the insanity of rage at the edge of Demarius's mind. It scared her more than she could process.

Zarzy gently pried the bitten hand out of Kiera's mouth. "Ease up now, Kiera. It's okay. It's okay."

Kiera looked up into Zarzy's eyes and started crying again.

"It's okay."

Zarzy lifted Kiera into a sitting position and wrapped her arms around the weeping woman. Kiera sobbed and sniffled into Zarzy's shirt and wished she could curl up tighter in the woman's embrace. As though reading her mind, Zarzy's arms tightened around her.

It felt like a lifetime passed before Kiera pulled away, finally in control once again.

"Sorry. I ruined your shirt."

Zarzy laughed, low and gentle, as she cupped Kiera's cheek. "Well, yes. You know, you really are the strangest Skyan I have ever met."

Kiera nodded. "Where's Levison?"

"He left."

"He *left*?" An ache caught in Kiera's chest, somewhere between her own heart and Tamin's.

A dragon's heart beats in my chest.

Yes, Tamin said, such sadness in so small and insignificant a word.

"He flew off. I have not seen him return."

Kiera nodded. She supposed it was safer, being away from Guardians, from Skyans, from the monstrous human race.

"Kiera?" Zarzy asked.

"What?" she snapped. The fury returned. She would forever mourn the deaths of the majestic creatures, but right now she wanted the anger. It fueled her fire.

"Why are you angry at me?" Zarzy snapped right back, as she stood up from the medical bed.

"You knew there was a dragon's heart inside of me all this time. Jayson told you, didn't he? When you were children, he told you that inside of all the Guardians were dragon hearts." Kiera stood, shaking her head, still finding ways to fit the pieces of the puzzle together without the full picture. "Every single Guardian carries around the massacre of the dragons. But instead of believing him, you stood against him, healing those who hurt him."

"That's not fair! I will not apologize for being a Healer. I don't have the power to judge who deserves to live and who doesn't."

Kiera tried to calm her breathing but the pounding in her chest would not ease. "You're right."

Zarzy's hands were on her hips as she faced Kiera. "You don't even know what you're talking about."

"Then tell me."

Kiera's chest continued to rise and fall rapidly as she stepped closer, the two women barely a foot apart, staring each other down. She wanted to run, to hide from it all, but she felt the pull of truth. She was so close. She knew it like the feel of her skin in the rain.

"The Guardians only have shards in their chests. There isn't enough of the heart to communicate. They don't know. It was a story told to me by my grief-stricken brother. How could I ever believe something so fantastical?"

"But you made him feel like a liar." Kiera's chest burned within her, tears pricking at her eyes. "What chance did Jayson have with no one on his side?"

"You can't understand how it was right after she died! Jayson was obsessed, withdrawn, not sleeping, manic at times. No one understood what my mother had been doing. It was only years later that he told me what he thought the experiments were actually for."

"And that was?"

"Finding a way to communicate with the dragons." Zarzy's words were thick and heavy. "And with their help, to find more crystals."

The idea was bile at the back of Kiera's throat. "More *crystals*?"

"You know the history." Zarzy sniffed back whatever emotion Kiera had felt from her and straightened her back again. "You probably know more than me."

Kiera stepped back. "I think I'm starting to."

"We were kids, Kiera. Why would I think what he was saying was real? Our father, Blue, told me Jayson hadn't been experimented on. He said they had him examined after he started talking about it all. I had already lost my mother, and my brother was raving like a lunatic. I was lost. I wish I had believed him."

The words floated around the room, and for a moment Kiera's chest hurt to the point of bursting.

"I'm sorry. I can't imagine how hard it's all been for you."

"No..." Zarzy's lips pursed. "You can't. You don't get to judge me, or anyone else. You left, and we had to live here knowing more than any of us wanted to about our own family."

"I should never have come back aboard. I should have left with Levison."

"And I should have tipped you overboard the first chance I got," Zarzy said, but as Kiera met her eyes, the corners of her mouth twitched.

Kiera shook her head and laughed. "I'm sorry."

Zarzy shrugged, a smirk on her lips. "I'm a convenient scapegoat."

"It wasn't fair of me. But please, I need to know everything you do."

"I can't tell you much—"

"Another attack by the Void."

Silana cut off whatever else Zarzy might have said as she raced in, wrapping a white apron around her middle.

"Shit." Zarzy reached out and brushed a single finger along the back of Kiera's hand. "We could use your help, and then I promise to keep fighting with you afterwards."

Kiera smiled, unable to ignore the electricity that zipped up her arm from Zarzy's light touch. "Help with what?"

"With the wounded," Zarzy answered. "It's the third Void attack in as many weeks."

"What are the Void?" Kiera asked.

"The real enemy." Silana's words were crisp and allowed no more questions.

CHAPTER 28

The first of the wounded were brought in on stretchers carried by others who wore the same Healer attire as Zarzy. Blood, torn clothes and stained bandages were more visible than the people beneath.

"What can I do?"

Kiera clamped her mouth shut as soon as the words were out. She had to swallow down the anger and rage. She had been so caught up in things she still didn't completely understand, things from the past, and yet here were people being attacked and left for dead. At least, that's what she had heard one Healer say as he transferred a burned child onto one of the tables.

She would not waste more time on self-pity.

Silana held out a set of keys that sounded more like wind chimes as they danced from her movement. "Take these."

"Okay."

"There are three other Healer rooms. Open them up and guide the next wave of stretchers through to them."

Kiera nodded and headed toward the door as more Healers walked in and out. She turned away from the stairs to the deck and found the other rooms. Once opened, lights came on to reveal one room larger than the medical bay and two others more like the medical room where she had been locked with Zarzy and Silana.

Once all the doors were open, she headed back up to the deck. More Healers and crew than Kiera had seen on Hesperus moved and filled half the space. She suspected their absence had not been coincidental.

They all walked, confident and with purpose. They knew their roles. And Kiera breathed heavy at the weight of how familiar they all were with the recent attack and this aftermath. With a determined breath, she began leading Healers and their wounded patients down to the rooms below. Before long, a wave of purpose stole through Kiera and the intimidation of these Skyans broke beneath the need of the patients. Her feet ached, and the sensation bolstered her sense of purpose.

"Zarzar?" A small girl wept as she clung to a small toy that looked suspiciously like the egg of the headquarters city. "Where is Zarzar?"

Kiera smiled at the girl but spoke to the Healers carrying her. "There's space with Zarzy."

The Healer nodded and began moving.

The girl's hand gripped Kiera's. "Please don't leave me."

Kiera looked around the deck. The stretchers had stopped coming, and the Healers on deck were finding places to sit and rest.

Kiera nodded and smiled again. "Okay."

"My name is Meeka."

"Hi, Meeka. I'm Kiera. You know Zarzy?"

She smiled and her eyes sparkled. "I know everything."

Kiera liked the kid already. "So, what happened?"

"The Void came." Her voice trembled.

"Meeka, you need to lay down," the Healer carrying the end of the stretcher insisted. "You've had a big shock."

"I don't need to be here," Meeka whined, but lay back on the stretcher.

"I've never seen a Void. I don't even know what they are."

"Are you stupid?" Meeka asked, disdain of a child much older than what she seemed dripping from her words.

"Meeka!" the Healer scolded.

"Sorry."

"It's okay," Kiera insisted. "I kind of am. Can you tell me?"

"The Void are the beasties of the skies. Way worse than the dragons, or the fae, or the phoenixes."

"Wow, all those creatures are real?"

"Yes." Again, Meeka was unimpressed with Kiera's lack of knowledge but her fingers gripped tighter as a coughing fit overtook her.

Kiera stayed silent, helping where she could to get the stretcher down the stairs.

"I got told the Void was just a story, just a fairytale to scare little kids." Meeka's voice was little more than a whisper. "But then they started attacking. My parents died the first time they attacked our home."

"When was that?"

Meeka held tighter to the egg toy. "Two years ago."

"Where did they come from?"

"No one knows. The Guardians are fighting them as well as the other beasties, but they didn't make it on time."

Tears welled in the corners of her eyes as she pulled her toy closer to her chest and squeezed Kiera's fingers in a vice grip.

Zarzy rushed over as they stepped into the medical room. "Meeka!"

Kiera's hand was unceremoniously dropped, and the girl sat up and let Zarzy wrap her arms around her.

"Her lungs?" Zarzy asked, as soon as she picked up the girl and placed her on one end of a bed.

"She went back for the younger kids."

"Meeks, what am I going to do with you?"

"I couldn't leave them."

"Your lungs aren't as strong as others. You should have told someone else to go in."

"It was my job," Meeka said, and the argument was over.

Movement above deck told Kiera another way of stretches were coming aboard. She left quietly, but confident in her job as new information whirled around in her head.

"Come sit."

Zarzy walked into the largest of the medical rooms where Kiera was collecting bloodstained material and putting them in a large calico bag she had found in one of the drawers. The similarities to the year and a day she had worked at the hospital weren't lost on her.

Kiera threw a glance over her shoulder, not really taking in much of Zarzy as she stood in the doorway. "I'm nearly done."

"Now. Before you fall down. Healer's orders."

Kiera let out a breath, her shoulders sagging as she dumped the last of the stained material in the bag. The floor still needed a clean but it could wait a few minutes.

Turning around, Zarzy offered her a granola bar with one hand as she crunched on another from her other hand. Kiera burst out laughing and only laughed harder when Zarzy raised a single eyebrow.

"I would have thought with all this magic, you would have found something nicer for food."

Zarzy looked down at the bar in her hand. "I like these. It's quick, convenient and easy."

Kiera smiled and munched on her own bar.

"I'm sorry," Zarzy said.

Kiera looked up and furrowed her brow, her mouth still full of granola.

"I'm sorry for yelling at you before."

"Me too," Kiera managed, as she swallowed, the food scratching painfully down her throat.

Real smooth, Kiera.

"It matters to me, you know," Kiera said, once she had finished eating

"What does?"

"That you didn't know."

"Of course I didn't know. But... I think it's all starting to make a bit more sense now."

"Want to share with the class?"

"Jayson is determined to return all the shards to the dragons. To give them back their hearts."

"Okay, so he is killing the Guardians to remove the shards. I'm with you so far."

"So, that's troubling enough..." Zarzy smirked. "...but there is more to worry about than just having another homicidal person in the same family."

Kiera laughed and nodded. "Okay. You've got my attention."

"So, Skyans don't have any magic of our own. We only exist up here because of the shards. They are in everything, our ships, our cities, our Guardians. Once all the shards have been collected and returned, then I believe our magic will end. Everything up here will end."

"Wait, what does that mean?" The granola bar now seemed like a bad idea, stuck in Kiera's chest. "Does it all just disappear? Will you fall from the sky?"

"I don't know." Zarzy looked at Kiera and the worry in her eyes made Kiera want to wrap her in her arms and steal her away from this place. "And that's the problem."

The bed they sat on shuddered beneath them.

"They've found us."

Silana came in, and the electricity that was swirling between Kiera and Zarzy dissipated in an instant.

"Fuck."

Zarzy seemed to like the word. Grudgingly, Kiera admitted she liked hearing it from her lips.

"Who has found us?" Kiera asked.

"The Void," Silana answered.

Kiera's skin vibrated and the heart inside her chest, the dark obsidian one, ached like it never had before. "Okay, so what now?"

Zarzy's lips lifted in a small smile, as though shyness had overtaken the ice-strong Healer Kiera had come to know. "Does that mean you are staying?"

When she was younger, not long after her parents' crash—except that never happened—she remembered standing at the top of a playground slide with a tunnel over the top, curving away to places she couldn't see. She'd imagined all kinds of things, her favorite being the portal to another world halfway down the slide.

But, even with the excitement of that portal in her mind, the minute she pushed off, there was a moment, just a fleeting second of fear, where she didn't want to go forward anymore, but it was too late to stop. The relative safety of the top step was gone.

That was how she felt now.

Too late to go back, and there wasn't any portal to whisk her away from the truth she had to face, about herself, and about the world between the clouds.

"How could I leave now that I know all of this?" Kiera smiled. "I can't turn my back on this. I'm not a monster."

For a moment, Zarzy looked slapped. Kiera wanted to explain, to make sure the woman knew it wasn't an attack on her. But then Zarzy's jaw clenched, and she turned to her grandmother.

Frozen again into that impenetrable wall of ice, Zarzy led the way to *Hesperus*'s deck, Silana a half-step behind. Kiera hurried to keep up with them.

As they got to the deck, half the starboard side was filled with Healers staring at the ship that had scraped along their side. They held swords in front of them and Kiera felt the unease of the sight down to her bones.

"What? You think we haven't learned how to defend ourselves?"

Zarzy twirled a sword in her fingers and Kiera laughed, because why not? She was on a ship in the sky, with a hottie of a doc who turned her on and drove her crazy, about to fight fairytale monsters.

The three looked over to see Jayson standing on *Zephyrus*'s deck. The twirling sword stopped, and Kiera's mouth dropped open.

"You said the Void?" Zarzy asked Silana, who simply nodded before she turned and walked toward a huddle of crew chatting amongst themselves.

"Behind him, Zarzy," Kiera whispered.

Behind Jayson were pulsating blobs of darkness.

"Oh, fuck," Zarzy said. "So, are they controlling him or is he controlling them? How? One we could take, but both?"

"Wait, the Void was a myth, until recently. Yeah?"

"Yeah, so?" Zarzy asked.

"He's created these monsters," Kiera said, pieces falling into place. "He's created them. They aren't the Void. Not like the fairytales."

"How does that matter right now?" Zarzy asked, hands wrapped around the handle of a sword, breath coming in and out, audible but controlled.

"I don't know, but it does. It's all right there."

Kiera's words came in a rush. *Zephyrus* was coming back to ram them again.

"Brace yourselves!" Silana cried to everyone on the deck of *Hesperus*.

A sword was pushed into Kiera's hand by a Healer she had never seen before. She smiled and gave a small nod as she braced her legs and the two ships slammed together once more.

"You can leave with your lives, no casualties, and your cargo of the wounded can remain on the path to healing!" Jayson called, arms up at either side as though that was all that stopped the Void from jumping the railings and killing all who stood against him.

"What do you want, Jayson?" Silana asked, the authority in her tone turning all heads on *Hesperus* her way.

"Just one, tiny little concession."

"Then out with it, child," Silana snapped.

Jayson shrugged. "Give me the Earth-walker."

"Earth-walker?" Kiera furrowed her brows and looked over at Zarzy. She was already looking at Kiera, already shaking her head.

"Oh, me?" Kiera asked, her free hand tapping against her scar.

"Don't go, Kiera," Zarzy said. "We can take him."

"We need to know more," Kiera said, past the lump in her throat. "There are still too many pieces missing."

Zarzy grabbed Kiera's free hand in her own. "He'll kill you."

"Don't tell me you're concerned about little, old me?" Kiera smiled. "Besides, he could have killed me last time, but he didn't."

"Well, I *have* just learned to tolerate you." Zarzy tried to smile, but it fell short. "And maybe that's true, but that doesn't mean he won't this time."

"I'll be okay," Kiera insisted, with more certainty then she felt.

"Why would we sacrifice any of our people to you, Jayson?" Zarzy asked, not giving in that easily.

"Because she is *not* one of your people," Jayson said, like he was explaining that rain was wet.

"Are you scared to face us?" Silana growled.

"Oh, Grandmother," Jayson laughed, and let his hands drop, one heading toward the handle of his sword. The Void slid forward on the deck behind him.

"No!" Kiera screamed, and Jayson's fingers danced in the air above the sword hilt. The Void held position.

"Heroic to a fault, hey, K. Well, come on then. If you wish to save these people."

"Kiera!"

Zarzy gripped Kiera's hand until she moved out of reach and had no choice but to let go.

"I'll be okay." Kiera gave Zarzy a wink. "Trust me."

"Oh, sis, don't tell me you've finally gotten sweet on someone." Jayson laughed. "And her, of all people."

"You hurt her, Jayson, and I swear I will revoke my oath as Healer."

Jayson laughed as he stepped toward the railing, hand outstretched for Kiera to take it. "My, my. The power you have over my family continues."

Continues?

Everything about Zephyrus was wrong. Stains splattered the deck. Dust and neglect lurked. It gathered in every corner, hung between crates, and covered every surface. Every surface except the Pillar, standing next to the ship's wheel, clean and catching the light.

The silence screamed in Kiera's ears and sent shivers up her spine. When she had last been on the ship, there had been sound and movement, even with just herself, Blue and a wounded Winger aboard.

Jayson laughed and pulled Kiera sharply into this new, horrific reality. His laugh played with the dust bunnies and caught on the spiders' webs. He stood at the helm, one long-fingered hand wrapped around the wheel while the other, bone-white, pressed against his chest. His labored breath, rough and ragged, reached Kiera where she stood, back pressed against the ship's railing. He was even more drawn than their last encounter mere days ago. Or had it been hours? It might as well have been a lifetime.

"Did you see her face? I would love to see that perfect frozen facade cracking now. She never believed me, not even as children. She was just like everyone else." He slammed his hands down on the pillar. The dust that surrounded the ship wasn't the deep indigo with speckled stars that had intrigued Kiera before. It was deep black. Black that threatened to never return light again.

"As soon as Mother was gone, everyone just wanted to forget

about the 'horrible things' she did. Well, I'd like to see them forget now."

"Stop."

Kiera couldn't take it, the pleasure he took in Zarzy's pain. His own sister. His twin.

Nausea roiled in her stomach as the blackness swelled, surrounding the ship, hiding the decrepit aspects of it. For a moment, the darkness took away some of the pain and anxiety, but then Jayson's sneering laugh cut through and set her teeth on edge once more.

"You have chosen your side, K. Don't get all twitchy on me now. I have some friends to introduce you to."

"The Void?" Kiera looked around, only now realizing they had vanished the moment she stepped aboard.

"Oh, they were just an illusion."

"But you *do* control the real Void, don't you? They're the missing Guardians?"

Neither comment was really a question, but she had to be sure. All the pieces were fitting but what if she was wrong, what if she had missed something?

"Of course, they are."

He tried for nonchalance, but Kiera could see the preening glint in his eyes.

"Have you killed them?"

"Killed them? Why would I do that? No, I've had use for them and they've proven very helpful. Besides, they deserve this fate."

"You've killed innocent people. Did *they* deserve it?"

Kiera couldn't hold back the anger when she thought of Meeka, already an orphan, death and loss and fear already the norm to such a young child.

"No one is innocent."

"We were."

The silence between them was thick and heavy.

"They've stolen everything. Our lives, our sanity. They pinned us to walls and turned our own bodies against us. They do not deserve your pity, or your mercy."

"No, Jayson. They didn't do that to us. We are not the dragons."

Kiera felt the bubble rise in her chest. Surely, he wasn't actually delusional.

"Of course we are. Do you think the shell is what makes a dragon? It's the heart, K. It's *always* been the heart."

He's right, Tamin said.

What?

And he's wrong.

Kiera blinked and felt her legs lose some of their newfound strength. Going with Jayson had seemed like a good idea, the best course of action. She could save all those people on Hesperus and she could find the last pieces to the puzzle.

Kiera forced the words out. "Now what?"

"We find the rest of the bastards who have hidden from me and get those hearts back to where they belong."

"And what about your heart? The one in your chest?"

"She is dead. She told me years ago."

Jayson looked away too quickly from Kiera's gaze. There was more there. But Kiera wasn't sure she really wanted to know.

"So, you know where the cave is?" Kiera asked.

"Come, I have something to show you."

His smile was anything but warm as he ignored Kiera's question. And what made the shiver down Kiera's spine that much sharper was the revulsion she felt from Tamin as much as from herself.

The blackness surrounding the ship disappeared as quickly as it had appeared, and Kiera blinked against the brightness of the light, a glare she hadn't felt since she had last been on Earth. The thought caught in her throat like a gasp.

"Earth..." she whispered, as she turned and looked over the railing. The bright midday sun stung Kiera's bare arms within moments.

"Come on. We have a lot to get done."

Jayson jumped over the railing and landed with a heavy thump and, a moment later, a muffled groan. She followed him off the ship, landing a lot lighter and without the audible discomfort. She looked around and saw a warehouse cordoned off with wire fencing. The ground was dusty and dry.

As she followed Jayson toward the large building, her legs rebelled against the hard earth. It had no give, no lightness. She hadn't thought about it up there—there was always too much else going on—but now she noticed the weight of the world, the force of gravity pressing upon her.

She was home, so why did everything feel so strange and uncomfortable, like a once-comfortable jacket she had now outgrown but still tried to wrap around her shoulders? Well, she knew why, but how it could all turn upside down in such a short time in the sky, she would never understand.

The light, hard and harsh, made her lift her arm to her forehead to shield her eyes. It was an industrial area, with little movement or evidence of life. A weekend maybe? Kiera had entirely lost track of days.

Her arms prickled as she followed Jayson through the small opening in a second wire fence closer to the building. She hadn't noticed it on her initial scan of the area. The feeling wasn't painful so much as uncomfortable, and set the hair on the back of her neck to attention. Jayson didn't turn at her small gasp; instead, he increased his pace, and she could do nothing but follow.

It was cool and dark inside. Kiera would have been relieved by the absence of the sun's rays if it weren't for the oppressive sensation that suddenly came over her. She followed Jayson through the doorway and down a half-dozen stone steps before they stopped.

Her eyes took a moment to adjust to the gloom and, when they did, she wished they hadn't. Inside was one, large room. Jagged shards of concrete evidenced walls hastily knocked down to create the open space. Covering the floor, among the debris of destruction, were cages that reminded Kiera of dog transports.

But there were so many crammed into the space. There were even a few stacked one on top of the other. A thin corridor ran between them, only just big enough for Jayson's emaciated frame to saunter down. And saunter he did.

At the other end, he lifted his arms up and smiled that dreaded smile. How perfect a bad guy he could play. Except, he wasn't playing.

"How did you find this place?"

"Oh, I've had a scout on this stupid planet for months now. They are very willing to help. You'll find base creatures like the Void can be controlled with just the right motivation."

She wanted to ask what the hell was wrong with him, but fear of the answer made her shiver.

"Behold, my strength."

Jayson had reached the other end of the room and turned back toward Kiera, arms rising as he spoke.

"These are all of the Guardians? All those that have gone missing? I didn't realize there were so many."

All except your scout, of course. Or did your scout scurry back in the cage as well?

"Oh no, there are even more. These are just the ones I've found. But the ones I still seek number fewer than my own army. Even if they mount a retaliation, I have already won."

"Why do you need them, J? What war are you fighting?"

"I don't need them." Jayson snapped. "This is not my war. I'm just cleaning up their mess, finishing what they started."

Kiera couldn't keep herself upright any longer. She sat on the bottom step and stared at what swarmed in the cages. Darkness, beyond anything she could imagine, looked back at her. She glanced from one cage to another, unable to focus on the eyes that blinked open, ranging from one to over a dozen.

She truly had taken her chances with the Devil.

So why did that snake inside her stomach slither with more vigor and excitement than she had felt in years? What side was she on? And why did Jayson's anger warm her veins instead of burning them?

Just a little longer. She let out a long, slow breath. She could dance with the Devil just a little longer.

"I know it's a shock." Jayson sat beside Kiera and placed a gentle hand on her knee. She fought back the urge to either flinch away or lean into his side. What the Hell was going on with her? "I know it seems cruel but trust me, they deserve this, and far worse. There are more out there, and they continue to kill the dragons they can find, and they keep creating more of their army."

"The dragons were never a vicious race. But the one I... The one I killed. She'd already attacked Blue. She was going for the kill."

"Can you blame her? She sensed the stolen part of another dragon within his chest. Human nature corrupts everything it touches, even them."

"Why can't we just kill them?"

Kiera cringed at the plea she heard in her voice, but she wanted it over. Tiredness pressed on her limbs.

"Because they have their uses. Do not ask again." Jayson spoke slowly, as though trying to fight back his own anger. "You don't know what it's like to live a lifetime of their memories. The cruelty we suffered at their hands. Do you remember any of it?"

"I remember you, in the bed. I remember feeling my ribs being cracked open."

"No, not what my mother did. What the false Guardians did."

"No, J. The only horror I remember is that room."

"I hope that's all you remember. I remember every second of the dragon who died still pinned to that wall. And I will make sure they pay tenfold, for all the dragons they have killed and more for those that still survive."

"Oh."

"None of the other children lived. Did you know that?"

"Huh?"

There were other kids. She knew that in theory, but the truth hit like a punch to the guts.

His mother—Jayson and Zarzy's mother—was dead. She had paid the price for that room and her experiments. But looking around at the darkness, both inside and outside the cages, she had to wonder where the line separated Fang-Ripper's cruelty from his?

"You really have a lot to learn, girl. Lucky I found you before they could turn you into another mindless drone."

"Oh yes, my luck is apparent." Sarcasm dripped from her words. She was going to die anyway. Why pretend to be anyone but the person she had always known herself to be? "Nothing like being abducted and held hostage so I can learn how to torture."

Sarcasm twisted into rage at all the cruelty she had been forced to see since stepping into that first green storm. The rage bubbled over like a witch's cauldron.

Are witches real?

She shook her head. Now wasn't the time to get distracted.

"It's not torture."

His face, for just a moment, reminded Kiera of that small boy who locked eyes with her and helped her survive, and then a darkness fell over his eyes, like a curtain lowering at the end of a play.

"Why did you bring me here? You could have killed me just as easily on the ship. I have nothing to offer you."

She gulped back bile and reached out her mind, trying to find something safe to hold on to, to keep her from being lost in the darkness that surrounded her. The throbbing pain in the back of her head built and her thoughts turned to Levison.

Stay away from the ships and the Guardians. Be safe and stay away from all of this, Levison.

She had no idea of the range of the telepathy, or if the dragon could even understand her. Either way, she had nothing to lose by repeating the thoughts over and over in her head.

"They can't hear you," Jayson sighed.

"What?" Kiera asked.

"You're trying to reach Hesperus telepathically, yes?"

Jayson waited for an answer, and Kiera gave a small nod and swallowed audibly. She would take whatever advantage she could, and if he wanted to assume he was that clever, she would hope it would help with his downfall.

"I know you're scared but trust me. We are doing the right thing." He smiled and stood taller. "I need to attend to something. Stay here, or I will start to think I can't trust you."

He snarled on the last few words before turning and leaving. The metal door clanged shut and the noise echoed around the open space.

She had made a mistake, trusting herself and her quick-thinking to find a way out of this mess. Knowledge was power—she was certain she had heard that many times during her schooling.

Not that she'd really had a choice in the end. She couldn't let the people aboard Hesperus fight, and possibly die, over her. She was no one. But whether there had been a choice then didn't matter. What mattered was her being trapped on Earth with no idea where she was, and no idea how to contact, or even *who* to contact for assistance. Unable to escape, unable to fight back, and still missing that vital piece.

Because, what the hell did Jayson want with her?

Fuck this.

She would not go down without a fight. She would not leave things like this and roll over. No one was coming to save her, and since when had she ever given credence to those story tale endings anyway?

Move quickly. Stop thinking, just move.

She didn't know how long until Jayson would return, but she was betting on it not being long enough. On her feet, she started moving. She had to focus on what mattered, and that was not the past. Every single living creature deserved the right to die in peace. All deserved the right to die. Immortality had never been something she coveted; the mere thought of the loneliness broke her heart.

Not this way, K.

Tamin's return to relative silence had hurt more than she realized, and relief washed through her hearing his voice.

We need to find a way out while we can.

"I need to stop him using these creatures for nefarious purposes."

I did not keep you safe all these years so you could become a martyr now.

It almost worked. Her feet hesitated for a moment, but it was only a moment. She could think and walk at the same time.

The moment she took her first step, the silence broke and began to scream around her. Each new step was slow and difficult, as though a gale pushed against her. She took another step and then another, until she stood between the first two cages. The murmurs and heavy breathing from the cages were sucked back, stilled like a candle snuffed out. Her skin broke out into goosepimples and she shivered.

Kiera walked between them, ice seeping beneath her skin each time she brushed past one of the cages. Tendrils of darkness slipped through and tried to grip her, touch her. They were the braver ones. After three seconds of their exploration outside of the bars, a sizzling hiss emanated from the cages and a snap of electricity zapped at them. The tendrils were quickly withdrawn.

She reached the end. As she turned, the darkness to her left opened its eyes. There were three of them, and two were far too familiar. Kiera dropped to her knees in front of the cage.

"Oh god…"

Leave, K! Tamin demanded, loud and urgent, but she barely heard it. *This isn't worth it,*

Kiera had been so caught up with Jayson and finding the Void that she had left Blue's body in the doorway of the Guardian headquarters. She hadn't noticed it missing when they had left, but she couldn't remember stepping over it when she went outside. Had she done it on instinct?

Focus.

It didn't matter. All she knew was she hadn't thought about him or his body again.

"I remember." A haunted echo of Blue's voice hissed out of the Void's mouth. "I remember the feel of the heart inside me, and now I am nothing but darkness. Every moment, more of me, that man who lived on loss and grief, slips away. Every moment, I grow with anger, like a tumor, a disease that will win and take me under. I want to die. I just want to die."

Kiera swallowed and stood up. Blue—no, the Void that was once Blue—started sobbing. The sound wasn't right. There was a grating of rocks and a hard, brittle snap to the voice.

"I din't know. I din't take part in the defilement of children. I tried to keep me children safe, and instead I made monsters."

"I can help." Kiera nodded. It was the first step, walking the hard line between compassion and mercy. "I can end it."

Blue's voice scraped over the metallic edge of what he had become. "The spear."

"Spear?" Kiera asked, looking around and seeing nothing but cages. "What spear?"

A tendril slipped out of the cage and pointed back toward the steps. Quickly, Kiera walked back. No tendrils reached out to grab her this time, but the shudder that shot up her spine, like spider legs crawling over her skin, was far worse. She pushed back her shoulders and forced one step after the other.

The spear was easy enough to locate—a long, silver shaft with a sharp-looking arrowhead on one end. Taking a deep breath, she let it out slowly between pursed lips. As she turned back, she saw the glint of keys hanging on the wall beside where the spear had been.

Life wasn't something to take lightly, and killing had never been something she had considered. Now, she had killed a dragon and driven a sword through a man's chest. She had to finish what she had started.

Perhaps she wouldn't be able to live with herself if she killed the Void, and starting with Blue was all kinds of right and wrong.

Taking a resolute step back toward the cage was a much harder task. The new silence was the walk of a condemned prisoner.

"Are you sure you want this?" she asked, standing back in front of the last cage of the row.

"Yes." The word was stronger and Kiera nodded, lining the spear up to the gap between the bars. "I don't want to lose myself in the darkness. Please end me. But, not in this cage."

Kiera let out a breath and rested the spear tip on the cement floor. Looking down, she saw the stains of debris and torture.

Kiera, this is not a good idea. Please?

"I have to," Kiera answered.

She slid the key into the lock until she heard a loud click that bounced around the cages and the walls. The roof of the warehouse would have been high enough to have fit Zephyrus with room to dance.

The moment the door was unlocked, the Void threw the cage door open and flung her against the opposite cage. Too many things happened all in the same moment, and while her mind processed them, her body struggled to react. The lock fell with a heavy thunk to the floor, Jayson yelled from the stairs, and thick tendrils of the Void wrapped around her arms, legs and torso, holding her in place.

It took another moment for the rush of blood to ease to a dull roar in her ears so that she could hear Jayson's words.

"You have killed us all. You fool."

The Void that stepped out of the cage stood, a twisted facsimile of Blue. It blinked three eyes and when they opened again, there was nothing of Blue in any of them. As it stood in front of Kiera, it stretched higher and wider. Blackness pulled away from its sides and soon there stood a monster with a dragon's wings, too many eyes and an armored form that continued to solidify as Kiera stared.

"Thank you," the Void said, and it still had hints of Blue's voice. "You'll be me first feast."

"Blue?"

"Ah, yes, I am him. And I'm still just protecting my babies. I have had so many over the lifetimes. The Guardians, the flesh children, and now the Void." He laughed and his wings opened wider, shadowing the rattling cages, as the warehouse filled with hissing and demands for release. "We are the myth and fairytale come to life."

The Void that had been Blue picked up the spear and held it to the cage beside his former prison. He slammed the metal arrowhead into the lock and a chaotic chorus of snapping electricity raced around the room, the blue lightning running along all of the cages.

"Magic still works on earth." Kiera felt like slapping her forehead as she mumbled the thoughts aloud. "Of course it does."

"Find your way out, my children." Blue lowered his voice once more and stepped closer to Kiera, towering over her as it did. "It's time to take this world by force."

Without warning, the tendrils of darkness invaded Kiera's mind. It burst through her eyes. She choked as it forced its way down her throat. Death. Oh, how she begged for death, as her body and mind were violated.

As quickly as the tendrils had invaded, they removed themselves, painfully and with no care for the damage they caused. There was a scream. Kiera was uncertain if she was the one making it.

"Hold on."

Strong arms picked her up and she curled into the secure embrace. Fragments of her mind told her she was imagining it all. Her mind had broken and the woman who rescued her in this desperate fantasy could never have such warmth.

But she allowed her mind to embrace the fantasy, to find a haven in the hopes and dreams of life beyond this pain and agony.

She forced her eyes open just the once. The base of a neck with smooth porcelain skin made her weep, a small sound escaping her mouth. She caught dirty, purple strands out of the corner of her eyes before they fluttered shut once more, and her mind gave into the blackness.

CHAPTER 30

The blackness came and went, and alongside it, giving her a massive middle finger, was the worst pain she had ever endured. It receded like a tide; slowly, leaving remnants of itself behind.

The room was dark. Not quite black, but enough for it to take Kiera a few moments, and a couple dozen blinks, before her eyes adjusted. She recognized the room. Not the medical room, but the small medical area within Silana's chambers. Her eyes scanned the space from her raised position on the bed. It didn't feel like a pillow behind her head, but there was definitely something keeping her head raised. Was it the tilt of the bed itself?

"It's okay." Sleepy words drifted from the corner of the room followed by something soft dropping to the floor and shuffling closer.

"Zar—"

"Hold on. I'll get you some water."

As promised, Zarzy appeared in Kiera's sight, bearing a glass of water and a straw. Kiera wanted to laugh and cry, and after a few sips, a mix of the two came spluttering out of her mouth.

"Pain?"

"No." Kiera shook her head, but hissed as the pain Zarzy anticipated made its appearance. "Straws, up here. So ordinary when I've just destroyed the world."

"Hush. That won't help anything."

"You are being kind. I must be very broken."

"You are. But you are getting better. Faster than we could have hoped."

Kiera squeezed her eyes shut as the furrowing of her brow caused a stab of bright pain to sheer across her forehead. "We?"

"Silana. She has supervised your treatments."

Kiera felt a hot fist wrap around the shard in her heart. Shame at her actions, her stupidity, her choices.

"How did you find me?"

"It seems Hesperus is quite fond of you. I told her you were in trouble, and she found you."

"You can speak to your ship?"

"No, but I was told recently I should stop overthinking things, and the worse that could happen was I was talking to myself."

"I fucked up."

"Well, yes." Zarzy nodded, her face showing no anger or disgust at Kiera's own admission of being wrong. "But everyone fucks up at some point."

"I let them out. Does everyone else's fuck ups endanger two worlds in one blow?"

"No..." Zarzy's voice remained calm and still. "But from what I gathered from your rambling so far, you were trying to release them from their tortured existence or something."

Kiera laughed, hissed at the pain, and then Zarzy stroked the tears from her cheeks. Flames lashed inside of Kiera's chest. "Stop it. Stop turning me into someone innocent. I'm not."

Oh, good! Yes, anger will make it all better.

Tamin's voice carried its own anger, and so much pain.

"We're in the clouds again," Kiera said. It wasn't a question.

"Not for much longer. The last evacuation of the cities is happening now. Looks like this fight is going to be on Earth, and we have a hell of a lot of disadvantages."

"Because I let them out."

"Yes," Zarzy snapped, and Kiera met her eyes, "you let them out. You fucked up. It happens. But are you going to do something about it or sit there and wallow while the world burns?"

Kiera turned her head away from Zarzy. "I need to sleep."

"Huh," Zarzy huffed, footsteps moving away from Kiera. "Wallowing it is then."

When the room around her held the silence of emptiness, Kiera slowly lifted her hand and rested it on her chest. Even through the blankets and whatever scratching material she was now wearing, she could feel the heat radiate from her skin.

"Tamin? Tamin, are you still there?"

A faint movement in the corner of her mind, as though Tamin had lifted his head in response to her call. For a moment, she waited for him to speak. Instead, she was blasted with more pain and anger.

Kiera curled onto her side, pulled her knees to her chest, gripped the blankets in fists with the meagre energy she could muster, and sobbed.

Once the tears dried, Kiera sat up and nodded, as though the salt water washed away what was superfluous and left her with resolve and focus. Her eyes focused on the small, metal tale beside the bed and saw the wristband Winger had forced into her hand.

"That's it!" Silana's voice boomed from the door. "Enough of—"

She stopped mid-sentence. Kiera was already dressed as she turned and met Silana's gaze.

"They suit you." Silana hobbled in, leaning heavily on a cane. Something in Kiera's face must have given her away because Silana shook her head. "I'm fine, child."

"Okay." Kiera nodded, unconvinced but respecting the woman's wishes. "And the clothes *should* suit me. Apparently, I was born to this."

Kiera looked down at the clothes she'd found in one of the cupboards. Her wrist tingled, like numbing gel fading away, beneath the pressure of Winger's band.

She had dressed slowly, accepting each new piece as her own. They were hers, and she was ready to accept the responsibility that came with them, the weight of the knowledge that so many Guardians had been denied before her.

"And here I was told you had chosen wallowing."

Silana's words were filled with amusement as they pulled Kiera back to the now.

"Only for a little bit." Kiera winked at the older woman, "I did set the world on a course of blood and fire."

Silana rolled her eyes. "Yes, and I birthed the woman who killed an entire generation of our people."

"Exactly." Kiera laughed, feeling the hysteria bubbling in her chest but confident enough to be able to control it, for now. "So, who better to lead the charge? And I have a plan."

"You really are quite strange," Zarzy said, as she stepped through the doorway.

Kiera turned and her smile widened, a genuine smile. It might have been the first real one she had been able to give Zarzy.

"Are you in?" Kiera bunched the material at her chest, nerves zipping to her fingertips as she awaited the answer.

"Why do you do that?"

Not the answer Kiera had hoped for but she'd run with it.

"Do what?"

"Feel for the dragon's heart. Well, I assume that's what you are doing? It's like you're scared it might have disappeared or something."

"Oh." Kiera laughed and shook her head. Zarzy scowled and she hurried on. "I wish it was something like that. It's a bit of a habit really. Not many people have seen the scar, and when they do, things change. I'm suddenly delicate and fragile, someone to be pitied. And behind all that, there's the revulsion."

Zarzy's eyebrow raised. "Revulsion?"

"How it looks. No one wants to date a girl, sleep with a girl, who can't wear anything revealing and carries around a hideous wound that is a reminder of the night she became an orphan."

"Oh."

"What happened?" Kiera whispered, as Silana hobbled to the far side of the room, busying herself in a drawer Kiera couldn't see.

"She was hurt when we found the warehouse. It's nothing serious. She will be back pounding the boards in no time. She does like that cane though. It's marked the backs of a few legs already."

"Yours?" Kiera smirked.

Zarzy lifted her chin as she spoke, but Kiera saw the lift at the corners of her mouth. "I would never give Grandmother the excuse."

"Why do you call Blue by his name, but Silana Grandmother?"

Zarzy stopped and blinked a few times, slow and deliberate. Had Kiera managed to surprise and shake the unshakable? If so, her recovery was phenomenal.

"Because one earned the respect, the other has not. You can figure out which is which."

Kiera nodded. "So, you wanna hear my plan?"

CHAPTER 31

"Y ou are insane," Zarzy said, once Kiera had laid out her plan and filled in a few blanks about what had transpired before her rescue from the warehouse.

"Well, sure, but I think that kind of works to our advantage, don't you?"

"And you're sure of this?" Silana asked.

Kiera opened her mouth and shut it again, reconsidering the words that had jumped to her tongue, then opened her mouth once more.

"Hell no. I'm not sure at all. But he seemed certain there are other Guardians hiding from him."

Zarzy smiled, and Kiera was almost certain she was a hair's breadth away from laughing.

"So, he has established himself as their leader, but how is he controlling them?" Silana asked, cutting away the moment between Zarzy and Kiera to keep them on track.

"I'm not certain he does anymore. He was furious when he saw Blue out of the cage."

"But the scout?" Silana asked.

"He said they were pliant with the right motivation." Kiera felt her stomach roil. "Which probably means their hearts, right? I can't think of anything else."

"So, he's not returning them to the dragons then?" Zarzy asked, and Kiera sensed the sadness in her words as the two lines between her brows appeared for just a moment before smoothing back out.

"I don't know. Perhaps he still intends to."

They left Kiera to her thoughts as they began implementing Kiera's action plan.

Kiera's own question, trumping all the others for dominance in her mind, stayed behind her closed lips, fear stopping her from voicing it aloud.

Where is Levison?

Kiera and Zarzy leaned on the railing, forearms resting on the smooth wood as they stared out at the world before them. The world that, depending on whether her plan failed or succeeded, might not feel another sunrise shining through the clouds.

"What's happened?" Kiera's voice didn't shake, and that was a surprise.

Zarzy's word was a whisper. "Look."

Kiera came to stand on her other side. There were tears slowly making their way down Zarzy's cheeks. Actual tears. In that abandoned building, the darkness that had forced its way into her had been terrifying and painful, but there was no deep-seated fear that could match this.

Forcing herself to turn and follow Zarzy's gaze, she saw the flames and heard the howling on the wind. Screams and the sounds of chaos floated to them. Behind the orange and red flames, behind the heat haze and smoke, a cluster of broken eggs, broken cities, flashed in and out of darkness.

"The Void?" Kiera gasped. "They aren't all on Earth?"

"Apparently not. At least, not anymore. And it seems my brother may still be leading them."

"Why do you think that?" Kiera asked, head cocked, but eyes still caught on the destruction going on in front of her.

Before Zarzy or Silana could answer, Kiera saw for herself. Jayson's form was fast and almost liquid in its movements. He sliced through a man defending his home with little more than a wooden stick.

"We can't leave these people for dead."

Kiera's disgust at the suggestion couldn't have been hidden, even if she'd tried.

Zarzy's voice was edged in hard ice. "There's no one else left to stop the Void. We've reached out to all our contacts, but no one has come, Kiera. The plan was good, but if there are other Guardians hiding from Jayson and the Void, they have no intention of coming out of the shadows now."

"Okay, so plan B, if we stop Jayson then—"

"It stops nothing," Silana spoke up. "You said yourself. His control may not be as absolute as he had you believe. We can't rely on the idea that stopping him will stop the Void."

"There are people, our people, dying in front of us."

Zarzy's soft words were accompanied by a gentle hand on her shoulder. "Our priority is to stop the Void."

"Fine, then let's get going." Kiera turned away from the destruction blazing in front of them. "I'm ready."

"Not yet."

Silana held up the sword she had left on Zephyrus—the one Blue had trained her with—in one hand and a pair of green boots in the other. Seeing the sword made Kiera's shoulders relax. Seeing the boots rose them to her ears again. They were made in the same style as Kiera's old purple Doc Martens, and she had no idea where they'd ended up.

"What are they made of?" she asked, but something turned uncomfortably in her stomach, and she knew before Silana answered.

"It's dragon hide."

"From the dragon I killed." Kiera's voice began to rise. "You expect me to wear the skin of the dragon I killed?"

"Yes," Zarzy said. "It is tradition. We don't waste any of the kills. But more than that, it's fireproof and has the best chance of protecting you against the Void."

"So why aren't we all decked out in dragon scale armor? The dragon was a lot bigger than a pair of boots."

Kiera flicked at the brown leather vest she wore over the soft, white shirt and baggy sleeves, just like a real pirate. She even had the brown leather pants like Blue's. Looking at the green boots, her stomach flipped for the first time wondering what the vest and pants were made from.

"Because it was stolen before we could get anything more made."

"Stolen by...?" Kiera asked, but she knew the answer before the question had left her lips.

The three all spoke as one. "Jayson."

"Of course it was."

Kiera let out a huff and gingerly took the boots from Silana. She would take any help, any small advantage, real or imagined. She did not have high hopes for this fight, but she knew she would go out fighting, no matter what.

The boots were surprisingly light. If she didn't think too much about it, she could even pretend the twist of revulsion in her stomach wasn't there.

"Now, it's time you learned how to fly, my baby."

"What? Hell no, I jumped onto Zephyrus by accident once and the migraine was days from buggering off."

"That's because you didn't ask permission."

Kiera's mouth flopped open, words failing her.

CHAPTER 32

Outside a small apartment block, under the pouring rain, Kiera slipped her new, green boots silently between the puddles. She forced their origin away from the forefront of her mind once again.

Her legs, so quickly accustomed to the air ships, now wobbled, unsure of the drag of the Earth's gravity and the strange, spongy throb of the ground beneath. She ignored the pull to get back on the ship, to get back to Hesperus, sitting immobile and grounded in the shadows of the building further up the hill. She had followed one of the oil-slicked trails from the warehouse to this home.

Only weeks had passed since her eyes were first opened to the world she had been born into, yet it felt like years. Lifetimes. She remembered the job she hated, all the jobs that had never fit her right. Nothing had fit her right, not once in the life she remembered.

With Aunty Em, she had almost felt as though she belonged, but the woman had always held Kiera at arm's length. As a teen, Kiera had convinced herself it was the reminder of her dead parents. But that history was all a lie.

Once the Void were taken care of, she would be having an awfully long talk to the woman she called Aunt Em.

Shaking her head, she pushed it all aside. The life she had before the green storm had been an ignorant one. Nothing more than a holiday from the truth. Now, her eyes were open and there was no closing them. She had a job to do.

A small sliver of her, a small voice barely audible, wished for the ignorance once more. But wishes weren't going to give her answers. And the sliver was easily crushed under the rush of adrenaline coursing through her.

She held the handle of her sword out as an extension of her arm, the way Blue had taught her, and stepped silently across the rain-soaked bitumen. The Void had already slipped inside the building. The blackness dripped from the windowsill like a Dali painting. This creature sought death and destruction. Kiera tasted the desire on the tip of her tongue, like metal and ozone.

She slipped through the same window, fighting her gag reflex as the smell of rot and decay mixed with a thick, cloying smell like a jar of cloves left out in the sun.

Movement from the corner of her eye made her turn, sword up and ready to attack. What she saw was arguably more frightening than a Void. Her reflection in the mirror attached to the wall blinked and stopped.

This latest adventure—she scoffed at the idea—had added years to her face. She was gaunt, and her skin looked scarred beneath the surface, like tattoos that had grown skin over them over lifetimes.

Whatever the Void had done to her, their mark was beyond the internal damage, and undoubtedly irrevocable.

Pushing down the morbid curiosity, she moved forward, following the black ichor. It steamed, small tendrils of discolored mist floating up into the cool, wet air.

Upon entering the room, she took in the Void, hunched over the bed. A thick vibration came from her throat. A growl, letting the creature know of her presence. A small whimper from Tamin broke her isolation.

"Hush." Kiera spoke over the fear, hoping the strength in her words, the faith in her ability to win, would help ease the damaged heart within. "We will take him together."

The Void laughed, and in that moment, Kiera lashed out. No hesitation, no wavering, as she thrust the blade of her sword through the black belly, rounded and swollen with the life it had stolen.

Its wings reared, talons aiming for her head. It was so much more than a Guardian with its stolen heart removed. It was a twisted, mangled creature, as though it no longer remembered what form it should take—human, dragon, or something else entirely.

With a sucking slurp, Kiera pulled the sword out of its belly and flicked her wrist, once, then twice. The movement, fast and efficient, relieved both wings of their monstrous and deadly claws. The Void howled, even as the blade thrust forward again, this time through its open mouth, past jagged teeth and out the back of its elongated head.

"You should have died when your heart was removed," Kiera said.

It screamed as the reality of its death began to wrap its wings, binding them around its leaking body. It thrust and gyrated against its own form, desperately trying to release itself from this inevitability.

"You can't beat us all, Fang-Ripper. I am but one. We will find it in the end, and we will win."

Its laugh, edged with its own fear, filled the room as it disappeared.

Fang-Ripper?

The mere idea caused goosepimples to cover her skin. The mass of ichor on the carpet smoked slightly, harmless but still something she was not keen on touching. Kiera stepped carefully over it and her eyes focused on the decimated body of the man on the bed. No skin remained. Organs were likewise gone, consumed by the Void. Bones bore small scratches, as though the flesh had been gnawed off, which Kiera conceded was most likely the case.

Forcing down the bile that was rising in her throat, she grabbed an unbloodied corner of the bed sheet and wiped the ichor from her blade.

There was another crack of thunder outside the apartment, loud and rattling the glass in the window frames. She turned on her heel, forcing the guilt aside. She could wallow over this man's death later. Right now, the fight was just beginning, and she was happy to let her instincts take over.

Five steps and she stood on the window ledge.

Below, darkness between the pooling rain pulled together, the sound like tearing material and flesh. Voids. So many of them here already. But why here?

Her actions had led to their freedom. Getting them back into cages wasn't an option. This was their last hurrah, Kiera would make sure of that. Even if it killed her. The world would suffer if she was not faster and stronger than them.

Her heart raced as pools of darkness took shape, creatures of nightmare, the Void.

As if they had been waiting for her to call, three ships, powered on magic and wind, broke through the thickness of the clouds covering the sky. All three bore white lines on the bow, a small marking Kiera now realized were indicative of Healer vessels.

"Three."

Kiera focused on the middle ship and smiled when she saw the twin figures of grandmother and grandchild standing on its deck.

She had expected fewer ships, but she had still hoped for more. Disappointment washed over her until, behind them, another three emerged from the clouds. The formation of the six reminded Kiera of migrating ducks.

But, more important, the second trio of ships didn't bear the small, white lines that identified them as Healer ships. If that weren't enough, the Guardians standing on the deck sold her, as the ships drew closer to the earth.

It took Kiera several deep breaths and stern mental berating to get her breath under control, or near enough. Her heart refused to be quelled.

It wasn't fear. The fear had fled the moment she decided they would ultimately win, no matter the cost. Despite the life she had been handed, even the one filled with lies, she still believed in the happily ever after, at least for the world at large.

She imagined she should still be scared, but death had lost its hold on her. She had begun down the path of destroying the Void believing her life would end, win or lose. She hadn't yet embraced the idea that she might survive the night, despite the small spark of hope that ignited inside her.

Jumping from the windowsill, Kiera screamed a war cry that would have woken all the inhabitants of Earth, if they had bothered to open themselves to the reality of a world beyond what they knew.

Soon, they would have no choice.

"You must be Kiera." A man, tall and thin with a grey beard and a bald head, jumped over the railing of the ship to the right of where Zarzy and Silana still stood. "Name's Jericho. I hear you're the one taking on the Void."

"You know what they are?"

Kiera didn't need a fighter who would be spooked if one of the Void remembered him, talked to him, knew his weaknesses and tried to exploit them, catching him unawares, just as Blue had with her.

His lips were a thin grim line. "We've been told. They ain't my fellow Guardians, not anymore. But yeah, I know what they *used* to be."

Kiera looked over as they disembarked and her wonder increased. "Does everyone else?"

She had assumed the Guardians who had hidden from Jayson's capture were nothing more than a handful of rebels. How mistaken she had been. Over three-dozen had already jumped over the railings of all three ships and settled a few meters from where she stood, conferring with Jericho.

"They've been briefed." Jericho gave a sharp nod of emphasis as he spoke. "We follow your lead. Goal is to stop the Void, right?"

The idea of being their leader was as unsettling as a root canal without anesthetic, but she preferred this to a bunch of yahoos looking to be a hero or pissing contests about chain of command.

"We need to kill them. Stopping them won't suffice."

"Aye."

Jericho spoke loud enough that his Guardians—her Guardians now, she supposed—all fell in line behind them.

Despite the tattered clothes and scruffy hair, the need of all of them to bathe, they gripped their swords as extensions of themselves. The fire and fight burnt bright as they lifted the points of their weapons into the sky and echoed a raucous, "Aye!"

"The Void aren't going to go easy on you." Kiera didn't know where the words came from, but they were like releasing a wild animal from a cage. They roared out, the freedom as powerful and natural as though she were born to this. "So don't go easy on them!"

"Aye!"

The chorus was louder this time. Swords pumped again toward the clouds.

Not a single sword shook, in the firm grip of the determined Guardians. Kiera supposed they had been the hunted for the first time in their lives and the instinct to survive was primal. She could understand that.

She looked over at Hesperus and was rewarded with slow nods from both Zarzy and Silana.

"Let's do this!" she screamed, as a clash of thunder boomed around them.

She stood taller, her own strength bolstered by the energy from the Guardians at her back, and Jericho at her side.

Her blood roared and her chest screamed a war cry as the smoldering flames burst alight with a new accelerant. The battle had begun.

CHAPTER 33

Time lost all meaning as the fighting took over. Around her, Void and Guardian clashed. The sound of skin and bones being sundered mixed with the clang and clash of swords against black armor and talons. The air shuddered with each thunderclap, and torrential rain washed the horror of it all into a warped version of reality.

Blood spread in blossoms over Kiera's white shirt. The brown jacket had been slashed to ribbons, her vest clinging together by its last threads. Her skin was soaked in the thick black ichor of the Void's blood.

The ooze mixed with her own blood and found passage through wounds she'd collected in the innumerable collisions with the Void—wounds numbed in the presence of the adrenaline—and every devoured drop filled up the darkness that clung to her, inside of her. Each time her sword sliced through the body of another Void, the thing inside of her stepped a little further out of the dark corner in her mind.

Still, Tamin remained silent.

The slurping suck of her sword came free from another collapsing form bothered her less and less. Still she turned away, unable to watch as the Void spasmed in its last throws of life. Kiera searched her surroundings for the next kill. She stood halfway up the hill, in the middle of the road. Houses were now spaced apart, dark within. The apartment building where she had fought her first Void lay somewhere down the bottom of the hill, lost in the shadows of the night and the looming Healer and Guardian ships.

"I was hoping I would get to be the one to run you through."

The voice came from the shadows to her left. She shuffled her fingers on the sword's grip and bounced on the balls of her feet as she turned toward the sound. The voice was thick and heavy like hard bread dragged through sticky molasses.

"You have the wrong person, pal," Kiera hissed, "but I'm happy for you to try."

"Hmm..." The voice didn't sound affected in the least by her challenge, chatting as though they were old friends catching up at a café. "You've the boots of the dragon you slaughtered. You really did have such potential, just like that little bitch I sired. But this..." Blue— the Void's twisted version of him—stepped out of the shadows. He opened his arms wide, black wings with sickly, mottled cartilage visible beneath stretched membrane, to take in the carnage around her. "I didn't even have to teach you to enjoy the kill."

"You aren't Blue." Kiera's voice dropped the name like an anvil.

Tamin screamed, and they both felt the shadow memories of the invasion, of this Void's tentacles forcing their way inside. Kiera slammed her teeth together and squared her shoulders. The anger and fire raged inside her and it warmed Tamin's fear.

The Void and Kiera circled each other. She fought against closing her eyes.

"Let's see what you've learned."

It spoke so much like Blue had during that time in the clouds, that a sob almost escaped Kiera's lips. She bit it back barely in time.

It's not Blue.

So let's put this bastard down, Tamin's voice said. It wasn't the strong force it had been, but hearing it ignited something primal in Kiera.

She nodded and took a slow breath as she relaxed her shoulders and bent her knees.

The thing that was no longer Blue snarled, but Kiera saw the oversized head nod. What passed for a smile on a beast like this, completely devoid of warmth, revealed sharp teeth reminiscent of prehistoric sea creatures.

Waiting would only deplete what little energy she had remaining. Kiera stepped forward and aimed at the monster's head. It blocked, its own blade deflecting hers. The sight of a Void wielding a sword was unnerving, but she would not show how amusing it also was. Soon, the world around them disappeared to the clang of their swords. Blue left a small nick in her forehead, and sweat and blood ran down her temple.

"Getting tired are we?" it mocked.

"I'm good, old man," Kiera replied.

"I remember you. I remember when you came to visit with my beautiful Fang-Ripper. She wrote everything about you and her hope of making you useful, since your parents abandoned you on the steps of the Guardian Headquarters. She hoped you'd be better than the others. Our own children had disappointed her, unable to wield the true strength of the crystals. But you were never useful. You were just another disappointment." He continued on his soliloquy of torment as they began to circle each other once more. "I never thought about you, not once during the trials. I didn't care if you were one of her experiments. You simply disappeared from all thoughts, and no one here ever missed you."

Not Blue!

"Your beautiful Fang-Ripper was a psychotic bitch!"

Her voice wavered despite her efforts to keep the effect of his words suppressed as she threw herself at him again, both hands swinging the sword out of exhausted desperation.

At first, she thought the bastard was doing something, because a new darkness mottled his flesh. It took three more heavy swings for her to realize that what she was seeing was a circling shadow, small and distant. A smile tugged at the corners of her mouth as the shadow grew and, oh, how she recognized it. What turned the tugging grin into a full smile was the Void's lack of attention to it as it raced over its dark skin.

"You finally cracked?" It laughed at her, but Kiera saw the concern in its three eyes, all blinking separately so it never missed a second of watching her. "Whatcha smiling for? You're about to die."

Kiera's smile widened further as she took her right hand off the sword and made a swooshing sweep of the air, with just her left hand guiding her weapon. It was a trick she had learned during fencing lessons, the element of surprise. Why it paid never to tell someone you were ambidextrous until you could use it to its full advantage. She'd won many a bout.

But this time, it was purely a distraction.

"Your wife was insane, and her experiments were never going to bow down to her. She wasn't a scientist; she was a torturer." Kiera's words dripped venom as Levison drew closer, his shadow now flicking across the black tar of the road behind the Void.

"She was a visionary." The Void dropped its sword and began slashing at Kiera with its wing claws, one after the other. "She would have saved our people!"

She barely blocked each blow, ducking and weaving her head when his frenzy grew.

"Your people are dead," Kiera forced out, between blows of steel against bone and bone against steel.

"My people, my *true* people, are just rising!"

Thick lips pulled back to reveal those prehistoric fangs of nightmares. They glinted white in a flash of lightning. Fresh bone, Kiera felt certain of that. Not part of Blue, but from whoever this creature had killed since. She didn't want to know all the details. There was already enough gore and horror that would follow her the rest of her life. She didn't allow herself to linger on how long that might be.

Instead, she found the Void's rhythm and when it opened those deadly wings, pulling back for another strike, she threw herself into the swing. Her steel bit into the sinew between the cartilage of its right wing. The roar that came from its mouth was earth shaking.

"You will die tonight," the Void hissed.

"Maybe, but you won't be around to see it," Kiera sneered in return.

Before Kiera could strike, the Void returned her grin.

As though in slow motion, it turned, slashing upward with its undamaged left wing. Kiera saw too late that the Void had not been as oblivious to Levison's approach as she had assumed.

"Levison! Down!"

But Kiera's call was too late. Levison's scream was louder than all the chaos surrounding them. Her sword clattered to the ground as the hatchling, *her* hatchling, fell back to earth with a heavy thud, landing on his back.

"No!"

Kiera raced to his side, forgetting the danger, forgetting the Void.

"Back off!" Jericho's voice rumbled beside her, as she pulled Levison into her lap.

She looked up, teeth bared and ready to hiss, but Jericho was talking to the Void, swords held between them.

"Next time."

The Void directed his comment to Kiera and turned on his heel. Jericho was about to follow, but Kiera raised her voice. "Jericho, get Zarzy. I need help with Levison."

Jericho bounced on his feet, obviously indecisive in his next action. "It's a dragon."

"Get Zarzy, now!"

The fire in her words blistered her lips and Jericho nodded, sliding his sword back into its scabbard and heading toward the ships.

We needed him. Tamin's voice was hard and angry. *He knows where to find the caves.*

"We can find one of the others."

The rest are all dead.

The words were a one-two punch. All dead?

She looked around, hands still pulling Levison's sliced skin as closed as possible. Around them were the sludge and breaking bodies of the Void, scattered amidst fallen Guardians. Not as many Guardians as she had feared.

Among the debris and wreckage of death, figures stood like cracked tombstones against the dark sky. The rain had become a soft drizzle and she counted nine figures, nine Guardians. She had feared a big loss, but there were still so many missing. Slowly, they trudged closer to each other, some resting bodies and heads on the pommels of swords pierced into the ground.

"Tamin, can we find them another way?"

I hope so, he said, but there was not much hope in the voice.

"Thanks for coming back."

Thanks for bringing me back.

His words were comforting despite the confusion.

"I'm here."

Zarzy's voice pulled Kiera back from her mental conversation. She blinked, refocusing her attention on her fingers as they clutched useless at Levison's damaged hide. Her fingers ached and the color had drained to a bone-white.

"Help him? Please?"

Kiera locked eyes with Zarzy and she nodded, face stony in the dim light.

Silana was behind her, dragging a stained stretcher between her and a Healer Kiera had seen during the influx of wounded on Hesperus, only she couldn't remember his name. Had she ever known it?

"You need to move Kiera. Let us handle it."

CHAPTER 34

The medical room she had previously seen on Hesperus was full. Levison lay, sewn up and resting on his stretcher in the corner. Kiera leaned on the door frame and watched as Zarzy tucked stray hair behind her ear and focused all her attention on the next patient she attended to. A Guardian.

Warmth spread through Kiera's chest and she was impressed at her ability to acknowledge any sensation beyond the pain and fatigue. But that was where the acknowledgement ended.

Instead, she focused for a moment on the Guardian. They looked fractionally older than twenty and that was being generous. Despite the woman's ability to rile her with a simple look, Kiera couldn't stop her eyes from wandering back to Zarzy.

As though Zarzy felt the gaze upon her, she looked up and met Kiera with a weary glance. Her lips quirked.

"Levison is healing," Silana said softly, as she took Kiera's elbow gently in her hands. "It's time to look at your damage. Come on."

Kiera didn't argue, letting Silana guide her to one of the other, smaller medical rooms. They passed previously open doors, mirror images of the medical room she had known, all filled with the Guardians who had survived. There were more than she imagined, and the thought broke her.

There were more. The nine she'd seen were not the last of her kind.

"Sit."

Silana jerked her chin toward an empty bed and busied herself with supplies she laid out on the table. Despite the exhaustion, Kiera couldn't help wishing for a different Healer, a very specific Healer, to be treating her again. The warmth touched her cheeks, and she leaned into it.

"Take off your clothes. They're covered in blood and ooze, and I need to patch you. You can leave your underwear on."

Kiera slipped off her boots and what remained of her jacket and vest. "Okay."

"Reports are coming in."

"Reports about what?" Kiera asked, as she hitched herself up on the bed once more.

She leaned back slightly at Silana's hand-waving, allowing the Healer to wash down a cut on her stomach. It wasn't all too close to the scar, but still, Kiera tensed as Silana looked her over.

"The Guardians have started reporting in. None of them have seen, or at least recognized, the Four among the dead. Which I suppose we can count as a blessing."

"Why is everyone so concerned about them? I mean, sure, they are the leaders or whatever, but—"

Kiera hissed as Silana slathered a poultice over a particularly deep cut to her side. The older woman waited out the reaction without a trace of apology or discomfort.

"I do forget you didn't grow up in the Skyan world. Yes, they are our leaders, though the title has lost much of its power since my daughter and her group were killed. It wasn't the executions people found objectionable. It was the way the experiments had gone on for so long, and the Four never took action. Children had been going missing for some time and the council, the Four, waved the concerns away as though they were nothing. If they had only listened to the parents earlier, the damage would have been so much less."

"So why is everyone so concerned about finding the Four?"

"They have the knowledge from the very beginning of the magic. The magic given to us by the original Guardians."

"The dragons," Kiera interrupted, clenching her teeth and feeling her jaw muscles tighten.

"Yes. It is still hard to take in the new knowledge."

"Will they accept it? The new knowledge?"

"Perhaps, given time. Things never returned to a place of happiness after the trials, and that will be to your advantage."

Silana finished patching up Kiera's latest wounds and presented her with a new set of Guardian clothes. She dressed, watching the clouds through the small, round window. They were still dark and heavy, but the rain had stopped and there was movement above, movement that made her and Tamin tremble.

"Rest." Silana gently pushed Kiera to lay back on the bed. "There is still work to be done."

She must have fallen asleep because her eyes flew open with a start.

"I didn't mean to scare you," Zarzy muttered.

"It's fine." Kiera shook her head and sat back up, rubbing at her eyes. "What's going on?"

"The others are on their way, and Silana is getting Hesperus in the air shortly. They are coming to us, and we've found a place close enough for us to be there in mere moments."

"What others?"

"The other Guardians. The ones that Jayson hadn't gotten to."

"The ones who fought?"

"No." Zarzy's smile was gentle and patient. "The ones from the far side lands. Earth and Skyan have a similar structure of land masses. Thankfully, Jayson had only been concerned with those closest to home."

"Why are they coming here?" Kiera asked.

"Mostly the space." Zarzy chuckled softly under her words. "But also, they believe the messages I have sent about our past, and they have some theories about finding the cave."

"Oh. It's not really over yet, is it?"

Kiera wanted to say more but feared doing just that.

Zarzy's cheeks pinked and she tucked a stray hair behind her ear.

"No. I think it's only just beginning."

If Kiera's mind weren't preoccupied, she might have enjoyed the stoic woman's obvious embarrassment and possible flirting. But even Kiera's interest in the cave was overtaken by a far more pressing matter. A question that she wanted answered first.

No, a question she *needed* answered.

How had she escaped that room with the mirrors and the experiments?

She had been asked by all of them now, asked if she remembered, but there was nothing to remember. Not from Skyan.

There was someone who must have a better idea. Someone who might even remember. A person they didn't even know to ask.

Kiera pressed her lips together to stop any mention of Aunt Em from slipping out.

CHAPTER 35

Within hours—hours that felt like days as Kiera paced the boards of Hesperus, fighting with herself about what she would do next—the ships from the other side of the world arrived.

When Hesperus had touched down on land again, Kiera went up to the deck and laughed at the large sports ground. She didn't know exactly where they were, but it didn't matter. It seemed all sports grounds were similar, though this one was certainly larger than the ones she had gone to as a teenager.

She rested her forearms on Hesperus's railing and looked at the netball court with the ring bent and rusted just below her. She hadn't stepped on the decks of the other ships. Not because she had not been invited, but because of the idea she might find something that reminded her of Blue, or of Jayson. She wasn't ready to face that. Not yet.

"There's too many questions," Kiera said, before Zarzy reached her. Kiera had long ago learned the sound of the woman's soft but confident tread, no hesitation.

"I agree," Zarzy replied.

"Jayson said something about sending a scout to Earth. I assumed he meant to find the warehouse for the Void."

"Now you suspect that wasn't the case?"

"I think it was only part of the case."

Kiera looked over and smiled at Zarzy. The features she had once seen as ice cold and bitchy took on new depths as she got to know the woman behind the statuesque features.

"You have an idea what the other part is?"

"I think it's the same thing I need to find."

"So, you have made up your mind?"

Zarzy's voice was confident in all the ways Kiera wished she could master. No emotions were betrayed in the cool clip of words.

"I can't go with them. I'm not a Guardian. I'm not part of your society." She met Zarzy's eyes and begged for the woman to understand. "Besides, they've got it handled."

Zarzy's voice was low, and softer than Kiera had heard it before. "What does that mean, exactly?"

"It means…" Kiera turned around, leaning against the railing. She bent her right knee and planted the sole of her boot against Hesperus's side. It still amused her that she'd thought a sky ship could ever be flimsy. "…that I'm going to go and visit family, and hopefully get a clue as to the caves. I can't let them stay there. I get the Guardians are scared, and I get they want to find a way to move forward. But Zarzy, if they come after me, I will kill them."

"Us."

Kiera's shoulders dropped a little, her mind scrabbling to catch up. "What?"

"I believe she said 'us', Kiera."

Silana stood a meter or two back, arms crossed over her chest, the stress of the last few weeks had caught up in the lines on her face.

Kiera felt like she should understand now, but still nothing made sense. "What 'us'?"

"We are coming with you."

Zarzy's patience had reached its end and Kiera could do nothing but stare at her with furrowed brows and a wide mouth, as her head turned back and forth. She imagined she looked as creepy as those midway clowns, waiting for you to toss a ping-pong ball through their plastic lips.

"Hurry up." Zarzy turned and headed down into the bowels of the ship. "Hesperus is eager to get going."

Kiera shook her head with more force, pushing herself off the side and taking several steps toward Silana. "No."

"Yes. We are a Healer ship. They will make contact if they need us. And besides, Levison isn't big enough to carry you yet."

As if hearing his name, Levison's shadow flew over them. He hadn't flown too far since his injury, and Kiera felt his presence more comforting than all the Guardians and Healers surrounding her.

His shadow was little more than the size he had been when he first wrapped his wings around Kiera's arm. She looked up into the sky, blinking against the brightness, but he was already gone. Hiding nearby but always close.

Kiera smiled.

She liked the idea of riding a dragon into battle.

THE END.

About the Author

Neen Cohen is an Aussie. She writes sapphic speculative fiction and while she tries to take things seriously she thrives being the hyperactive bookworm who rarely stops smiling or laughing. If she had to decide between never reading or never writing again she simply wouldn't. Rules were never her strong point. When not writing or working the day job, Neen loves nothing more than dancing, nerf wars with the boys, playing the latest PS obsession, and crafting wild and crazy things sometimes for the kiddo, other times because she can.

AUTHORS NOTES:

THE VOID has gone through many changes since its humble beginnings. Originally two short stories were written and submitted to Eerie River Publishing. While Michelle (you are amazing) enjoyed the sorties they didn't quite fit the horror feel she had been looking for. The stories were rejected with a counteroffer of embarking on extended them and making a series. My first full length novel series. There have been changes and upsets, sickness, ups and downs but the learning and growth for both myself and this book has been epic and fantastic. I am so proud to have The Void out in the world. I can't wait for you to meet Kiera, Blue, and Zarzy. Not to mention the other delightful characters who demanded their time on the page. I hope you enjoy reading it even half as much as I have enjoyed writing it. Thank you.

Neen Cohen

AVAILABLE FROM EERIE RIVER PUBLISHING

NOVELS
They Are Cursed Like You
Helluland
Shades Of Night
Untamed Night
Gulf
NOTHUS
SENTINEL
Infested
Miracle Growth
Storming Area 51
In Solitudes Shadow
Path of War
Beyond Sundered Seas
Dead Man Walking
Devil Walks in Blood
A Sword Named Sorrow

ANTHOLOGIES
Blood Sins
Of Fire and Stars
Monsters & Mayhem
AFTER
Last Stop: Horror on Route 13
It Calls From the Forest: Volume I
It Calls From the Forest: Volume II
It Calls From the Sky
It Calls From the Sea
It Calls Fromt the Doors
It Calls From the Veil
Elemental Cycle Series
Darkness Reclaimed
With Blood and Ash
With Bone and Iron
Forgotten Ones
Dark Magic

COMING SOON
The Void
Rotten House
At Eternity's Gates

EerieRiverPublishing.com

More from Eerie River

Eerie River Publishing, is a small independant publishing house that is devoted to uplifing Indie Authors and releasing quality dark fiction novels, novellas and anthologies.

To stay up to date with all our new releases and upcoming giveaways, follow us on Facebook, Twitter, Instagram and YouTube. Sign up for our monthly newsletter and receive a free ebook Darkness Reclaimed, as our thank you gift.

https://mailchi.mp/71e45b6d5880/welcomebook

Interested in becoming a Patreon member?
Patreon membership gives you exclusive sneak peeks at upcoming books, early chapter releases, covers art as well as free ebooks and discounts on paperbacks.

https://www.patreon.com/EerieRiverPub

EERIE RIVER PUBLISHING PRESENTS
THEY ARE CURSED
LIKE YOU
TRAILER PARK WITCHES   BOOK ONE
HOLLEY CORNETTO & S.O. GREEN

HELLULAND

A NOVEL

A GIFT AWAKENING
A LEGEND REVEALED

C.R. LINDSTRÖM

EMPIRE OF RUIN
1
IN SOLITUDE'S
SHADOW
DAVID GREEN

A dark fantasy
LGBTQIA+ anthology
OF FIRE
AND STARS
EDITED BY S.O. GREEN
EERIE RIVER PUBLISHING